M

Thank you for supporting & spreading the message of Down Thru Love! I have seen you grow & now seeing you become a mother is so amazing!

I miss you

#Restart

With Love,

FriesenPress

One Printers Way
Altona, MB R0G 0B0
Canada

www.friesenpress.com

Copyright © 2022 by H. B. Pierre Simon Jr.
First Edition — 2022

Contributing author: Elijah Pierre Simon

All rights reserved.

No part of this publication may be reproduced in any form, or by any means, electronic or mechanical, including photocopying, recording, or any information browsing, storage, or retrieval system, without permission in writing from FriesenPress.

ISBN
978-1-03-910826-4 (Hardcover)
978-1-03-910825-7 (Paperback)
978-1-03-910827-1 (eBook)

1. FICTION, FAMILY LIFE, GENERAL

Distributed to the trade by The Ingram Book Company

DOWN THRU LOVE

THE 21ST JOURNEY

H. B. Pierre Simon Jr.

Table of Contents

PART I   1
CHAPTER 1 The End Before the Beginning   3
CHAPTER 2 Happy For Now   11
CHAPTER 3 Decisions   33
CHAPTER 4 The Unknown   41
CHAPTER 5 Acceptance Going Down   61
CHAPTER 6 Back and Changed   71

PART II   85
CHAPTER 7 Peyton Love   87
CHAPTER 8 A New Life: A New Journey   97
CHAPTER 9 A Glance Back, A Look Forward   109
CHAPTER 10 College and the NP's Spiral   117
CHAPTER 11 Jasmine's Path   123

PART III   135
CHAPTER 12 Rain and the Forgotten Lights   137
CHAPTER 13 Voicemails   157
CHAPTER 14 Beantown: Two Loves   165
CHAPTER 15 Forgiveness Begins   189
CHAPTER 16 Time's Gift   203
CHAPTER 17 Love's Hope: God's Plan   225
CHAPTER 18 Purpose Fulfilled   239

About the Author   251

PART I

CHAPTER 1
THE END BEFORE THE BEGINNING

A battered brown suitcase opens, yet it is almost impossible to make out the contents within. Though the outside is covered with random stickers, pins, and obscure markings, the inside contains an old journal, a single sheet of paper, and two photos taped to the underside of the suitcase's lid.

A shaky hand slowly grazes the sole sheet while a soft, arrhythmic sob pushes through the deafening silence. As a man looks up toward the sky, a lone tear races along the crevice of his nose and continues down his cheek.

The tear appears to travel with purpose, halting only to fill the well created by a dimple of sorrow.

The suitcase closes...

"Sometimes, I just don't understand. I did everything right, just as you said

...I found him, Mom, forgave him, and now this. This? What am I to do now?"

Standing up from the dew-covered grass, a short man slowly walks away from the crowd. Tightly clenching the handle of the suitcase, he walks aimlessly and without purpose, almost as if he has absolutely nowhere to be, or that even the very notion of time has forsaken him.

Walking away, he wipes his free hand on his faded, brownish-green corduroy pants. In harmony with his increasing sobs, his steps become slower and without direction before drawing to a halt.

Faint sobs escape his lips. White knuckles grip the antique handle of the suitcase. His grasp gets tighter and tighter with each uncontrollable sigh...

Disoriented steps become more staggering as the countenance of sorrow and pain upon his face becomes overwhelming.

He falls back to his knees, suitcase now clutched to his chest, looking back to the funeral.

As the funeral staff begins to lower the casket, which threatens to fall from sight, the man looks back, as if to give one final goodbye. Only a few words are spoken. Sorrowed gestures and visions of farewell exist within that moment...

He is left standing in the dewy blades of grass with only the tears that fill the corners of his eyes.

As the casket slowly disappears from sight, the crowd, which is no longer a part of the man's focus, begins to disperse.

The troubled man whispers, "As we say goodbye, thank you... thank you, love!"

With final embraces, the crowd moves toward their vehicles and prepares to leave the grounds.

Yet one remains, his eyes so filled that tears blur the casket's final visible moments.

Peyton weeps as he opens the old beat-up journal, and reads from a torn-out page he has folded and stapled within:

What is love? A question that has been debated for centuries yet very few have laid claim to a true answer. Can it be found? Does it teach forgiveness? Does it enter and leave our lives, giving us but a snippet of its true form, just to remind us that there is something more out there? Or is it merely the desire to feel an attachment with one other, as we go through this life? The answer is yes, it is all of the above.

It is all-encompassing. It is fear. It is hope. It is the feeling of finally finding the one who understands you. It exists within the fleeting moment of losing one's grandmother after a lifelong example of what a woman should be to a family. It exists within the moment one feels accomplished after crossing the stage of graduation at the ripe age of forty-two, just because they wanted to set an example for their family. It exists within the short-lived moments of young infatuation, when one first feels the flutters of care and admiration.

However, in its purest form, it exists from the moment a mother feels her child clench to her from within, and the bond of love is created forever. Divine love!

    As a tear falls from his cheek, Peyton kneels and draws something in the wet grass with his index finger. It could be coincidence or fate, but the tear drops directly in the middle of his sorrowful illustration.

    His drawing finished, Peyton looks up toward the cloudy blue skies, just sitting there, contemplating life, and what his purpose will be from that point forward.

The Beginning—Nearly Thirty Years Before

"Yo, Tommy, what's Jasmine's story? Is she cool? Is she single?" Mark asked his new friend. He'd been watching Jasmine during homeroom since he transferred in from Atlanta. She kept to herself, did her work, and quickly left at the sound of the bell. Unlike many of the other girls, she hadn't even given him a glance when he'd arrived.

Tommy gave Mark Love a side-eye coupled with a smirk, and Mark knew he'd enjoy a future "lover boy" nickname for quite some time.

"Man, I don't even know, M. She pretty much stays to herself and doesn't talk to many people. Apparently, she's like the smartest person in the school. I haven't seen her with any guys, though. I dunno, man. She could be single." Tommy shrugged.

Throughout the semester, Mark tried to find opportunities to talk to Jasmine. Eventually, fate seemingly showed up, as Mrs. Opry placed Mark in the same group as Jasmine for their STEM project. Meeting after school with the team, the two got to know each other quite a bit. He saw her in a new light, and for the first time, Jasmine began to open up to him.

"So, after we work on the project, would you like to go and grab milkshakes with me?" Mark asked.

"Umm... are you asking me out like on a date-date?" Jasmine replied.

"I mean, I just figured we could go grab milkshakes at the UC. Don't make it weird or anything." He laughed.

The deafening silence seemed to last an eternity. Jasmine looked up at Mark and replied, "Yeah, I'd love to. I mean, I *am* pretty hungry."

Mark was relieved and excited, but of course, due to his pride, he couldn't let that show. He simply smiled at her. "Cool," he said softly.

Things were a bit awkward during their "first date," but they both eventually opened up and began to enjoy each other's company. Mark ordered a cookies and cream milkshake, while Jasmine proved to be more adventurous, ordering "the works" milkshake.

The two were there so long that Jasmine brought up the idea of splitting a large order of fries. Mark smirked a bit and let out a small laugh.

"What's funny?" Jasmine asked.

"Umm, umm, oh nothing. I… I…was just thinking about something Tommy called me a while back. Oh boy, if he could see me now."

"Oh, really now." Jasmine smiled and asked, "And what did he call you?"

"Lover boy," Mark said with a smile.

The two leaned toward each other and laughed.

The truth was, Mark wasn't actually laughing at what Tommy had called him. He was laughing because Jasmine had unknowingly saved their "date." He didn't have that much money left after buying their milkshakes, and Jasmine's timely suggestion to split the French fries saved his manly pride.

Hours later, as the sun was setting, Mark placed his left arm around Jasmine and looked at her for a moment. He sighed and pursed his lips. "Jeez, you're beautiful."

Jasmine blushed, looked down, then back up at Mark. "Thank you. You're not terrible to look at either."

They laughed at Jasmine's little dig to Mark's pride.

"Well, I guess we better be heading home soon, huh?" Mark asked.

Jasmine looked at her watch. "Oh wow, I didn't even realize it was getting this late."

"I guess when you're enjoying a 'non-date' so much, you kinda lose track of time," Mark joked as he gave Jasmine a side-eye, raising and lowering his eyebrows.

"Oh, someone is confident, I see," Jasmine joked back.

The two kids finished their fries, and Mark took Jasmine home. It was a perfect night.

As the semester went on, Mark finally worked up enough courage to ask her to prom. He had everything planned out. He'd convinced the principal, Dr. Watkins, to allow him to interrupt the pep rally before their big regional match against Westfield.

Getting down on one knee and "proposing" to Jasmine, asking her to be his prom date, had sounded a lot easier when he was planning it with his mother in the kitchen at home.

It turned out to be a complete mess of a proposal. Mark's entire lacrosse team entered the gymnasium, horribly singing Musiq Soulchild's "Love." Co-captain Arthelis pulled Jasmine out of the crowd and brought her to the center of the basketball court.

Even though Jasmine was shy, she weighed the cost of being pulled out of the crowd versus having the entire senior class watch her and not "go with the flow," so she accepted Arthelis's "invitation."

Walking to the floor, Jasmine could see Mark in the middle of the lacrosse squad's huddle as they continued with their tone-deaf rendition of the song, "Love."

When they finished, Mark leaped out front and grabbed the microphone. "Jasmine, I'm so glad I've had the opportunity to meet you. You're smart, you have a beautiful smile, and you're *drop-dead gorgeous*."

The entire senior class let out a mixture of oohs and ahhs.

Jasmine stood there, shy and clenching her face in her hands.

Mark took a knee. "I want to know if you'd make me the happiest man in the world by being my date to the prom?"

At that moment, Arthelis took the microphone from Mark and held it in front of Jasmine.

The entire gym was silent, awaiting her answer…

"Yes, yes, I'd love to," she replied

"*And she said yesss, and the crowd goes wild!*" Arthelis screamed into the microphone.

The entire senior class cheered and clapped.

Though Jasmine was shy, she was so happy at that moment.

Mark stood and picked Jasmine up, spinning her around. She hugged him, kissed him, and the entire crowd seemed to fade away. They were both elated.

Senior year was a blur, but Jasmine and Mark were never more than a stone's throw from each other. From playing in the park to going to prom, to Jasmine watching him continue their dominant lacrosse season, to Mark coming to her chess tournaments, to arguing about foolish topics, to making up, kissing, and even almost having sex, the two were inseparable.

One night, the two were out with friends, and Jasmine was tired. Mark took her home, and since her parents were out of town, she invited Mark inside. As the two watched TV, Mark kissed her neck, and Jasmine reciprocated by holding his face and kissing his forehead.

"I want to, Mark. I want you, but I'm just—"

Mark stopped her. Being the perfect gentleman, he said, "Baby, I'm in no rush. We can wait."

She kissed him. "Thank you, babe. I just don't want you to

think that I don't want to. I just want us to wait, you know."

"Jas, I'm OK with us waiting. I love you."

"You do?" she asked, shocked.

"I do. I've felt this for quite some time, and I didn't want to wait any longer to tell you."

"Mark, I love you, too," Jasmine said as she leaned toward him.

They kissed and enjoyed the remainder of the night, laughing and watching TV.

Throughout their senior year, their lives together began to take shape and unfold. They shared many memorable moments in such a short time.

From meeting for the first time, their first date, passing perfectly folded notes back and forth, their first kiss, and Mark getting made fun of by his friends for being a "lover boy," it was as if their love was moving a million miles per hour with no brakes.

Graduation was right around the corner and both Mark and Jasmine had applied and been accepted to Boston University. The two lovebirds wanted to stay as close as possible, so they agreed they'd both attend BU and continue their relationship.

At graduation, they threw their caps into the air and hugged. Jasmine whispered something into Mark's ear. He smiled, caressed her shoulders, softly placed his hands on her cheeks, and kissed her. They were in young love, and now that love would face the challenge of college.

CHAPTER 2
HAPPY FOR NOW

Driven and very ambitious, Mark and Jasmine were studying to finish their undergraduate degrees at Boston University. They spent hours studying. Well, Jasmine would spend hours; Mark would spend an hour studying, and the rest of the time, he'd sneak photos of Jasmine via his Polaroid.

Mark was headstrong on going to law school and becoming the world's greatest personal injury lawyer. Jasmine had other plans. She wanted to save the world, one patient at a time.

They knew that falling in love in high school had its advantages, but it was rare to see that love last forever. Right now, Jasmine and Mark were happy, by all societal standards. They were truly in love, growing in life together and seeing each other change and become adults.

Jasmine grew up in a very religious household and although her father hadn't initially approved of them moving in together, he came around because he liked Mark and felt like he was a standup guy.

This approval didn't come with ease, however. Mark often joked with Jas that her father actually sat him down and had "the talk." You know the one. The one where he basically asked, without asking, "Are you trying to marry my daughter and make her an honest woman, or do you just wanna get your rocks off at will?"

Mark and Jasmine had done everything together and they were in love, but the two continued to practice celibacy. As Jasmine put it, although Mark reluctantly agreed, they were holding out for marriage—a marriage that Jasmine had hinted at more and more as the years in high school transitioned into college.

They were both active in their university community. Jasmine was the president of the National Association of Hope, Delta Sigma Chapter, an organization she had created. Its focus and mission were volunteering with at-risk youth, specifically education about early prevention of life-altering diseases. She held this position for two years, and in her words, "Focused on saving one child's future, *today*!"

On the other hand, Mark was an apprentice for Crawford & McCray associates, and he held this position while studying for the LSAT and mostly volunteering to beef up his résumé.

Ambitious as they were, they weren't all business. To Jasmine's dismay, Mark annoyingly carried around a Polaroid camera at all times, capturing "the beauty within the world." He took picture after picture of Jasmine and taped them on the walls of their cozy, 921-square-foot apartment. Some of the photos were not so flattering.

"Why do you put these ugly pictures up of me, Mark?" Jasmine laughed as she ran through the hallway, pulling down Mark's recent photos.

For every picture she ripped down, Mark captured two or three equally terrible candid photos of her, which somehow found themselves taped onto the walls the next morning.

She'd often wake to the sound of him shaking a freshly taken Polaroid of her as she slept, slobbered, and snoozed in what she called the most "unappealing fashion."

"Babe, what do you wanna do for dinner?" Regardless of how meagerly they lived, they always ate together in their small apartment, talking about school, the day, and what was happening on campus. Many of these conversations would quickly turn into Jasmine discussing her plans to save her next child and Mark reviewing old LSAT exams.

"We can do whatever. I just know that I'm tired of Chinese food," Jasmine replied.

"Well, excuse me, Ms. Fancy. Chinese has treated us well... annnd we can afford it," he said sarcastically. "I mean, look at these guns!!! You don't get these eating fancy steaks and juicy lobster, do you?" Mark flexed his biceps, though very little muscle protruded from his limbs.

"What guns? Those things wouldn't scare a six-year-old off the playground," Jasmine teased.

"Easy, easy now. These guns didn't have any trouble getting you to notice me, did they?" Mark said as he squinted, giving her side-eye.

"Boy, relax. I was young and dumb, and now I'm just used to you and don't want you to be stuck out in the cold lonely, with those... large guns." Jasmine chuckled.

"All right, I'm going to order our usual," Mark yelled from the other room.

"That's fine," Jasmine replied. "After we eat, you wanna go back to the library and study for a bit? I have this stupid anatomy exam I have to cram for."

"Yeah, we can go, but if those clowns are in our spot again tonight, they have to move."

Every night, Jasmine and Mark studied together in the same place in the library—the third floor of the Cynthia Michelle

Memorial Library on campus. It was *their* spot.

Jasmine laughed. "You can get them to move with those large guns of yours." She smirked.

"Haha, funny. I mean, I've said it a million times, you don't even need to study for those exams. You crush them with ease. You would make sooo much more money just switching to pre-med and being a full-on doctor."

"And I've told you time and time again. It's not about the money. It's about—"

"I know. I know. Saving the world, blah blah blah." He cut her off.

"Yes, *finally*, you get me," she replied.

The two argued for a bit on whether or not Jasmine should follow her passion for "the money," or simply "changing lives," but in the end, Mark accepted Jasmine's love for people, and he admired her for it.

Ring ring...

"I think that's the food."

"I'll get it," Jasmine replied while walking to the door.

After eating, they set off to the library. "Hurry up, I don't want our spot to be taken, plus I want to get in there and knock out this practice exam," Mark said.

"Boy, don't rush me. I'm coming," she replied.

At the library, they went directly to the third floor. Mark was peeking around the corner, hoping that their spot was open.

Jasmine saw him looking. "Why do you look so worried? You're going to make them move right if they're in our spot? With those large guns, correct?" She could barely talk for making fun of Mark and his puny arms.

"Shut up. I have this covered, woman."

Their usual library location was available, so they sat down, pulled chairs together, whipped out their laptops, and began studying.

At about an hour into studying, Jasmine sighed as if she had something on her mind. She looked toward Mark slightly, yet as he looked toward her, she turned away.

He could tell something was on her mind, but he just shrugged it off and continued studying.

"Where do you think we'll be in five years?" Jasmine was all the way invested in him, but it was evident that Mark was still unsure of what he wanted for the rest of his life, including their relationship. From planning their date nights to ensuring that her schedule accommodated his, Jasmine always prioritized their relationship.

Mark sat back in his chair, rolled his eyes, and loudly exhaled as if preparing for a long verbal fight that he'd experienced before. "I don't know, Jas. I'm just trying to focus on doing well on this LSAT so I can set my life up." He shook his head in annoyance.

Jasmine's face quickly changed as she leaned closer to him. "Don't you mean *our* lives?"

Tilting his head to the side, lips clenched together as he nodded yes, Mark acknowledged her frustration, but quickly blew it off by leaning back in his chair and covering his face with his hand. Shaking his head, he said, "Jasmine, stop. You know exactly what I mean. Don't start this again. Pleeease!"

"I'm not starting anything, but if we're truly in this together, and are planning a family one day, we need to discuss *us*, don't we?" She leaned in and reached for his arm.

Mark pulled away and leaned farther back in his chair. "Jaaas, stop with the marriage stuff. We're happy. You bring this up almost every conversation now. We are happy. We are good. Let's just be that for now... *happy*." His voice began to escalate with annoyance.

"We are happy, and we are also good, but I don't think there's anything wrong with looking forward, right?" she asked rhetorically as she turned back toward her book.

"No, Jas, there's nothing wrong with looking forward, but let's focus on *the now*. What's coming will come. We are fine." Mark pulled away from her, and his body language changed.

Jasmine realized he was upset. She didn't want them to end up in a heated, weeklong debate, so she decided to drop the conversation and continued her studying.

Junior Year

Mark and Jasmine were both in their junior year of undergrad at BU. Both studying for their prospective exams, living together, spending every day together, yet the question remained... What would become of them once they were accepted, and if they were accepted at different locations?

The fall semester came and went. Jasmine continued to volunteer at nearly every health clinic in the city while maintaining her 3.8 GPA. School was easy for her.

She didn't really need to study, but she did because anything less than a hundred percent on any exam was unacceptable in her eyes.

Mark was taking his LSAT in just a few weeks, so he was quite stressed. Studying every night and what seemed to be all day, he took practice exam after practice exam.

Jasmine was also studying for her entrance exam into nursing school.

One morning, while studying together in the library, Jasmine said, "You know you don't have to stress, right? You are going to do well, likely a 170 or better, plus your resume is phenomenal."

"Yeah, but in order to get into Harvard, Princeton, or Thurgood Marshall, I have to be better than phenomenal. And

I don't have a family legacy at either. I just feel like I'm at a disadvantage to some of the other candidates already, you know?"

"Yeah, but you can't think like that. You'll take the LSAT, do as well as you can, and what will be, will be. Besides, remember you're not practicing law just to have a plaque from Harvard or Princeton. You want to practice law to help those who've been injured and would likely fall prey to a system that's meant to protect corporate greed. Right?"

"Yeah, buuut I also want the prestige and the plaque," Mark replied jokingly.

Jasmine always had a way of putting things into perspective for Mark. Her father was a pastor back home, and her mother was a longtime teacher. Because of the discipline she'd been taught from a young age, education was always a top priority. But beyond education, she'd been taught the true value of effort and accepting outcomes as they are.

As she often told Mark during their conversations about the future, "I've lived on the other side of the tracks where people wondered where their next meal would come from or where they were too poor to go to the doctor for proper medical treatment."

Having seen first-hand what it was like to struggle through life fueled her desire to work hard in school and accomplish her dream of working in healthcare, providing service to the underserved.

Test Week

It was test day, and Mark had been stressing all week like never before. Jasmine woke up early to make him a French press cup of coffee with two eggs and peppered turkey bacon. It was his favorite, plus she wanted him to be calm for his exam.

Mark woke to the smell of peppered bacon. He smiled and yelled, "*Why is this woman so good to meee?*"

From downstairs in the kitchen, Jasmine just smiled and yelled back, "I know. You definitely don't deserve me. Now get your ass in the shower and get down here!"

"Yeeesss, ma'am," he replied.

While it was Mark who was taking the LSAT, Jasmine was a wreck for him because she knew how badly he wanted to do well on it.

As Mark was coming down the stairs, Jasmine ran to the bottom and met him with a folded note and a kiss.

"Don't open this until you get on campus, OK?" she said with a smile.

"Why not? Now I'm going to be thinking about what's inside."

Being the thoughtful person she was, Jasmine had had his entire family write brief messages wishing him good luck, giving him words of encouragement, and telling him just why they all knew he would do well on the LSAT. She had been collecting these short messages from everyone for quite some time, and knew it would mean a lot to him.

He kissed her. "Please tell me why you're so good to me."

"Because you're mine. If you do well, we do well." She smiled and kissed him back, then the two walked to the kitchen. Jasmine didn't eat. She just sat with him, present, there, and in the moment.

"You don't want any?" he asked.

"Nope, I just made it for you. You are going to smash this exam. I'm not even worried. You've prepared, studied, and you know your shit." She assured him with confidence.

The two sat as Mark ate, just there, just them, just in that moment, simply present with each other.

"All right, babe. I gotta go. I'm going to be late."

As he took one last bite of his beloved peppered bacon,

he buttoned the top buttons of his shirt, hugged her goodbye, grabbed his backpack, and ran toward the door.

"Baby, aren't you forgetting something?" she asked.

"Uuuggghhh," he said jokingly, as he ran back to her to give her a kiss.

As he came in for a kiss, she put her hand in front of his lips. "No, crazy man. You forgot to zip your damn pants!"

They both laughed, then he hugged her and whispered in her ear, "You're right, I'm going to kill this exam. Not because of me, but because of you. Thank you, Jas. You're a true queen... my queen!"

They were there, then, in the moment, present. Happy. In love.

Mark arrived on campus early, ready to take his exam. He walked in to find it was only him and the proctor. "Is this the right location for the LSAT?" he asked.

"Yes, sir." replied the proctor, "but you're either really ready or really nervous because you are about an hour early."

"Is it possible to be both?" he smiled at the proctor before choosing a seat right in the middle of the auditorium. He sat down and seemed to exhale and soak in the moment. Thoughts of everything that brought him to that moment flooded his mind. He began to recite affirmations to himself.

"I know I can do this. This is meant to be. I will do as well as I know I can because I'm ready. I've prepared. I've studied. This exam is mine for the taking."

He sat in the nearly empty auditorium, looking around, checking his watch, and nervously adjusting himself in his seat a million times. Then he remembered the note in his back pocket that Jasmine had given him. He pulled it out and began to read.

Son, first off, I'm proud of you. You have worked your tail off up to this point, and everything that you receive from here on isn't an accident. You set a goal, put a plan in place to accomplish that goal, and now you are here. Here at your moment of greatness. Just know one thing: the outcome of this exam doesn't determine your greatness. That was predestined from the moment your mother informed me she was pregnant with our little blessing. Do your best, take your time, and know that we all have your back.

~ Dad

Hey Mark, I just want you first to know that I love you. You have made me so proud for so many years. I know you are going to do well on this exam. You will have the choice of whatever school you want to attend, and whatever school doesn't offer you, it will be their loss because you are a rare breed, my breed. Do your best and remember, no matter what, Mom loves you. Oh, and you better bring your grown butt to dinner Sunday, or you'll be getting a call from me. Love you, Mark. Now stop reading and get ready for the test.

~ Mom

Mark, you have been a proven leader to the team. You work hard every day, and you have accomplished to the fullest everything that you set your mind to. This damn exam will be no different. Kick ass, and you'd better not be late to practice after. :)

~ Coach

> Big bro, when Jas asked me to write a few words to you on this big day, I didn't know what to say. I don't know anything about an LSAT exam, but I know it's important. So, just wanted you to know, on this day, how important you are to me. I've always looked up to you. I know I can always call you with my silly questions, and you're always patient and answer them with ease... Maybe because you're going to be a lawyer, and y'all always at least pretend to know the answers, LOL. Anyway, I love you, big bro, and I want to wish you good luck, and I know you're going to pass with flying colors.
>
> ~ Jon Jon

And then, Mark saw Jasmine's handwriting. He was nearly in tears from the love he felt coming off the pages. He was hesitant to continue reading because he wanted to remain focused, and he knew she'd likely bring him to tears with her message of affirmation.

> Mark, I thought hard about what I would say to you before the biggest exam of your life. All I could come up with was, "I love you." I don't love you because I know you're going to ace this exam. Instead, I love you because of your fear of not acing it.

Mark made a face. *Where in the world is this going?* He thought.

> Fear can either be an obstacle that holds us back in life or a challenge that, if we meet it head-on, makes us stronger, wiser, and better for facing it. And that is exactly what you did. You set your goal to become the world's best personal injury

> lawyer, and even in the face of the fear of not being good enough, not passing the LSAT, not getting into the school you wanted, you've persevered. You are an example to me and all those that will come behind you.
>
> I love you and I know you are going to not only pass this exam, but make this exam your bitch... well, not your bitch-bitch, because that's me, LOL. I love you, baby. Best of luck!!!
>
> ~ Jasmine

He slowly folded the letter exactly how Jasmine had given it to him and looked up. The room had filled with eager souls ready to put their dreams into action. He took out his pencils... He was present, in the moment, and ready.

"Ladies and gentleman, you will have three hours to complete your exam, please fill in your name... You may begin," the proctor announced.

Feeling confident, Mark realigned his pencils on his desk, opened his exam

...and he was off.

Jasmine waited at home on pins and needles as though she was awaiting the results of her very own LSAT exam. She sat in the kitchen and thought about how Mark was doing, wondering if the note she gave him encouraged him or put more pressure on him.

To keep her mind busy, she started to clean the apartment, which seemed to help. As she was cleaning, she saw one of Mark's long-sleeved shirts and a pair of his lacrosse socks on the top of the clean laundry. She took off her shirt, put on his and his socks, and continued cleaning.

She cleaned the entire apartment, put up the leftovers from

breakfast, fell into the bed, and dozed off. Everything was as it should be... perfect.

"Jaaas," Mark yelled from the front door. "I smaaashed it. Where are you? *Baaabbbeee!*" he yelled as he rushed around downstairs, frantically searching for her.

Jasmine was still asleep, but woke abruptly when she heard him yelling. "I'm upstairs."

"Did you hear what I said?" he yelled. "I smaaashed it."

Jasmine ripped off the blanket and ran to the top of the stairs, still wearing his long-sleeved button-up lacrosse shirt and his socks. As she stood there, smiling atop the stairs, Mark began running up to her.

When he saw her, he stopped halfway up the stairs and laughed. "Look at you. I like the outfit, and the place looks great. I fucking killed the LSAT, babe. I just know I did!"

Jasmine screamed. Mark screamed. They were screaming together.

He raced up the last few stairs. When he reached the top, he picked her up and spun her around. They both just laughed and screamed into each other's faces. Then Mark stopped and kissed her softly on the forehead. "We gotta celebrate, Jas."

"Ok, what do you want me to cook? Or we can get a bottle of wine and order Chinese food."

"Oh nooo, ma'am, I'm taking you out to dinner," he said. "We're going to celebrate this the right way."

"OK, OK, When do you get the results?" she asked.

"I don't know. I don't care, I'm just glad it's over, and I feel really good about it, babe. I'm going to make a reservation. Can you be ready in like forty-five minutes? I'm going to see if Tico's has some open tables.

"Ooo yes, Tico's! I love that place," Jasmine yelled from the closet, as she hurried to find something to wear. She was so excited for Mark, so it was imperative that she find the perfect outfit for this celebration.

"Hey, you know what? Maybe we should shower together. You know, to conserve water and all," he said, giving her side-eye.

"Boy, get your butt in the shower. I already showered. I'll be ready. Call and see if they have space for us first, though."

So, Mark called Tico's and made a reservation. They both got dressed and headed out for the night to celebrate Mark's excitement about finishing his LSAT.

Mark held Jasmine's hand the entire taxi ride to Tico's and all through dinner. "Jasmine, I want you to know that you're the reason I even made it this far. Your drive, your passion for life, your zeal to help people, namely me. I don't even feel like I deserve you."

That night, he said all the right things.

Jasmine loved it. This was the emotional side she'd wanted to see from Mark all along. At times, Mark could be somewhat cold, never allowing himself to be vulnerable and speak his true feelings. *Even though he's probably just excited to be done with his exam, I'm glad he's opening up,* she thought.

They toasted with champagne and spent the whole evening talking and laughing. Just after ordering dessert, Mark stood up from the table and held his hand out to Jasmine. "Dance with me," he said, as the live jazz band played Kenny G's "Songbird."

"WHAT? Are you crazy? Everybody is eating, boy. They'll look at us like we're both crazy."

"I don't care," he said. "I'm happy, I smashed that damn exam, and I have the most beautiful girl in the room next to me. We can't lose. Hell, let them look. Let them laugh. It doesn't matter. Get up, Jas. I want to dance with you."

It was rare, but when Mark showed emotion, it was a beautiful thing. Jasmine loved it. He made her smile inside. They were there. They were happy, then, in the moment.

When Jasmine stood, Mark wrapped his arms around her and slow-danced in the middle of the restaurant to the band's soft tones. They were happy.

Even in their shared happiness, Jasmine was still shy and embarrassed. When Mark could tell that she wanted to sit down, he pulled her closer. Feeling her heart racing with embarrassment, he whispered in her ear, "Look at me. We're the only ones here. Nobody else is here with us, just you and I."

His voice calmed her as she looked into his eyes and slow-danced. After a few minutes, Jasmine's shyness kicked in again, and she laughed and kissed Mark on his cheek. "You know, I love when you're sweet, babe."

Mark smiled at her. "Well, I guess I can be sweet sometimes. Maybe I should be this way more."

"Uh, you think?" She chuckled.

They sat back down, toasted with their champagne, and finished their desserts, which had arrived mid-dance.

The entire taxi ride home, Mark held her hand, slowly intertwining their fingers as she rested her head on his shoulder.

When they arrived back at the apartment, Mark said, "Hey, let's walk the block. It's a beautiful night."

The stars were out, the weather was great, and they were both stuffed from their meal and happy. Walking the block turned into the two of them walking the entire complex, holding hands, and enjoying each other's company. When they finally made it back to the apartment, Jasmine hugged Mark and kissed him. "Thank you for an amazing evening. I'm so proud of you."

They walked inside, and Mark turned back to lock the door. As Jasmine was preparing to go upstairs, Mark grabbed her hand and pulled her back. He kissed her passionately, caressed her face, and slowly pushed her against the wall. She held his face, caressed his back, and kissed him as if it would be their final kiss.

He pulled back, looked her in the eyes and whispered, "I *want you*. I know we said we'd wait, but—"

"What if I don't want to wait? I love you. I always have. I want you too." Jasmine interrupted him.

"I need you. I want every piece of you, all of you!"

She grabbed his hand and slowly walked up the stairs. They'd waited so long to have sex because they'd both wanted it to be the right time.

"Baby, are you sure?" Mark asked cautiously.

"No, I'm not sure, but I *am* sure about us," she whispered softly.

As they slowly walked to the room, Jasmine turned around, and Mark picked her up. He could feel her breath increasing and her heart racing more and more the closer they got to the room.

"Are you OK?" he asked. "Are you sure, babe? I'm OK with us waiting."

"No... I want you. I have wanted you for so long. But babe, you gotta take it slow with me, OK," she whispered.

So many times before, they'd wanted to break their celibacy. In those times, either Jasmine would lean on Mark to be strong for the two of them or vice versa... But not this time. The moment had come, and their internal decisions were made.

Jasmine was nervous, but she loved him and knew she would spend the rest of her life with him.

Walking slowly to the room, Mark held her, kissed her, and rubbed her back as she kissed him and caressed his face.

Her gasps increased more and more as she moaned in anticipation. "Baby, I want you so much right now. Make love to me. Make me yours. I want it all," she whispered in his ear.

"J, you're turning me on so much."

She locked eyes with him, crawled her fingers down his body, and grabbed him. "I can tell I am, and I want it all, baby. Give it all to me."

Laying her down on the bed, he kissed her, intertwined their hands, and started to kiss her neck. "Let me take care of you," he whispered.

"Wait, take my heels off." She laughed.

"Nah, babe, leave them on. You look amazing in them." Mark pulled her dress up, kissing every inch of her body as she moaned and grabbed the back of his head.

"Baby, don't stop. Just like that. Make love to me." She moaned.

"I'm not stopping. I need you. Now turn around for me."

Her dress halfway off, Jasmine turned around and quietly watched the love of her life kiss down her body.

She looked over and noticed their silhouettes in the full-length floor mirror. "Wait a minute, baby."

She got out of the bed and went to the bathroom with her dress halfway up. As she began to pull her dress down to cover herself, Mark yelled, "Babe don't you dare pull that down. I wanna see it all. Just keep walking in those heels."

Jasmine smiled, bit her lip, and continued toward the bathroom.

"What are you doing in there?" he asked.

"Mind your business."

Jasmine grabbed three candles. Before she returned to the bedroom, she looked into the bathroom mirror as if seeking affirmation. She was going to make love to Mark. They were there, then, now, present, with each other.

She walked back to the room, and Mark stood from the bed to meet her. "Sit down, babe," she said.

She leisurely walked around the room, and as she did, Mark began to undress. She lit the largest candle on the floor next to the full-length mirror, looked at Mark, and whispered, "I want to see everything."

Walking past the door, she closed it gently, placed a second candle on the dresser, and lit it. She took the third, placed it on the bedside stand, lit it, and looked at Mark.

As she climbed into the bed, Mark grabbed her and began kissing her entire body. Rolling her over on her back, he removed her dress, kissing every inch of her as he raised her dress higher and higher.

Jasmine allowed only the sweetest of moans out of her mouth and their breathing was nearly in harmony with each other. Intertwining their hands again, Mark whispered, "Babe, should we use a condom?"

"No, babe. We're fine. I've been on the pill for months. I want you now, like now! I want to feel it all... *everything*," she said with assurance while looking into his eyes.

Mark kissed her, and Jasmine kissed him back. They were in the moment, and it was perfect. All was perfect. As he entered her for the first time, she whispered, "Take care of me!"

"That's all I want to do, tonight and forever," he whispered back.

He slowly entered Jasmine's body and soul, and she moaned louder and louder with every stroke. As they made love, Jasmine gazed over at the mirror, watching the synchronized movement of their bodies. "Look," she said, drawing his attention to the mirror. "It feels so amazing, baby. Go deeper. Deeper baby!" Her breath faded as it escaped her.

Mark went deeper and deeper... faster and faster, as Jasmine gripped and clawed at his back. She yelled in ecstasy. "Baby, make love to me. Ugh, this shit feels so good. Give it to me. Give it to me, baby," she moaned.

"Wait, baby, it feels too good." Mark gasped, trying to hold on longer and longer before pulling out.

"Where are you going? Don't stop, baby. Please don't stop. I want it all. Give it to me. I want you to cum for me!" She grabbed at his hips, pulling him back inside.

"Not yet, baby. You just watch the mirror." Mark started to kiss down her body. He kissed her chest, her nipples, her side, and then went farther down.

"Baaaby," Jasmine moaned.

"You just watch that mirror, J." As Mark continued down her body, he kissed her stomach and licked her thighs, all while Jasmine was rubbing his back and moaning louder and louder. He began to kiss her clit, and she arched her back as his tongue touched the tip of her, and she moaned in full ecstasy.

"Are you watching?" he asked.

"I am, baby. I am."

She was trying to follow instructions and watch "the show," but it was nearly impossible to keep her eyes open as Mark gripped her body and tasted all of her.

Jasmine watched their silhouettes in the mirror. Moaning, scratching his neck, and convulsing, she screamed with every stroke of his tongue.

He kissed her clit, and went deeper and deeper inside her, tasting all her love as it dripped down his face. She grabbed the back of his head and began to control his movements. She watched as he softly kissed her thighs, clit, and brought her closer and closer to climax.

"Baby, you're going to make me cum," she whispered.

"Not yet, baby. Not yet," Mark replied.

As he continued, and she came closer to climaxing, she pulled him up. "I want you inside of me now!"

As he came up, she grabbed his face, bit his chin, and tasted every bit of her on his beard and face. Mark turned her around and continued making love to her.

"Baaaby, you're so deep inside of me."

The two of them looked into the mirror as the candle burned just bright enough for them to see their silhouettes and their shadows on the wall. Grinding slowly inside of her, gripping her hands, kissing her back, and biting her neck, Mark brought her to another place in time.

Jasmine looked back, kissed him, and moaned in his mouth as he climbed into her soul. "Baby, you're about to make me cum," she said.

"You're going to cum for me?" he asked rhetorically.

"Yes, baby. Yes, baby. YESSSSS!" she screamed as she winced in pleasure.

"Then cum for me, J. Cum for me!" Mark ran his hands over her head, then gripped her hair, pulled her head back closer to him, and repeated, "Cum for me, J. I want it. All of it. Give it to me!"

"OK, I'm going to cum. I'm cumming, baby, I'm cummm…" Jasmine climaxed and screamed as if they were the only two humans on the planet. They were there, then, present, making love, and it was perfect.

As he moved slowly in and out of her, her moans began to subside. She looked at him and said, "Lie down. I want to be on top of you. I want to make you cum. I want you inside of me. All of you."

Mark complied, and Jasmine climbed on top of him. As she slid down, she gasped, and leaned her head to the side of his neck, "Mmm, baby, it's so deep." Grinding slowly and moaning, she grabbed Mark's hands and placed them on her breasts. She put one hand on his chest and the other on his inner thigh. Jasmine moved with purpose, up and down, more and more vigorously with each thrust. She watched him. His face said it all. "Tell me how you like it, baby," she said while watching his body respond to each of her movements.

"Just like this, Jas. Don't stop. This feels insane."

She leaned down and kissed him as she continued pleasuring him. She bit his ear and whispered, "I want all of you inside of me. Give it all to me, baby. Don't hold back. I need it. I crave it. It's mine."

Mark grabbed her back and slid his hands down to her hips.

He leaned up in the bed to go deeper inside of her, and Jasmine's heightened moans confirmed that he had, in fact, accomplished that goal.

"Fuck, baby, you're going to make me go again." She gasped.

"Wait for me, baby. Wait for me. Same time," he said.

"OK, baby. I'm trying, but I'm really close."

"Me too, I'm... I'm... I'm... I'm about to cum." Mark said.

"*Me too*, I'm cuming again," Jasmine yelled while clenching his chest.

"Me too, baby. Here it comes!"

She pulled Mark close to her chest. He gripped her body as she trembled on top of him. They looked each other in the eyes, kissed, and they both came together. Both screaming, both holding each other close, and climaxing at the same time. It was perfect. Mark felt her drip down his body, while Jasmine convulsed each time he pulsated inside of her. Her mouth opened as she exhaled and moaned with each uncontrollable thrust from Mark.

Jasmine lay on his chest.

"Damn, baby, that was amazing." She sighed as he rubbed her back and ran his fingers through her hair.

"I love you," she said.

"I love you too, baby," Mark replied.

They lay there for hours, just talking, laughing, neither wanting to move or leave the moment. As the candles began to dim, Jasmine drew a heart on his chest with her finger. They fell asleep just as the final candle burned out and the smoke rose to the ceiling.

CHAPTER 3
DECISIONS

The semester was nearing its end, and Jasmine had been applying to several nursing schools. She wanted to stay in Boston, but she also wanted to be near Mark so they could make the transition together.

Though this decision was mostly out of their hands, she hoped and prayed that they'd end up near each other at least.

Jasmine was studying for her nursing school entrance exam while Mark awaited the results of his LSAT and continued to work at the firm. His plate was quite full as he was also the captain of the lacrosse team, and they were having a great season.

Mark planned to attend BU's Spring Abogado Mixer, an event that BU hosted, where prospective law students would meet with alumni and professors from law schools from all around the nation. BU's Sigma Gamma Law Fraternity had created the event five years prior, and Mark had attended the event two years in a row.

"Babe, I'm going to head to the mixer," Mark said.

"OK babe, I'm just going to stay here and study. I'm taking the exam tomorrow. I feel good about it, but I just want to get some last-minute review in. My classmate Jessica helped me make these index cards, so I want to make sure I get good use out of them."

"OK, babe. Don't study too hard. You're ready, trust me," Mark assured her on his way out of the door.

While at the mixer, Mark went to booth after booth, introducing himself and handing the recruiters his résumé. While he talked to many recruiters, his focus was really on Harvard, Princeton, and Thurgood Marshall. When he walked to the Thurgood Marshall table, he looked down and noticed that there was only one blank sheet of paper on the table. He introduced himself and began to chat with the recruiter.

"So, what's the relevance of this one sheet of paper?" he inquired.

"Well, son, we at Thurgood Marshall believe that law, though it is written, is mostly blank!"

Though Mark had a puzzled look on his face, he found himself intrigued. "Blank? What do you mean? How can the law be blank even though it's written and pretty much black and white? No pun intended," he asked curiously.

"Well, if you look up the definition of blank, it means 'A space left to be filled.' You see, laws change, laws are interpreted, and laws are simply humans' way of trying to understand the universe. So let me ask you, how many planets are there in the universe?"

Mark paused and then began to name planets. "Well, there's Earth, Mars—"

"No, son," the recruiter said. "I asked how many planets there are in the universe, not just our solar system."

"Ahhh, true. Well, I can't name them all in the universe because I just know the ones within our solar system." Mark laughed as he pulled out the chair at the table and sat with the recruiter.

"That is the very point of this blank paper, young man. You can start naming the planets or masses in the universe, and even if you used Google, by the time you started to write them down, you'd easily fill up this entire blank sheet of paper.

"That's what law is like. When I asked you, you immediately began to name what you knew based on your understanding, but just as laws change and we have to interpret said changes, our knowledge of the universe and our laws are ever evolving. This blank sheet of paper simply aims to explain what we are looking for in a candidate. Someone who can see this blank page as not just a blank page, but rather a canvas to expand their mind to what currently must exist and be interpreted and someone who sees this blank page as endless opportunities. The question is, are you that person?"

This simple conversation intrigued Mark. An hour later, he was still there, discussing the law, interpretation, torts, and what angles of the law meant the most to him, as well as those clients he'd one day represent.

After the conversation, he was sure that Thurgood Marshall School of Law was the law school that he wanted to attend.

"How was it?" Jasmine asked as Mark opened the door.

"Damn, babe, can you kiss me first? What does a guy gotta do to get some love around here?"

"Boy, shut up and just tell me how the mixer went."

"J, honestly, it was amazing. I met sooo many representatives, talked to all of them, and I am even more excited to go to law school now than before... barring, of course, that I didn't bomb the LSAT."

"What did I tell you about putting bad vibes in the universe? You're going to do amazing, clown." Jasmine was always giving Mark affirmation. She always supported him but also continued to pour positive vibes into his cup of doubt.

"I met with Harvard and Princeton, and it was amazing. Their programs and what each has to offer are so inspiring. Like, if I got in, it would be amazing and perfect for the type of future I aim to build. I literally talked to everyone. It was a phenomenal event for sure."

"Babe, I'm not surprised," Jasmine said. "They're both really good programs. You can't lose with either of those. So, which one gave you the most rhythm?"

"I feel like they all did, but I gotta be honest, Thurgood showed me things today that I wasn't expecting."

"Showed you things? What do you mean?"

"I don't know exactly how to explain it. It was just like they saw past the law and torts . . . They spoke to me, like *really* spoke to me. We talked about the purpose of law. Honestly, it expanded my thoughts of law school. It was about more. It was about me. It was about life. We talked about the true purpose of the interpretation of the law. Not just right and wrong. I was impressed. We sat for over an hour or so, just talking about what kind of lawyer I wanted to be. We discussed the power a true attorney could have over making someone's life better. It was as if they spoke primarily about purpose, and the fact that if purpose were found, the law would always seek it out and join it toward a just result. It was remarkable!"

"Wow, that sounds incredible. Plus, it has you talking like you're Plato or Aristotle, or someone," Jasmine joked.

"Honestly, that's how I felt. It was as if they looked past the law and discussed what it should truly mean to be an attorney, regardless of which type of law you practice. So strange, yet so refreshing," Mark said pensively.

"But wait, you already know you want to practice personal injury. I'm confused."

"J, that's what I'm saying. We talked about personal injury, corporate, contract, and even civil law. But I feel like they invested in me. Like me-me. They took an interest in me and showed me a whole different side of the law. It was so interesting. They had a blank sheet of paper on their table. I asked them about it, and this dude opened my eyes to a whole new idea of the law. There I was, thinking law was about black and white written text, and this representative sat down with me and truly opened my eyes. It was transformative!"

"So, what are you thinking?" Jasmine asked.

"I dunno, babe. On the one hand, I want one of the most prestigious universities, but then tonight, it all changed. I feel like they spoke to me in a way that others haven't. They spoke about more than law. They spoke about life, meaning, and what law could become with an open mind."

Jasmine was intrigued. Mark went on and on, and she just listened in support. She knew Mark wanted so badly to have degrees on his wall from Harvard or Princeton, but she was excited that he finally saw that law school was about more than just the prestige. She was happy that he saw what law could really mean.

They spent the entire night discussing options and why Mark was so excited about Thurgood Marshall Law.

Finally, Jasmine had had enough. "OK, OK, clown. Enough about that. Come here to me and make love to me, baby," she said as she took off her shirt.

"Oh, you want it like that?" He smiled.

"Well, if you wanna talk more about law, sure, we can do that, but I'm just going to get naked and lie here wanting you!"

"Your wish is my command, gal."

Jasmine stood up, grabbed the back of his neck, and pulled him down to the bed.

"Oh, you weren't playing, were you?" he said jokingly.

"Does it feel like I'm playing?" she whispered into his ear.

They stayed up all night... making love and talking about his time at the mixer and about Jasmine's upcoming entrance exam.

The next morning, Jasmine woke before Mark, so she grabbed

her backpack and went downstairs to study.

When Mark woke up, he went downstairs, saw Jasmine studying, kissed her forehead, and said, "I'll make us some coffee, babe."

"Thanks, babe. I feel ready for this exam, but I just want to ace it, you know. I don't want to have to worry about getting in or if I'll have to lean on my extracurricular activities. BU wants a score of 150 or better, which I'm certain I can get. I just want to do really well."

"Are you certain you want to go to BU, though?"

"I mean, I know the people. I already know the university. I just feel like it would be a smooth transition."

"Yeah, but what if I get accepted to Harvard or TG? Are you staying here or moving to Texas?"

"I mean, I would, but I just want to stay here. I guess I'm just comfortable here."

"So, what you're saying is you want to do long distance for two years? I mean, I won't be here, so how will we make that work?"

"You want to start that fight today, Mark? Really? Today, of all days?"

"I'm not trying to fight, but you don't think it's something we should discuss?"

"Yeah, but for me, it's not even a choice. In my mind, it doesn't matter where we go. You could be in Alaska, I could be in Wyoming, and it would not change my mind on what I want with us. I want to spend my life with you. So, two years of a long-distance relationship or even three doesn't change how I feel. Why are you so stressed about what might or might not happen anyway?"

"Jas, I'm not trying to fight, babe. I just think we should discuss if we really want to do long distance for years. I mean, if I am *all* the way on the other side of the country, and we're both studying like crazy, how can it work? I think it's worth discussing, babe."

"Cool, but it doesn't sound like a discussion, Mark. It sounds like you already know what you want to do. Like you want to just end it if we don't end up in the same part of the country."

"I'm not saying that, though. Damn, forget it. I just wanted to talk about the inevitable, and it's turning into an argument. Never mind. Keep studying. I'm going to go upstairs to shower."

"Baby, I'm sorry." Jasmine grabbed his hand, brought him closer, and hugged him. "I just don't like thinking that we're going to end just because our lives are changing. Mark, we've planned for this and always knew we would be apart at some point for a while, so it coming true doesn't deter me from what I want, and it shouldn't deter you either."

"I know, Jas, and I love you. I just don't want us to be studying like crazy and trying to keep us going and have it distract us from what we are trying to accomplish." Mark left the conversation cold, shaking his head as he turned away.

As he walked upstairs, Jasmine watched him walk away. She sat there, wondering what would become of them.

As Mark was nearly out of sight, he looked back and said, "I love you, babe."

"I know. I love you too." She smiled.

After that conversation, they rarely discussed the topic of where they would end up. Jasmine eventually took her entrance exam, and she knew she did well. She spent the remainder of the semester volunteering when she wasn't in class.

As the semester neared its end and they were both awaiting the results of their prospective exams, their relationship felt cold. Though they were still sleeping together, they never discussed the inevitable. Instead, they practically pretended it wasn't coming.

CHAPTER 4
THE UNKNOWN

Light rain fell onto the roof as mild winds blew past the bedroom window. At 2:43 a.m. on Tuesday, Jasmine's eyes began to open as she awoke slowly at first and then with a jolt.

Looking around in the dark until her eyes adjusted, she could feel her stomach churning. The feeling went from nausea to heartburn, and it was unrelenting.

Grimacing in pain, she clenched her pillow in her right hand, and her stomach in her left, trying to soothe the sharp pains that had woken her up. When that didn't work, like muscle memory, she reached out for her point of relief, Mark.

He wasn't there. Mark had received acceptance letters to the University of San Fran, Thurgood Marshall, and Harvard Law all in the same week. He was rightfully out celebrating with friends.

Gripping her pillow between her legs, she found temporary consolation, yet it rapidly dissipated. Tossing, turning, and wincing, she tried all she could to get these foreign morning pains to subside, yet nothing worked. She grabbed her phone and made a call.

"Hello," a sleepy voice answered.

"Mom, I'm in so much pain right now, and I don't know why."

"Baby, did you eat something bad? Have you been sleeping? Talk to me—"

She could hear the concern in her mom's voice because Jasmine rarely called for help.

"I don't know, I haven't been sleeping for a few days now, and this morning I just woke up with a sharp pain in my chest and stomach. I feel nauseous."

"Your stomach? Is it on your side? You might have appendicitis, love. Do you have a fever as well? Is the side of your stomach warm?"

"I don't know. I just know it hurts, Mama!"

"Where's Mark?"

"He's been out with his frat guys tonight."

"Well, Jas, grab that heating pad I got you and put that on your stomach. Peyton, wake up. Jas's stomach and side are hurting!"

"Nah, Mama, don't wake Daddy up—"

"Girl, he'll bring—"

"That's her?" her dad asked in the background.

"Mama, don't wake Daddy up. You know he'll worry."

"Here, give me the phone, Holly."

"Sweetie, talk to me," he said.

Jasmine had been restless a few nights on end, yet she figured the frigid Boston weather was finally catching up to her. It was merely her turn to weather the storm of influenza, which had seemed to spread throughout the entire city that spring.

She could hear the door being unlocked and Mark drunkenly fumbling around at the door.

"Baaabe," Mark yelled up to her.

"Is that Mark?" her father asked.

"Yes, sir."

"OK, you want me to bring Mama by? We can bring you some soup. Mama made her chili tonight."

"Nah, I'm OK. I just wanted to talk to y'all. I'll be all right.

I'm just in a little pain. Feeling nauseous." She downplayed it so as not to worry her parents.

"OK, Jas, well, we'll have our phones on. You call us if you need us, OK?"

"Yes, sir, I should be fine."

She hung up with her parents, as Mark came upstairs, reeking of alcohol.

"How was the party?" she asked.

"It was good. Derrick got way too drunk, but we had a good time. I just can't believe it's finally happening!"

"Well, you worked for it, so I never doubted it."

He kissed her, drunk and in good spirits. "Thanks, babe. I'm going to shower real quick, then lay down. I drank way too much."

She hadn't told him how she was feeling because she didn't want to spoil his mood.

"Wanna join me?" Mark asked with a side-eye.

"Nah, babe, I'm good. I already showered, plus I don't feel too well."

A few minutes later, Mark was in the shower, singing in drunken tones… "Reasons, reason that we're heeere…"

When he got into the bed, Jasmine rolled over to him, trying to cuddle up next to him for comfort.

"Babe, it's too hot and I'm drunk. Not tonight," he said, annoyed.

"I wasn't looking for anything. I just needed to be next to you," she replied.

"Baaabe, I don't feel great."

"OK… well good night," she conceded.

Jasmine rolled over. She lay there thinking about how all she wanted was for Mark to have a good night after his acceptance into Thurgood Marshall. She felt at that moment that she only thought about his happiness, but at every turn, he rarely put her first… rarely caring how his actions made her feel. She never asked much of him, but tonight she needed him. He couldn't make her feel better, but simply caring for her in the moment would have helped. Instead, she just rolled over and tried to sleep, yet she tossed and turned all night. Jasmine didn't know if his lack of concern bothered her the most or the pain and unrest she felt from within.

A long while later, she got out of the bed slowly so as not to disturb Mark. She placed her feet on the cold hardwood floor and took sure slow steps. Heel to toe, heel to toe, across the creaky floors until she reached the bathroom. Even with all the pain she was in, she was thoughtful of Mark. She didn't want to wake him since she knew he had practice in the morning.

When she got to the bathroom, she stared into the mirror as though looking for answers. Wondering what was wrong internally, she just stood at the sink, hands placed on both sides, mentally begging for the pain to subside. As she clenched her stomach and bent down over the side of the bathtub, her mouth began to water.

She had felt this feeling before, but it was usually after a long night of partying with friends, getting home, lying on the bed, and exhaling as the room would begin to spin. It happened on those nights when the cheap college alcohol was too much for the human body and had to come out.

Sure enough, Jasmine knew this feeling. She rushed to the toilet and began to vomit. Now she was worried.

Mark heard her moving around. "Hey, are you—" He dozed back off.

Jasmine couldn't hear him because she was vomiting.

When she finished, she went to the sink and began to wash her face. Out of the corner of her eye, she glanced at the partially opened medicine cabinet. There was an assortment of items, but the one she focused on was a little square packet with silver lining over the top of it.

As she reached for the packet, she immediately took her hand away as though she was fearful of what might be inside. Looking back into the mirror, Jasmine was worried. She slowly reached into the medicine cabinet and removed the packet. Pulling out the contents, she read the packet and lowered her head.

"No, no, no, this can't be. Not like this," she whispered softly to herself. "It's just a bug. It's the flu. I didn't miss that many. This can't be happening right now."

Finally, Jasmine's hand grazed the packet and revealed it was her birth control medication. Several of the pills were gone, but several remained. She had clearly forgotten to take several pills.

As she grazed her fingertip over the packet and began to count the days, her countenance became more and more worried. Trying to ignore the pain within her, she could only focus on whether her internal battle was somehow related to the number of birth control pills that were not supposed to be there.

"How did I miss so many? How?" she whispered.

She took the mouthwash out of the cabinet and swished it around, washed her face, and slowly walked back to the room. As she turned off the bathroom light, she felt a sense of calm in her stomach, so she figured all was OK and that her body had just needed to rid itself of something bad that she'd eaten.

Slowly lying back down so as not to stir Mark, she pulled the covers up to her shoulders and clinched the pillow close to her chest. Just as she began to doze off, this nauseous routine started all over again. She began to toss and turn...

"Are you OK? Damn," Mark asked, annoyed. He had little concern for her well-being in his voice. "Can you please quit moving? It's keeping me up, Jas," he said angrily.

In too much pain to reply, Jasmine simply lay there, still trying to balance her frustration with his lack of concern with the intestinal battle she was dealing with at the time.

She lost this mental battle. With little to no warning, her

stomach informed her that she would need to take an immediate voyage to the bathroom.

Nauseous, restless, and annoyed by Mark's lack of care, she slung the covers from her body, nearly removing him from his fluffy cocoon.

"What the—?" he yelled.

Jasmine ran into the restroom and began vomiting again. As she was at the toilet, she caught a glimpse of her birth control packet, still partially removed from the cabinet.

She reached for the sink, trying to find her face towel to wipe her mouth. Washing her face, she looked into the mirror again, hoping she was just sick with the flu.

"Lord, pleeease," she whispered.

Jasmine was up and down all night; meanwhile, Mark slept like a baby.

Perceived Yet Not Believed

Gradually opening her eyes the next morning, Jasmine took her movements slow, hoping that the pain she'd felt all night was gone. She rolled back the blanket, placed her feet on the hardwood floors, and looked across the room to the full-length mirror. Feeling the cold wooden floors beneath her feet, she curled her toes and sat there in contemplation.

Thoughts racing through the coils of her mind; she wondered how she would even broach the subject of what could be with Mark. He was clearly more concerned with what was going on with his life than with what would become of them after this year.

Should she get a pregnancy test or just wait to see if she started her cycle? Jasmine sat there at the edge of the bed for what seemed an eternity, just contemplating what could be and how she would handle this potential next phase of their lives.

She grabbed her phone and saw several missed messages from her parents.

> Dad: Call us when you get up babe.
>
> Mom: How do you feel J? You OK? Do you need anything?

As Mark began to wake, Jasmine pulled back the blanket and walked into the bathroom. As she leaned over the sink and began to wash her face, Mark entered, hugged her from behind, and kissed her cheek as he walked to the toilet.

"Somebody was up all night. Better yet, somebody tried to keep me up all night," he said with a side-eye.

"Yeah, I didn't get much sleep at all. I didn't feel well all night."

He touched her forehead to check for fever. "Don't get me sick now. We have a game coming up," he said jokingly.

Jasmine quickly turned a sharp gaze toward Mark, nearly allowing an eruption of rage to spew from her lips, but instead she maintained her composure, shook her head, and rolled her eyes in frustration.

"Whoa, don't look at me like that," Mark said, gesturing his hands defensively in the air. "I'm just joking anyway."

She tried her best to keep her feelings off her face, though that didn't take away from her internal disappointment at Mark's response to one of the worst nights of her life.

"You don't seem to have a fever, though, Jas. Maybe it was something you ate. Perhaps it's time we switched it up and laid off that Chinese food for a bit. It had me feeling queasy the other night as well."

She washed her face, brushed her teeth, and just kept her thoughts to herself. She knew that she had to tell him somehow, but how? When?

Knowing Mark had a huge lacrosse tournament that weekend, she figured she'd find out for sure first and then talk to him.

"I think I'm going to go to the clinic on campus just to get tested for the flu, just to be sure," she said.

"Yeah, at least they can give you something to help the symptoms," he replied. "Let me know how it turns out."

He kissed her, brushed his teeth, showered, and went back to the room to get dressed.

"You're going to stay in the bathroom all day?" he asked.

"Nah, I'm about to go. I just need a minute."

"OK, I'll see you later. I'm going to meet up with the fellas and get some last-minute catches in before the match."

Mark was the star attacker for their lacrosse team. The team had had a great season and would be playing in order to make it to regionals. This game meant everything to Mark, yet his heart was fixed on going to law school, and as he put it, starting his life.

"OK, I'll just see you later," she said.

"K babe," Mark yelled as he was walking out. "Ugh, I'm never drinking again!"

Jasmine wasn't actually going to the clinic to get tested for the flu. She was more concerned that her life, and their future lives, had been changed by a decision they would both have to live with.

When Mark left, she slowly climbed back in bed. Drawing the covers over her head, she lay there, hands clenched in the sheets. She started to cry because she knew she would eventually have to make a hard choice. She cried because her life seemed to be headed in the perfect direction, yet this could alter the very path of her journey together with Mark.

She grabbed her phone and texted her parents back. She didn't want them to worry.

I'm much better now, maybe it was the food I ate.

She lay there for hours, wondering if she should get a pregnancy test or just wait. Wanting to sleep to take her mind off her mental battle, she tried to calm her mind and eventually doze off. After a short nap, she woke to the sound of the mail slot toggling downstairs.

Walking down the stairs, Jasmine became a little light-headed and began to stumble, but she figured it was because she had been up all night vomiting and hadn't eaten anything.

She walked past the front door and saw several envelopes, a small package, and what looked like a newspaper full of coupons for the local grocery store. Since she wasn't in a great mood, she walked past the mail and headed into the kitchen.

Jasmine aimlessly walked to the kettle on the stovetop and turned on the burner. Moving sluggishly through the kitchen, she grabbed a teacup from the second shelf and a spoon from the drawer. After filling the kettle with water, Jasmine became so weak from being sick and not eating that she had to rest midway through the process.

Jasmine was clearly in mental anguish, talking to herself and placing her head in her hands several times, only looking up to wipe the tears from her face. She wasn't sobbing, but the tears just continued to run down her face as if they flowed with purpose. She needed Mark to be there for her, but he wasn't.

As the kettle began to whistle its completion, Jasmine finally mustered up enough energy to complete her daily tea routine. She grabbed her honey, chose a book from the shelf, and sat back down at the table. It was a weird routine, as Mark had told her many times. She would blindly reach, take a book from the shelf, and pick up from wherever she'd left off reading last. She wouldn't read many pages, just enough to progress in context from her last "tea sitting."

Weirdly enough, though, on this morning's "tea sitting," she'd unknowingly selected one of her favorite self-help books that focused on switching our outlook on life from *what if* to *what is*. A book that she'd enjoyed many times, *The Flight of the Phoenix: Living Forward*, was all about taking the hand you are either dealt, or that you deal yourself, and making the absolute best out of all situations.

"Fitting that I would blindly select this book." She chuckled a bit as she sat back down.

She'd made her favorite green tea with mint, two slices of lemon, and a tablespoon of organic honey.

As Jasmine slowly stirred her tea, dipping her tea bag in and out of her cup, she glanced down at the book she'd read many times. It was like she was reading the book without even opening the pages. She thought about one of her favorite chapters, "I'm Still Breathing," which encourages the reader to understand that as long as they have breath in their lungs, they have a chance at life and an opportunity to course-correct past failures or current mistakes.

But there she sat... not drinking the tea, just stirring and placing the spoon on the table, and picking it back up just to stir the tea again. It was as if she had no plans to actually drink the tea or read her randomly selected book, but something about continuing with her routine brought her some sense of peace.

Eventually, Jasmine drank the tea, placed the unopened book back on the shelf, and placed the teacup in the sink.

She grabbed her purse and keys. "I'm just going to go and find out," she whispered to herself. She walked to the front door, grabbed the mail that was hanging in the slot, and placed it on the banister.

The entire drive to the pharmacy, Jasmine's mind weighed heavy. As her tears flowed, all she could think about was how her life might potentially be changed in a major way. At the pharmacy, she looked in the rearview mirror to wipe away the remnants of her final tears and ensure her mascara wasn't running down her cheeks.

"Can I help you, ma'am?" the store clerk asked.

"Yes, ma'am, where can I get a... get a pregnancy test?" She hesitated.

"That'll be in the pharmacy section, in aisle 8."

She grabbed three pregnancy tests, paid for them, and went straight home. When she arrived, she grabbed the mail from the banister and rushed upstairs.

Sitting on the edge of the bed, she placed the mail next to her and gazed into the restroom with an empty stare.

She had left the light on before she left for the pharmacy, so her attention was drawn to the medicine cabinet, where she could still see her birth control packet.

Jasmine gathered the mental strength to get up and walk into the bathroom. Reluctantly, she took the pregnancy test, sat it on the toilet seat, and quickly went back to the room. She put her head in her hands and softly began to pray as she sat on the edge of the bed.

"Lord, please don't let this be. I know I messed up, but please help me. I just can't be pregnant right now."

Minutes passed.

Jasmine was so afraid to go check on the test. Several times, she stood up, started walking toward the bathroom, and then quickly sat right back on the bed.

Finally, she stood up, walked slowly to the bathroom, and grabbed the test...

As she looked down at the test, she just stared for what seemed forever. She was hoping it was a false positive, but it was so clear. She lowered her head, began to sob, threw the test away, quickly opened the second one, and immediately took it.

As she sat on the toilet, she took the second test, and sat it on the bathtub's edge. Minutes later, she grabbed it, saw that it was positive, and fell to the floor crying.

Where was Mark? She needed him at that very moment. So many thoughts ran through her mind.

Eventually, Jasmine pulled herself off the floor and went back to the bedroom. She decided it was time to text Mark.

Just as she picked up her phone to type his name, she noticed the mail, and saw a familiar symbol on the front of the yellow envelope...

It was Boston University's nursing program's crest.

As her eyes filled with tears, she grabbed the envelope, still holding the second pregnancy test in her other hand. She opened the letter...

> Dear Ms. Hopkins, it is our pleasure and honor to congratulate you and welcome you into Boston University's prestigious nursing program. Your work in the community, excellent references, and exceptional entrance exam percentile, along with your overall academic performance, are just a few of the reasons we are excited for you to join our team.

The congratulatory letter continued, but Jasmine stopped reading and began to cry heavily. This was meant to be one of the happiest moments of her life, yet it was overshadowed by the very test she held in her other hand. She was at a mental crossroads.

Broken mentally, crying heavily, she fell to her knees, gripping her stomach and crying to the point of nearly vomiting.

She eventually gathered herself, grabbed her phone, and walked over to sit next to the full-length mirror. She pulled up Mark's number and began texting him.

> How'd the game go?
>
> Where are you?
>
> When are you coming home, babe?

Just as she was about to press send, Mark walked through the door. Jasmine ran to the top of the stairs in hopes that she'd immediately find comfort in their love.

When she saw he was with some of his lacrosse teammates, she stopped at the third step, so Mark figured that he and the guys had woken her up from her sleep.

Nothing a little hug and a kiss can't cure, Mark thought.

Fresh off their regional lacrosse victory, Mark and his teammates were very excited because this win meant that they would move to the next round of the NCAA tournament.

All very excited, they were laughing and scream-singing Boston University's alma mater fight song.

As the fellas walked toward the kitchen, to no doubt raid the refrigerator for what little sustenance lay within, Mark began to climb the stairs in order to quickly apologize with a kiss for waking her.

As he began to walk up the steps to kiss and hug her, his excitement quickly turned to concern as he got closer and realized that she had been crying.

Wiping her eyes as Mark got higher up the stairs, Jasmine thought, *How in the world will I tell him this?* She literally had no idea what she should do. She turned and ran back into the bedroom.

Mark looked back toward the kitchen and yelled, "Yo, y'all go grab a beer, and get me one ready. I'll be right back." He left the guys to raid the kitchen.

One of his overly giddy teammates replied, "All right, man. You can *play house* later. It's time to party, bro!"

By this time, Mark arrived at the top of the stairs, and he could see the bedroom door open, with Jasmine's legs hanging off the edge of the bed.

As Mark walked into the room, his eyes were immediately drawn to the open yellow envelope sitting in the middle of the bed. Since Jasmine didn't say anything when Mark walked through the bedroom door, Mark figured this envelope had something to do with her somber mood.

He grabbed the envelope, saw the nursing emblem, and immediately thought that she didn't get into BU's nursing school. "Oh baby, nooo. It's going to be OK. It'll work out. This was just one school."

"Nooo, baby, no. That's not it. I got in!"

"Well, what's wrong, J? Talk to me. You should be on cloud nine right now, baby. This is amazing!"

She looked up to him with tears in her eyes, "I know. I know I should be but, baby..." She exhaled. "Baby, I fucked up, like I really really messed up," she said, panting and breathing heavily. "I don't even know how to say this—"

He knelt down next to her and replied, "What is it? Just tell me."

"Umm, OK, well, Mark, umm, I think I might be pregnant."

"Are you serious? How? When? We were so careful. I mean, J, you've been on the pill. We even used condoms most of the time. What the hell? How could this happen?" Mark nervously berated her with questions.

"Well, you remember I told you I missed a few of my pills. I mean, I was originally just taking them to regulate my hormones."

He began to rationalize. "What are we going to do? Let me have the guys leave."

"No, y'all go ahead and celebrate. I'm just going to rest, baby."

"No, this is way more important than some stupid game. We need to go get a test immediately, J, to find out. We will figure this out." Mark appeared really supportive at that moment.

Jasmine pulled back the pillow where she'd put the second test, "Baby, I already took two pregnancy tests, and they were both positive," she said as she lowered her head and handed him the test.

"I'll be back, babe. Let me get the guys to leave."

Mark went downstairs, frantic and rubbing his head with worry. "Hey guys, I hate to do this, but I need to deal with something."

"Awww, come on, man. We're here tonight. We're raging. You realize how big tonight was? We are going to the tournament, man. Yo, Jas, he'll come up in a bit," one of the guys yelled.

"Nah, serious, fellas. I need to deal with something. I'll hit y'all tomorrow!"

The guys left, and Mark ran back upstairs, nearly tripping on his way up, he was moving so fast.

They sat and talked through the pros and cons, the ifs and if nots.

"What is my dad going to say?"

"How are we going to pay for law school, nursing school, and raise a child?" Mark asked rhetorically. "What are people going to think of us now," he said. "Babe, how did this happen? You were on the pill."

"Yeah, but I told you several times that I had missed a few. I feel like you're blaming me for this, Mark."

"I'm not blaming you. I just don't know what we are going to do. Like how the fuck did this happen? And what is 'a few'?" Mark asked facetiously. "OK, OK, let's just take a moment. Let's figure this out," he said trying to calm the conversation down.

Mark grabbed Jasmine's hand as she began to cry. "Granted, neither of us wanted a child at this age, but we're adults, and I'm making decent money for now at the law office. I think we can be fine. I have no idea how, but I know we can figure it out. Do you want to keep it?" he asked.

"You mean, do *we* want to keep the baby, right?" Jasmine paused for his reaction.

Mark shook his head, and replied as if he was annoyed, "You know what I mean, Jas. Come on, now. Don't do that, please. I'm just asking a simple question."

Clearly upset that he'd even asked, Jasmine turned from Mark. As he reached out to grab her arm, she jerked away from him and shook her head.

"Hey, we're in this thing together. I'm just looking at all options here, Jas. What am I to do? I'm not ready to be a father. Are you ready to be a mother?"

"Well, it's funny how none of those questions came out when we were having sex, Mark." Jasmine stormed out of the room and went downstairs to the kitchen.

Mark chased her. Catching up to her before she reached the final step, he reached out to grab her arm in comfort. Look, I'm sorry. I'm just a bit overwhelmed by all of this. I didn't mean to upset you."

Jasmine pulled away from him still...

"It's not so much that you basically asked about an abortion. It's the fact that this is all I have been thinking about all day, and the moment I tell you, the moment I need you to just be here with me, now, right here... The very moment I tell you shit that changes both of our lives forever, that's one of the first things to come out of your mouth."

Jasmine placed her head in her hands and sighed. "I'm hurt because all I've needed all day was for you to talk this out with me, and it's like this was a total waste of time because all you can think about is a way out or how we got here. Like, have you even stopped to consider what I'm feeling right now?" Her voice escalated as she expressed and unleashed her disappointment.

"Baby, I said I was sorry. We can talk this thing out and figure out the best route for us, OK? I love you!" He grabbed her and hugged her. "Let's just figure this thing out, Jas."

Jasmine initially tried to pull away from Mark's embrace, but she eventually folded into the warmth and comfort of his arms, and just for a moment, everything was OK.

Jasmine and Mark spent the entire night talking, holding

each other, and trying to work out the gravity of what their lives would become.

Two Lines

"Hello, I'm Rachael Takareno, and I'm going to be taking care of you all today. So, what brings you in today Ms.... Hopkins?" Nurse Rachael said as she looked down at her paperwork, searching for Jasmine's name.

"Well, we're actually here to get a pregnancy test," Jasmine answered.

"Oh OK, well, let me take your blood pressure, weight, and height, and we can get you all set up and started."

Mark went with Jasmine to the appointment, but he sat quietly in the extra chair in the room, contemplating. Was this really going to be their lives, going forward?

As the nurse left the room, Mark stood up and walked over to Jasmine, who was sitting on the in-room med table. He reached out and grabbed her hand. "Are you OK?"

"No. How could I be OK, Mark? Are you serious right now? I mean, I took multiple pregnancy tests, and we're basically here just hoping that they were false positives. Like what are the chances that they will be?" Jasmine asked.

"Well... it happens, Jas. Plus, we're here to find out definitively so we can make an educated decision about our future."

"OK, but—"

The nurse walked back into the room. "OK, are you ready? I'm just going to take a few vials of your blood, then we'll send it off to the lab. You did the right thing, by the way. Blood is the most accurate way to determine if you are, in fact, pregnant. Now

I have to ask you some questions."

"OK," Jasmine replied.

"So, when was the last time you had unprotected sex?"

"Well, we've been having both protected and unprotected sex for quite some time, so I don't really know."

"OK, that's fine, but y'all have had unprotected sex after your last menstrual cycle, correct?" the nurse confirmed.

"Yes, ma'am, we have."

"OK. Are you on any oral contraceptives? I'm sorry, I have to ask these questions."

"It's fine, and yes, I'm on birth control, but I've missed a few pills. My doctor originally prescribed them in order to help regulate my period, but once we started having sex, we used condoms mostly, but sometimes we didn't. Stupid, I know!" Jasmine said as she lowered her head.

"No, no, no honey, you're not stupid at all. That's very common with couples, but let's not worry until we have to. We will simply send your bloodwork to the lab, get the results, and then we'll know for sure, OK? So don't worry, ma'am, we'll find out, and you all can go from there." The nurse was very reassuring.

Mark held Jasmine's hand as the nurse pulled out a thin rubber tube, wrapped it around Jasmine's arm, inserted the needle, and began filling the vials with blood.

She concluded, and said, "OK, Dr. Dixit will come in a bit and discuss how the blood test works, and answer any further questions you two might have."

Jasmine and Mark sat there in silence, Mark holding her hand while Jasmine pressed the cotton ball against the injection point.

Dr. Dixit entered. "Mr. and Mrs. Hopkins—"

"Oh no, we aren't married," Jasmine said, laughing.

"Oh, sorry," Dr. Dixit replied hastily. "Well, Ms. Hopkins, we've taken your blood, and we'll send it off to the lab for testing. Once we hear back, we will give you a call and inform you of the results. Now, my nurse said that you took a pregnancy test at home. Is that accurate?"

"Yes, sir, we did, but we didn't know how accurate they were."

"Well, you did the right thing. The blood tests are about ninety-nine percent accurate, so it's better to know for sure, so you all can truly know where you stand. Again, we'll get the results and give you a call in a couple days to confirm. Are you having any symptoms now?"

"Symptoms like what?" she asked.

"Well, let's start with, are you late on your menstrual cycle?"

"Well, like I told the nurse, I was taking birth control to regulate my period, but I missed a few. Plus, we were using condoms off and on, and my period has been irregular for quite some time."

Jasmine lowered her head, and Dr. Dixit reassured her, "Yes, birth control can throw off your cycle, especially if you miss pills. Again, let's not worry until we have to. We'll get the results and then we'll know, OK?" He clenched his lips and nodded.

"OK, thank you!"

"All right. My nurse will come in and get you all checked out, OK?"

"OK, thank you," Mark said.

The next two days seemed to be the longest of Jasmine's life as she waited for the phone call from the doctor's office.

Wednesday at 11:22 a.m., her phone rang from a number that she didn't recognize, so she just knew it had to be from the doctor's office. Afraid to answer and hear the definite results, she let it go to voicemail.

"Ms. Hopkins, this is Christina from Doctor's First Family Medicine, and I'm calling you because we have the results of your bloodwork. Please give us a call at 617-330-8004 at your earliest convenience so that we can review your results. Thank you."

She listened to the voice mail and immediately texted Mark. *Babe, the results are in, they left me a voicemail, but I haven't called them back yet. Can you let me know when you're coming home? I'd like to call them back with you.*

Mark responded quickly. *OK I will be there after practice, babe. See you soon.*

Jasmine couldn't wait, though. She had to call...

"Ms. Hopkins, you are, in fact, pregnant. From your hCG levels, the lab estimated that you're about six weeks pregnant. Would you like to come in and speak with one of our counselors?"

"No, thank you. I'm good. I just needed to know for sure. Thank you for calling."

Jasmine hung up the phone and fell on the bed, clenching the pillow between her legs. She wanted to cry, but she'd cried all the tears she had. Instead, she lay there, waiting for Mark to get home.

How would she tell her parents? What would she do? Would they keep the child? Would they abort? So many thoughts clouded her mind, but no answers came.

When Mark got home, he dropped his gear at the door and ran up the stairs.

Walking into the bedroom and seeing Jasmine's countenance, he could tell she had something to tell him.

"Well, it is official, babe. I'm pregnant. The results came back, and I couldn't wait. I had to know." Jasmine said softly and emotionless.

Mark sat down on the bed in silence. He leaned his back against the head board and closed his eyes, while Jasmine placed her head on his chest, and the two were there, in silence, until they drifted off to sleep.

CHAPTER 5
ACCEPTANCE GOING DOWN

Over the next three weeks, Jasmine and Mark had many heated discussions, yet ultimately settled on keeping the baby.

Meanwhile, Mark had been accepted to TG Law, and Jasmine was finally excited that she was accepted to BU's nursing program.

A few of her friends wanted to throw her a party in celebration, not knowing all that she and Mark were dealing with at the time. She turned it down, telling them she wanted to focus on finishing out her semester, but really, she just wasn't in the mood to celebrate, considering all she was dealing with.

They were approaching what Mark referred to as "the point of no return" in her pregnancy. So, two weeks later, Mark and Jasmine decided to go back to the doctor and have Jasmine tested to ensure everything was OK with the baby.

Though Mark wasn't on board with having a child this early in their careers, he was supportive, and they both agreed that they could figure it out somehow.

During the appointment, they checked Jasmine's uterus, poked, prodded her, and ran every blood test in the book. Since the office had recently purchased and set up their very own in-house diagnostics center, they were able to run her blood test and provide results within the hour.

"So, just so you all know, as you get further into your pregnancy, we also have the ability to run genetic testing on the fetus, Ms. Hopkins," the OB resident said.

"What's the purpose of those tests?" Jasmine asked, perplexed, leaning back on the table.

"Well, we usually run these tests to identify if the child is predisposed to any genetic illnesses or if the child has a chance of having certain developmental deficiencies like Type 2 Osteogenesis, fetal infections, and other potential defects. Think of it as a risk assessment for you to have all the necessary information for your pregnancy. We offer these in case the parents want to know more so they can make an informed decision on carrying to term or terminating the pregnancy. Now, you're only at about eleven weeks of your pregnancy, so we'd wait until you're fifteen to sixteen weeks to perform the tests, in order to ensure accuracy...so about a month from today. But today, we'll focus on your bloodwork and make sure everything is going well with you."

"Oh no, we don't need those additional tests," Jasmine quickly replied.

"Wait, Jasmine... don't you think we need to know these things going in?" Mark asked, moving closer to Jasmine.

"I'll give you two a few minutes to think it over so you can discuss it with Dr. Dixit and get more clarity," the OB resident said as she exited the room.

Jasmine and Mark talked about the pros and cons of the tests as the doctor left the room.

"Why would we need to know the results of potential defects, Mark? Like, what value does that hold for us at this point?" she asked.

"Jas, are you serious? We need to know because this could be potentially life-changing for both of us. We need all the facts in order to make the right decision. Don't you think?"

"Mark, there's no right decision to be made here. Our lives are already changed. What will a test tell us that will change our minds about whether to keep the child or not? Will we even be able to abort the pregnancy at that time, anyway? I mean, I'd be nearly four months pregnant at that time, and there's no way I could go through with an abortion."

"I'm not saying that. I'm just saying that we need to know, babe. Like the resident said, it's so we can make an informed decision and not just a decision."

"OK, OK, Mark. If you think that is best, then sure." Jasmine, simply mentally exhausted from discussing the issue, gave in. "Yeah, that's fine. This is all just too much for me right now, babe," she said as she lowered her head.

This should have been Mark's cue to back off, but staying true to form, he rarely acknowledged Jasmine's needs, and proceeded. "I know, babe, but we're in it together, so let's just have all the facts so we can make an informed decision together."

A few minutes later, Dr. Dixit entered the room. "So my resident let me know that she told you all of the additional screening and testing that we offer. To put your mind at ease, we don't offer these tests to scare anyone because there is a great chance your baby is growing just fine. We offer these tests because technology now allows us to be fully informed and as ready as possible to bring a child into this world or make decisions that are best for all parties involved."

Dr. Dixit sat down next to Jasmine. "To be clear, there is absolutely *zero* pressure for you to have any additional screening. You two have come today to ensure that everything is in order with you, Ms. Hopkins, and I have those results. So, you're already on the right path," he assured her as he reached out and grabbed Jasmine's hand in comfort.

"OK, thank you so much for putting my mind at ease, Dr. Dixit. Mark and I talked it over, and we think we'd like to move forward with the additional testing or screening, but would like more time to think it over. Is that OK?" Jasmine looked at Mark, and the two nodded in agreement with each other.

"Absolutely, I believe that's an excellent idea, and that you all have made the right decision. There is no harm in being fully prepared. This is a huge change to your lives, so why not have all the information? Take the time that you need to discuss it. Give my office a call sometime next week, and let my staff know what you all decide, and we'll be with you all every step of the way."

Jasmine smirked at Mark, since she felt the doctor agreed with him, and said, "OK."

"So now let's focus on your blood test results for today, and then my nurse will come in and discuss the process for the next appointment, should you all decide to move forward with additional testing. OK?"

Jasmine and Mark nodded.

Dr. Dixit continued, "Reviewing your labs, it looks like everything is in order. Your bloodwork looks clean, you're healthy, but your cholesterol slightly concerns me as it is a little high for your age, but it's not terrible."

"Probably all that Chinese food," Mark whispered as he pulled his chair closer to Jasmine and held her hand.

While Dr. Dixit continued to deliver the good news, Jasmine and Mark both took turns sighing in relief as they looked at each other and smiled. When the doctor finished, he asked, "Any additional questions for me?"

"No, but thank you, Dr. Dixit, for taking the time to explain everything to us. We're clearly new at this," Mark joked.

Dr. Dixit laughed. "The funny thing is, sir, every parent was new at this at some point, myself included!"

As the three of them laughed and enjoyed a lighthearted

moment, Dr. Dixit waved goodbye and left the room.

Mark and Jasmine waited patiently and quietly for the nurse to re-enter the room and discuss the next appointment.

Though the two sat in silence, the thoughts in their minds were loud enough for Mark to look up and see the mental anguish upon Jasmine's face. Standing from his chair, he grabbed Jasmine's head softly, and laid it on his chest, stroking her hair. "Everything is going to be just fine. Do you know how I know? Mark asked.

"How, Mark? How do you know?" Jasmine asked with a smirk.

"Because you are YOU, and that has always been enough!" Mark reassured her.

She kissed him. "Thank you, babe," she said.

As the nurse entered, she explained the procedure to them and then discussed the timing of the test and potential outcomes.

"So just give us a call next week, and confirm if you want to keep this temporary appointment that I'm going to set for you all, which will be a month from today. Ok?"

The two nodded in unison.

The nurse continued, "The exams usually take an hour, and the results usually take about a week to receive. Once we have all the results, we'll bring you back into the office, and Dr. Dixit will walk you through them and answer any questions you all might have, OK?

"OK, that sounds good," Jasmine and Mark both replied.

The two didn't wait an entire week to decide, but, rather, discussed the additional testing the entire way home and into the night. After a night of discussing their fears about the possibilities, they ultimately decided to call the next morning and confirm the appointment.

Those four weeks of waiting were among the longest four

weeks of Jasmine's life. All she could think about was the test and the potential that something would be wrong with her baby. Although Mark did his best to reassure her, nothing seemed to comfort her enough to focus on the positives and the chance that their child would be perfectly fine.

Their relationship seemed bleak as the potential of raising a child while in school weighed heavy on both of them. The strain was taking its toll. Throughout these four weeks, they simply coexisted, barely studying together and barely speaking about the upcoming doctor's appointment.

Mark had received a date for his interviews down in Texas, and Jasmine received additional acceptance letters for nursing schools, though none in Texas had accepted her yet.

Finally, it was the week of Jasmine's additional screening, and she received a call from the doctor's office early Tuesday morning as she and Mark were sitting at the kitchen table.

"Ms. Hopkins, we're very sorry about the inconvenience, but we need to reschedule your appointment. We can still fit you in this week, though. It would just have to be on Thursday instead of tomorrow. Does that still work for you?" the office administrator asked.

"Yes, ma'am, that still works with my schedule, thank you," Jasmine replied.

"Babe, don't worry, I'll cancel the interviews. I can always go and interview." Mark whispered while Jasmine was on the call. He'd received an invite to fly to Texas and participate in a round of interviews for a law clerk position, so he set up his interviews to ensure he could go to the original Wednesday appointment with Jasmine and fly out the next day, Thursday.

"No, it's fine," she whispered back as she covered the phone's receiver.

She gathered her new appointment time, thanked the staff member, and hung up the phone. "No, it's fine, Mark. I can go to this appointment myself. They're just doing some testing, plus I don't want you and your weak stomach to see all of this anyway." Jasmine laughed.

Mark leaned over and kissed her forehead. "You're the best. You know that, right? But OK, I'll literally be right back Friday morning, and I want to hear all about it."

Jasmine shook her head. "Trust me. I've looked up what the testing includes, and you definitely won't want to know everything." She laughed.

When Thursday came, the day flew by. Mark headed to the airport, and Jasmine was going to the doctor's appointment like it was another regular day. Before leaving, Mark kissed Jasmine. "I'll call you as soon as I land to check on you. OK, babe?"

"OK, babe. I'm sure it'll be fine. Dr. Dixit, for some reason, is very comforting and has a calming presence."

"Yeah, he is, right?" Mark asked rhetorically, nodding his head.

After a tight embrace, they parted ways in two separate taxis. Jasmine decided to take a taxi to the appointment instead of driving because she didn't know what to expect afterwards...and of, course, she couldn't ask her parents to take her because they were still oblivious to the entire situation.

As she expected, Dr. Dixit was as comforting as she'd remembered, and he greeted her with a big smile. "OK, Ms. Hopkins, I have you in the hands of my best tech, and she'll get you all prepped for the procedure. I'll come back in a few minutes, and we'll have you all done in no time, OK?" Dr. Dixit smiled and rubbed Jasmine's shoulder.

"Thanks, Dr. Dixit," Jasmine replied.

Jasmine was all prepped, and Dr. Dixit and his team were starting the amniocentesis. He walked her through each step, but her mind drifted off as she lay there, thinking how much she wished Mark was by her side.

"Now you might feel a little pressure, but you shouldn't feel—" Dr. Dixit continued walking her through the procedure step-by-step, while Jasmine's mind was elsewhere.

As she allowed her mind to drift, Jasmine looked over and saw an empty chair in the procedure room. She flashed back to her last appointment when Mark was there with her, and just the thought of him being there brought her some comfort.

"OK, we're all done." Dr. Dixit said. "Not so bad, right?"

"No, it wasn't nearly as bad as I thought. Thank you, Dr. Dixit," Jasmine said in relief.

"Now, my nurse will come back in and explain what you can expect for the next few days. We'll monitor you here for an hour or so, and then we'll call you once we have all the results and bring you back in, OK?" Dr. Dixit was very thorough.

"OK, thank you, Dr. Dixit. About how long should I wait before I call to check on the results?" she asked nervously.

"Well, they can take up to two weeks, but we usually have them back in a week. Don't worry yourself with calling. We'll make sure we call you as soon as we have the results and get you back in, OK? Don't worry, my staff and I have you covered."

Jasmine thanked the team, and after an hour and half, they were ready to discharge her. Since Mark had already flown out, Jasmine had the staff call her a taxi home since she hadn't even told her parents that she was pregnant yet.

A part of her had waited so long to tell her parents because she worried about what they'd think of her, and the other side of her waited because she knew she and Mark were still unsure about keeping the child.

The next day, Mark returned, took a taxi to the apartment, and immediately ran into the house. "Jas, I'm back," he yelled before he could even get the door open.

"I'm upstairs," she replied from the bed.

Mark dropped his bags and ran up the stairs as if he were late for the final match of his lacrosse career. "So, how did it go? Are you OK? When do we get the results? How do you feel?" He peppered her with questions, concern in his eyes.

"Babe, relax. I'm fine. Everything went smooth and they'll call us back in when the results are ready," she replied as she waved him over to the bed. "Now come here, lie with me, rub my back, and tell me all about Texas." Jasmine always had a way of calming Mark down.

"Yeeesss, ma'am," Mark replied with a goofy smile on his face.

The two lay there and talked all night about the appointment and Mark's trip to Texas.

After getting clearance from his boss, Mark stayed home with Jasmine. They decided not to mention the tests again and just to help each other wait patiently for the results. They spent the week looking into childcare, baby shower ideas, and figuring out how they'd finally tell their parents.

Six days later, they received the call. By this point, they were both relieved to finally have the results. Hanging up with the doctor's office, Jasmine called for Mark, who was downstairs making breakfast. "Babe, they can fit us in today for all the results."

Mark could hear the excitement in Jasmine's voice. He ran upstairs, hugged her, kissed her, and said, "Perfect, and I know everything will be just fine! When can they see us?"

"They said we can come now because we are just getting the results, and they could fit us in," she said with a smile.

"Even better. I'll shower up and get dressed, and then we can head out," Mark replied as he rushed off to the bathroom.

It was like a mental weight had been lifted off their shoulders. They both breathed a sigh of relief.

CHAPTER 6
BACK AND CHANGED

Back at the doctor's office, Jasmine was more nervous about these results than she had been when she'd taken the first pregnancy test.

The nurse came in. "Well, the doctor is going to be in to share the results with you all and answer any questions that y'all might have."

"Do you not have the results?" Jasmine asked nervously.

Mark looked over and noticed Jasmine's hand was shaking quite a bit, so he reached out and grabbed it to comfort her. "All is going to be fine, Jas." He pulled her hand toward his face and kissed it.

The nurse reiterated, "Well, the doctor is more knowledgeable about these tests, so he's going to come in and go over them with you."

Jasmine and Mark sat in the room for what seemed an eternity, just holding each other's hands, wondering what results the doctor would walk in with.

Minutes later, two knocks on the door, and the handle began to turn... Jasmine's heart raced.

"So, Ms. Hopkins, great to see you two again," Dr. Dixit said as he shook Mark's hand.

"I have your results. From the Osteogenesis Type 2 test, it looks like we don't have to worry about that. The fetus seems to be growing just fine. That said, based upon your diagnostic exams, both the amniocentesis and the percutaneous umbilical blood sampling, it appears that there's a very high chance that your child will have Down syndrome. The way these tests are run, there's really no way of us knowing a hundred percent this early, but the fluids forming around the brain, as well as the—"

Jasmine tuned out because all she could hear was that not only was she pregnant with a child before she and Mark could start their lives, but that the child growing inside of her would have Down syndrome.

She was numb—no emotion, no tears, no facial expressions. She just sat, silent… as Mark squeezed her hands each time Dr. Dixit started a new and unfortunate sentence.

The appointment came and went, and all she could remember was hearing Dr. Dixit say, "Listen, this isn't the end. We have options, and you don't have to make any decisions today."

Mark and Jasmine left the appointment in silence and were silent the entire ride home. As they got closer to their apartment, Jasmine began to sob softly under her breath. Mark tried to console her, but she just leaned toward the door with her head pressed against the window, curled up in the passenger seat, crying.

This had become their reality… This was their now. This was their lives. In Jasmine's mind, life as they knew it had been not only changed but thrown a curveball that neither could see themselves escaping.

When they arrived home, Jasmine said, "Go ahead, I'm going to sit here for a bit."

"No, babe, I'll sit here with you," Mark replied softly.

"No, it's OK. I just need a moment, baby."

Jasmine sat in the car, crying while clenching her face within her hands. She pulled her shirt up, looked down, and touched her belly. She traced the outline of a heart as her tears ran from her face, down to her hands, now resting upon her stomach. She eventually got out of the car and went inside.

This was her life now. What will I do? She thought. *How will I survive this?* Thoughts poured through her head, yet no answers ensued... No feelings of encouragement, just the dark brisk night with her mind in turmoil.

The next two days were quiet, though the tension was high as unsaid thoughts filled the air of their apartment. Jasmine and Mark barely spoke, even though they both knew they needed to discuss the results and how they would move forward with their lives... yet no conversations were had. They just went to class, returned home, and barely broached the inevitable.

It was like they both were pretending the results didn't exist, as if they'd wake up from a dream, a nightmare that had altered their paths.

The next morning, when Mark woke, he could see Jasmine brushing her teeth from the bedroom. "Are we going to discuss this or just pretend that we didn't receive those results?" he asked. "I mean, at some point, we have to—"

Jasmine pretended as if she didn't hear him. As she continued her morning routine, Mark opened the door and stood in the doorway. "Babe, you didn't hear me?"

"I did, Mark, but I just don't know what to say right now. I don't know how to feel. I just feel like I'm just here, floating through life, with no ground to stand on. I feel empty. I just need you to be here right now, and I honestly can't tell you what that entails."

"I understand, babe, but we need to discuss our options, don't you think?"

"We do. I just can't now, babe. I just can't. I don't even know where to start. Just tell me what you want to do. You clearly have an agenda or an idea of what you want to do."

"I don't, though. I just think we need to discuss this. I mean, it's kind of important," Mark said, raising his eyebrows while walking farther into the bathroom.

"Mark, you don't think I know that?" Jasmine yelled. "I haven't even told my parents yet because this whole time, I knew you never really wanted to keep this child. So how can I tell them that their daughter is not only pregnant but that she's also having an abortion?"

"Whoa, whoa, I didn't say anything about that yet. Jasmine." Mark raised his voice.

"Yeah, yeah, but you may as well say it because we both know you're thinking it," she yelled.

"Well, I'm thinking it because the doctor said we didn't have that much time to decide on our course of action, seeing as you're nearly four months pregnant."

"Again, Mark, don't you think I know that?"

"Yes, I know you know that, Jasmine, but walking around pretending like we don't have to make a decision doesn't take away the fact that a decision must be made."

The two spent the remainder of the night going back and forth until Jasmine finally gave in, ran into the restroom, slammed the door, and got in the shower. When she turned on the water, she stood under the shower head, lifeless and saddened, allowing the water to hit her face and run down her body, masking her tears.

She was broken.

The next day, they went on and on, weighing the pros and cons. The more the conversation continued, the more Mark leaned toward terminating the pregnancy. While pointing out all the cons, it was as if Mark wasn't even considering keeping the child, but rather, he pushed and pushed Jasmine toward termination of *the situation*; as he put it.

Jasmine never made it clear what she wanted to do, but Mark knew she wanted to keep the child and figure it out.

Night after night, they began to argue more until they concluded terminating the pregnancy would be the best. Jasmine finally gave in because she feared losing everything that the two of them had created together, afraid of losing Mark and all they had built over the years. Mostly, she was mentally exhausted and had little fight left in her.

"Jasmine, this will be difficult for both of us," Mark said, "but I believe we can get through this, and this is the best for us right now and where our lives are going."

She barely responded when he discussed ending the pregnancy. Nonetheless, she was exhausted with the idea and tired of discussing a never-ending battle.

They called the clinic to set a date for the abortion, but due to how far along Jasmine was in her pregnancy, Dr. Dixit had ensured that she had a direct contact with a physician at the clinic who was prepared to walk them through the process.

She initially dialed the number, but when the help desk agent answered the call, Jasmine threw the phone down onto the bed, and began to weep.

Mark picked up the phone and set the appointment, but Jasmine would later have to take over the conversation, as patient privacy prohibited Mark from fully scheduling the appointment.

Jasmine concluded the call, looked at Mark, then turned around with her back to him, and went to sleep.

As the termination date quickly approached, Mark and Jasmine barely spoke. Their relationship was as cold as a brisk Boston night, as if they were two complete strangers cohabitating out of habit as opposed to choice.

The First Dual Heart

The night before Jasmine was supposed to have the abortion, she felt internally broken. She'd wanted to be a mom all her life, but she feared that now wasn't the time.

Would she be judged? Would there be protestors at the clinic, making her feel worse? How would she tell her father that she'd aborted a child within her? How had she become the girl who did everything right, yet these were the cards she'd been dealt, or the hand she'd dealt herself to play?

Though her initial morning sickness had passed, night after night, she woke in tears at what she had hesitantly agreed to do. Random times during the day and night, she'd rub her belly and trace the outline of a heart upon it, as it brought her some sense of peace.

As Jasmine lay there in the quiet Boston night, she raised her pajama shirt and looked down at her growing belly. She had done this several times before, turning away from Mark and proceeding with her nightly routine. It was like her alone time with the very child she had reluctantly agreed to terminate.

She began to feel more and more connected to the child growing within her. As she reached her fingertip closer to her belly to rub her baby bump for what would be the final time, she closed her eyes.

She began to trace the outline of a heart and imagined what it would be like if the child growing within met her finger and traced the outline with her. After completing the first side of the heart, she began to trace the outline of the second side of the heart. Jasmine was now imagining so hard that she felt what she thought was a little finger from within, joining her in the nightly routine of love.

Chills ran over her body. She jumped out of bed, ran to

the full-length mirror in the corner of the room, and began to sob. Whether it was in her mind or simply a flutter within her stomach, Jasmine knew then that her little one deserved a chance.

She believed and felt that her little one had reached up and traced the heart with her from within, imploring her to give them a chance.

"Is that you? Are you in there, little one?" she whispered rhetorically.

As she sat alone on the cold wooden floor, she wept. She thought about the life she wanted for herself. She pondered the life she wanted with Mark, and then she thought about the life within her.

How can I be a proponent of taking on life as it comes, with obstacles, and facing it head-on if I face my largest challenge and turn away from it? she thought and mouthed quietly.

This mental battle lasted hours, as she bounced back and forth between being confident in the decision she and Mark had reached, and *Should I just tell him I changed my mind, and I want to keep the child?*

She reached down again to trace the heart on her bump, hoping or praying that she'd feel the flutter again, as though it would be the sign from above what she needed to do.

However, no sign came, no flutter, just her, there on the floor in tears, contemplating the most significant decision of her life. She was in utter mental disarray.

As Mark slept, Jasmine remained awake all night, wrestling with the choice that had to be made the very next morning.

Flutter-esque

Jasmine woke just minutes before her alarm was supposed to go off. Opening her eyes, wondering if she would start crying, she just lay there for a minute. She was all cried out and exhausted from Mark and her staying up multiple nights discussing the future.

She reached for her phone in the dark, grabbed it, and turned off the alarm before it could sound. As she slid from under the blanket, she placed her feet on the wooden floor and whispered, "Mark can we talk? Mark, babe, are you awake?" she continued softly.

Mark laid there silent, so Jasmine nudged him. "Babe, wake up. I need to talk to you," she said.

As Mark began to stir, Jasmine stood up and walked to the other side of the bed. When she sat at Mark's side, his eyes opened. She grabbed his hand, and Mark asked, "What's wrong, Jas?"

She laid her head on his chest and began to cry.

"What's wrong, Jas?" he asked as he stroked her hair.

"I just don't know if I can do this. Something happened last night, and I have no clue how to explain it to you."

"What do you mean 'something happened,' J? We talked about this. We can't keep going back and forth. Like, we have to make a decision and stick to it," Mark said as he began to sit up more attentively.

"Well, I just don't think it's that simple, though. Like, I don't know how to explain it to you, but I just think that we should discuss this again. I don't know if it's something I can go through with! Last night I was touching my stomach, and, and—"

"And what, J? Like, what do you mean 'something happened'?" Mark's tone was becoming increasingly annoyed as he was now fully sat up in the bed.

"Well, I was rubbing my stomach and tracing a heart on my

stomach, and I swear I felt a finger trace the same heart with me!"

"Jasmine, that's not even possible at this point in your pregnancy. Like, come on, you're allowing your mind to play tricks on you. Seriously."

"No, Mark, I'm telling you, I'm not. I know what I felt, and even if it was in my mind, it doesn't take away from the fact that I feel like the baby has the right to live."

"OK, Jasmine. Well, you tell me. How in the world do we pay for law school? Nursing school? Raise a special needs child—"

She cut him off. "Potentially special needs child."

"OK, you want to take that chance based on potential? Really?"

"No. I don't know Mark. I just know we need to talk about it some more." Jasmine began to cry harder and stumble over her words. "I—I... mean, it seems like your mind is already made up, so I'm just wasting my breath. Just forget it," she said in disgust, walking away.

"So, what do you want to do, Jasmine? You want to risk our entire futures on 'potential'? We already discussed this, and we came to a decision together. I understand what you're saying, but I don't want to have to worry about law school, us, and also a special needs child."

Jasmine quickly turned back to Mark, cutting her eyes at him, "You're unbelievable, Mark. How can you be so 'matter of fact' about this?"

"Stop it. That's not fair. I'm just speaking rationally and discussing what we already agreed to, damn!"

"Well, I'm changing my mind. This isn't what I want anymore. I can't do this!"

"Jasmine, what about my life? What about our lives?"

"Mark, what about the child's life? Do we just selfishly ignore that?"

"No, but it's early enough, and we aren't in the position to raise a child, let alone a child with special needs. Don't make me out to be the bad guy when we've already discussed this. Now you wait until the morning of the appointment to do this. To make me feel like I'm the bad guy for not wanting to ruin our lives."

The two argued all morning, and Jasmine had finally had enough. Mark had worn her down. Hours had passed, and they went from arguing around the room, to finally back in bed, still discussing the impending decision.

Eventually, they both got out of bed and went to the bathroom to shower. When Jasmine got in the shower, she closed the door before Mark could get in with her. She was so disgusted with his lack of willingness to budge on the idea, she didn't want him to shower with her.

Mark took the signal, turned to brush his teeth, and left the bathroom after. "I'm going to get dressed," he said.

Jasmine heard him but didn't answer. She had reluctantly agreed yet again to abort the child within her, and she just needed peace and quiet. As she walked to the room, neither of them spoke. They just got dressed, got in the car, and started the journey to the Planned Parenthood clinic.

The entire ride, they sat quietly. Mark tried to grab her hand and hold it, but Jasmine pulled back, turned toward the window, and just stared outside.

She had so many thoughts going through her head. All she could do was weep and whisper silent prayers of strength.

As expected, as they got closer to Planned Parenthood, they began to see protestors holding signs.

Kids Deserve Life Too…

What if your parents made this same drive, would you have wanted them to turn around?

You don't know when life begins, so why decide when it ends?

The signs went on and on. Jasmine looked at Mark and said, "Turn around. I can't do this. I just can't. I can't do this, Mark."

"*Uuuggghhh, Jasmine*," he yelled. "We talked about this. This is not the life that I want. We can't do this. We are not in a position to make this work. This wasn't the plan."

"Yes, we can! We can figure it out, babe. We didn't plan it, but we can figure it out. I just can't do this. Please turn the car around." She begged with watery eyes.

"Jasmine, I'm not turning around. We planned this. We talked about it. We've already decided."

With tears in her eyes, she turned to Mark and yelled, "Mark, let me out of this damn car now. You don't have to turn around, but I'm not doing this. I can't. I just won't!"

"Jasmine..."

"*Just stop the car, damn it!*" she screamed.

Mark stopped the car, barely making it to the side of the road before Jasmine was unlocking the door.

Jasmine got out and ran in the opposite direction on the sidewalk. As she was running and crying, a protestor approached her to provide her some comfort.

"It's going to be OK!" the white-haired woman said.

"Get away from me. You clearly don't know what I'm going through and have no idea how I feel or if things are going to be OK," Jasmine yelled.

As she ran away, Mark turned the car around to get her. Pulling the car up beside her as she walked on the sidewalk, he yelled, "Jasmine, get in the car, babe!"

"No, Mark, I'm not doing this. I'm just not!"

Mark was angry, "Fine. Then I'm not doing this, either. This isn't what I wanted." He sped off, leaving Jasmine there.

She sat on the curb and placed her head in her hands. "How did my life get here?" she whispered as her tears fell to the ground below. She sat there for nearly an hour, then grabbed her phone and saw a text from her father...

> Just wanted you to know that we love you, and we are rooting for you. Let us know when you hear from BU's nursing school.

Jasmine hadn't even told her parents that she had been accepted into nursing school because her mind was so clouded with her current situation.

She didn't respond. Instead, she called a taxi to take her home. When she arrived, she realized that her life really was about to change forever. Jasmine walked up to the door and was hesitant to walk inside, as she had no clue what awaited on the other side. As she opened the door, she could hear Mark rummaging upstairs.

"Mark, I'm home," she said.

Mark didn't respond. He just kept rummaging around.

As she sat at the base of the stairs with her head down, Mark started to walk downstairs. She looked back and noticed he had a suitcase in his hands.

"Oh really?" she asked sarcastically. "So, you're just going to leave like this?"

Mark threw his free hand up and shook his head, "Well, it doesn't seem like I have a say-so in this situation, plus this is *not* what I want Jasmine, and you know that."

"I don't want to worry about all the school we're about to be in and worry about raising a special needs child. Sorry, a potentially special needs child," he said with air quotes.

"You are such an asshole. I have stuck by your side through everything, and then this happens, and you're packing your bags that quick? Are you kidding me? What kind of man are you?"

"I'm just going to stay with my boys. I just need some space right now."

"*SPACE, REALLY?* What about what I need right now, Mark? I'm the one that you were basically pushing into getting an abortion, not your boys!" she yelled.

"So, you went back and had the abortion." Mark paused.

"Fuck you, Mark. Seriously, fuck you. No, I didn't go back to have an abortion alone. I told you, I can't do this, and I'm not doing this."

"Well, Jasmine, you know this isn't what I want, so I have to leave. I need some space right now to figure out my life. This isn't what I want."

Jasmine and Mark continued to argue. As Mark was about to walk out the front door, Jasmine grabbed him, pulled him closer to her, and pleaded with him. "How can you just leave me like this when you know this is difficult for me?"

"I told you already. This isn't what I want. I have to go."

"No, Mark. No, you don't. You're being a coward. You're choosing to walk away."

Mark placed the suitcase down. "I'm not a coward, but we had a plan, Jasmine," Mark raised his voice.

"Yeah, but plans change. Things happen. It's called LIFE, MARK!"

They continued to argue until Mark had had enough. He yelled, "*I'M DONE WITH THIS, AND I'M NOT THE VILLAIN BECAUSE THIS ISN'T WHAT I WANT.*" He stormed out of the front door, got in his car, and drove off in a rage.

Jasmine watched from the front door window as he drove away. Heartbroken and in disbelief, she sat down on the bottom step of the staircase, placed her head in her hands, and wept.

PART II

CHAPTER 7
PEYTON LOVE

Jasmine's parents were traditionalists and had never really liked the idea of Mark and Jasmine moving in together. However, this was the least of her worries. She knew it was time they knew her situation.

She called her mom, crying. "Ma..."

Her mom immediately knew something was off with Jasmine. "What's wrong, baby? Why are you crying? Talk to me."

"I need to talk to you and Dad."

"Well, your father's at work. What's going on?"

"Can I come over? I need to talk to you."

"Of course you can. I was just about to go to the grocery store, but I can go later. What's wrong, Jas?"

Jasmine just sat on the phone a while, crying. Her mother didn't pry, trying instead to calm her daughter down.

"Ma, I just messed up. I messed up big."

"It's going to be OK, baby. Whatever it is, we'll work through it. What's going on, Jas?"

The words were nearly impossible to say, but Jasmine got them out. "Mama, I'm pregnant... Mark and I got pregnant." As the words escaped Jasmine's lips, a deafening silence ensued. The two sat on the phone, Jasmine crying, her mother trying to piece together what to say to her daughter. Holly was disappointed in Jasmine, but she also just wanted to be there as a comfort for her.

Finally, Holly broke the silence. "How, Jas? I thought y'all weren't having sex, baby?"

"I know. We weren't, Mama, but then we did, and we continued. It just happened."

"Weren't you on your birth control for your period?" Holly asked, then she stopped herself. "You know what, that doesn't matter, baby. Come over, and we'll figure this out. Where's Mark?"

As her mother asked about Mark, Jasmine put the phone down and began crying hysterically.

"Jas, Jas, Jasmine, baby, pick up the phone. Talk to me. Baby, can you hear me?" It broke her mother down to hear Jasmine so distraught. Holly's eyes began to fill with tears as well.

Finally, Jasmine picked the phone back up. "I'm fine, Mama," she said through her tears, "but Mark left."

"He left? What do you mean he *left*?"

"He just left, Mama. We had a big fight."

"A big fight about the pregnancy? When was this, Jas?"

"Mama, I've been waiting to tell you all. It's still kind of early, but we've known for a while now. And… and… and he just left because I didn't want to have an abortion."

"An *abortion*!" Her mother gasped.

"It's been so much drama, Mama. It's not just the abortion. When we found out, I went to the doctor to get a blood test to confirm the pregnancy test. The blood work came back positive. I was, in fact, pregnant by about five weeks or so. We sat on it for a while because, yes, we discussed everything. Adoption, keeping the baby, and I'm ashamed to admit, even abortion. I wanted to keep it, but Mark was concerned about being in law school and me being in nursing school, trying to raise a child. After we talked, we agreed that we would keep it and tell y'all once we got 'outta the woods.'"

"So, what changed, Jas? How did y'all go from there to... to Mark being gone? Baby, I'm sure we all can figure this out. Mark will be fine. He will come back. He probably just needs some space right now."

"No, Mama. It's literally over, like over-over."

"Baby, don't get yourself any more worked up. Just come over, and when Dad gets off work, you, me, and him will discuss this and figure out what needs to be done."

Jasmine hung up with her mom, and just lay on the bed, crying.

Later that afternoon, when she arrived at her parents' house, her father was sitting at the kitchen table, and she could tell that her mother had already informed him of the situation. Her father looked up with tears in his eyes. "Come here, baby," he whispered.

Jasmine ran to him. No matter what was going wrong in her life, she knew she could always fall into her father's arms for comfort. She ran to her father.

He stood up and wrapped his arms around her. "It's going to be OK, baby. Everything is going to be just fine, Jas. Everything is going to be just fine."

Her mom stood at the sink. "Baby, let me make you some tea."

"Here, take a seat, and tell me what happened, Jas. What happened between you and Mark? How far along are you?" her dad inquired while rubbing her back.

"I need to tell you all everything that happened. I'm nearly sixteen weeks along, and I waited so long to tell you because we weren't sure what we were going to do." Jasmine bit the side of her lip as she continued because she knew there was so much to finally tell her parents. "After days and weeks of discussing our options, the doctor's office offered a test called an amniocentesis where they can basically identify certain genetic disorders or growth defects with the baby."

She began to cry. "We were planning to keep it, I swear. I swear we were, and then everything went wrong, Dad."

"Yeah... like what?" he asked. Because of his furrowed brow, Jasmine knew he was concerned, but his soft, deep voice gave her comfort to continue.

Her mom sat down and placed the cup of tea in front of her. "Here, baby, drink this."

"Thank you, Mama."

"Well, we got the test results back, and the doctor informed us that there was a very high chance that the child would be born Down syndrome."

Her dad's eyes began to fill with tears. "Baby, it breaks my heart to see you hurting. Come here," he said as he pulled her chair closer to his, and she rested her head upon his shoulder as he consoled her.

Her mom rubbed her back. "Oh baby, those doctors don't know everything, plus only God can determine that."

Jasmine continued, with her head now buried in her father's chest. "And then everything changed between Mark and I. It was like Mark wanted nothing more to do with the child. All he kept saying was, 'We can't pay for law school, nursing school, and raise a special needs child. Special needs this, special needs that. It's like his mind was made up from the moment we received the results.'"

Jasmine lowered her head onto her dad's shoulder.

"It's OK, baby. It's OK," her dad reassured her.

"What makes matters worse, and I'm ashamed to even tell you all this... I agreed to get an abortion after seeing how adamant Mark was about it."

"Jaaas..." Her dad sighed.

"Daddy, I know. I know. But I love him, Daddy. Plus, I don't even know how I can do this. Like, how in the world am I going to be able to raise a child, let alone a child that could have Down syndrome, and make it through nursing school? Everything is messed up, and it's all my fault."

Her dad rubbed her head and pulled her close. "Baby, we're going to figure this out, I promise you. We love you, and you won't deal with this alone."

"Come here, Mama," her dad said to Holly. They sat there, holding and comforting Jasmine as she cried in their arms.

Jasmine raised her head to look at her father and mother. "Wait, there's more. We set an appointment to have an abortion, and I wasn't even going to tell you two because I didn't want you to be disappointed in me."

Her father clenched his lips together, and shook his head slowly. "Jasmine, you know we can be disappointed, yet it would never change our love for you. You're our daughter. We will forever be with you, through the good and whatever else life brings you. You're our baby." He leaned in to kiss Jasmine's forehead.

"I know, Daddy... The morning of the appointment, I told Mark that I didn't want to go through with it, but he was persistent. I accepted it, and we went to the clinic. Daddy, it was so horrible. People were protesting, yelling at the car, throwing things. It was horrible. I told Mark I couldn't go through with it, and I got out of the car. When I got home, he was packing up his suitcase, saying he didn't want this, saying that he was leaving. We fought, and I begged him to stay, and he just left, Mama. He just left." She turned and said to her mother, teary-eyed. "Mama, he just left. He just left me. I can't believe it. He just walked out, like the last few years didn't mean a thing."

It was hard for her parents to see her like this, distraught and broken. "It's OK, baby. Just move back in with us. I'll get all of your stuff and we'll figure this out together. Everything will be OK. We love you, baby."

They spent the rest of the night consoling Jasmine, being there for her, and occasionally wiping the tears from her face. They discussed what it had been like when her mom was pregnant with Jasmine and how scared they were as well.

Jasmine found comfort in her mom's experience and her dad's fear that he wouldn't be an adequate father when they found out. Her parents had also been in college, married, with very little money, but they found a way.

Later that month, Jasmine moved back in with her parents as she was preparing for nursing school and the baby's birth. She told them about her acceptance to the BU Nursing Program.

They were excited for her and tried to comfort her as much as possible throughout the pregnancy, even going to every doctor's appointment with her. She was finally there, present and feeling at peace throughout her pregnancy. All seemed as though it would be fine.

The World's Love

As Jasmine entered the final weeks of her pregnancy, she realized it had been months since she'd heard from Mark. Although her parents were extremely supportive, a part of her still longed for Mark to be there with her. She missed the days they'd spent together, the moments they'd lie in bed talking about absolutely nothing, just holding hands.

Occasionally, she would text him updates about her pregnancy, yet Mark never responded. Jasmine always kept her mind focused on preparing to bring her child into the world, so she rarely let it bother her too much. Jasmine pushed through, juggling both nursing school and her pregnancy, even though Mark wasn't there for her.

It was an early brisk autumn morning, and Jasmine woke, washed up, and went downstairs to have breakfast with her mom. The two of them didn't say much that morning, but as Jasmine made it to the breakfast table, she leaned over and kissed her mom's forehead.

"Mmm, that's nice," her mom whispered softly as Jasmine smiled.

"Morning, Mama," she replied.

The two sat and enjoyed each other's company in near silence. It was a good morning.

Jasmine finished her breakfast, took one final sip of orange juice, and slid her chair back to stand. As she stood, she felt an unfamiliar sensation... her water broke.

She looked at her mother with a smile, which quickly turned into overwhelming panic. "Oh my God, oh my God, Mama, Mama, it's..." Jasmine said frantically.

Her mother quickly stood up from the table, and hurried to Jasmine's side. "It's OK, baby. Let me call Daddy. It's finally time. We already have the bag ready. Oh my God, oh my God, it's happening," her mother yelled in excitement, then hugged Jasmine, kissed her cheek, and whispered to her, "You can do this. We got you, baby."

Holly called Jasmine's dad, and let him know that it was go time, so he left work and rushed to meet them at the hospital.

Jasmine grabbed her mother's arm, and looked her in the eyes. "Mama, I wanna call Mark to let him know."

Her mother frowned, turning her head to hide her expression from Jasmine. "Baby, we haven't heard from him in months. This is your time. This is going to be a beautiful day." She didn't approve, but she also knew Jasmine wanted to call Mark. "Honey, I guess I just don't want this day ruined by someone that hasn't been here at all to support you through this. You are strong, beautiful, and Daddy and I have your back. This is your day!"

Even though Holly wanted Jasmine to focus solely on the beautiful life she was about to bring into this world, she could see Jasmine's countenance souring with each mention of Mark not being present over the last few months. Her mother knew that

Jasmine felt that she at least needed to attempt to contact Mark, so Holly quickly changed her tune. "You know what? You're right, Jas. Call him. He should know. I'll go get the car started and pack all the bags in the car."

Jasmine called Mark, yet like many calls before, he didn't answer; so she left a voicemail. "Mark, it's me, Jasmine. I just wanted you to know that I'm going into labor. My water broke and my mom is taking me to the hospital. We'll be at Boston Methodist in the delivery ward if you want to come. Please come. I need you there. We need you there."

A part of Jasmine hoped Mark would show up, but the other part of her feared that he wouldn't. She had gone this long without him. She was stronger now and determined that she'd do this with or without him.

Jasmine was in labor for hours, yet at 2:23 a.m., the love of her life was born. When she held him, she cried and said, "Hello, you. I knew you'd be this beautiful. It's me, little one. I'm your mother."

As her parents came back into the room, she looked at her dad, "His name is Peyton, Peyton Love." She had given Peyton Mark's last name because she still held out hope that Peyton would one day have his father return to his life.

Her father began to cry because he had no clue that Jasmine would name Peyton after him.

As her parents came closer to the bed to see little Peyton, Jasmine looked up and smiled at her father.

"I chose Peyton because you're the best man that I know, and if he grows to be half the man you are, Daddy, I will have succeeded as a mother," Jasmine said softly, tears in her eyes.

Jasmine and her father made eye contact as his lips pressed together. He nodded in appreciation, and accepted her words with pride.

As his eyes teared up at the notion of his grandson being named after him, his heart was also broken because he could hear the pain in his daughter's voice. Pain because of the absence of Peyton's father and pain because it was finally official.

Peyton Love, born six pounds eight ounces, was born with Down syndrome. Jasmine wasn't sad because Peyton was born with Down syndrome. She was hurt because the love of her life couldn't imagine the same beauty in their child that she could finally see.

The family spent the entire night taking turns holding little Peyton and kissing his forehead. They didn't speak much about Peyton being born with Down syndrome. Strangely enough, Peyton being born and finally knowing that their little angel was healthy with Down syndrome brought them all a sense of peace.

The nurse came in. "Mama, you've been through a lot. We can take baby Peyton to the nursery so you and Grandma and Grandad can get some rest. Congratulations, by the way, Grandma and Grandpa!"

Jasmine's parents didn't even take their eyes off little Peyton as they responded to the nurse. They just smiled and said, "Thank you!"

After a few minutes, Jasmine's dad finally looked up at the nurse and said, "You know she named him after me, right?" He had a huge smile on his face as though Peyton was his son and not his grandson.

They all just laughed and smiled.

As the nurse was preparing to take little Peyton to the nursery, Jasmine said, "Wait, let me kiss him one more time, please."

Her dad placed Peyton into Jasmine's arms. She kissed him, hugged him tightly, and lifted her finger to his forehead. "You're my little prince." She traced a heart on his little forehead as Peyton looked back at her. She was there, present, happy, and at peace.

CHAPTER 8
A NEW LIFE: A NEW JOURNEY

The tumultuous months came and went. Everything that Mark and Jasmine had feared about being in nursing school and raising a child with Down syndrome, Jasmine was facing alone.

As Peyton and Jasmine's new life together took shape and began to unfold, things were quite difficult at the onset.

Jasmine stayed up many nights trying to calm and soothe Peyton to sleep, all while balancing nursing school, volunteering, and studying.

Peyton had many ailments that affected him from birth. He immediately needed eye surgery in order to correct his strabismus. After multiple inner ear infections, the ear, nose, and throat surgeon, Dr. Carolyn Watson, recommended that he receive tympanostomy tubes. This simple procedure would bring both Jasmine and Peyton some relief, as his ears would now be able to drain properly.

He also had difficulty breathing at night, so Jasmine was always afraid that he would stop breathing altogether. For the first few months, she barely slept. Her parents helped where they could, but she knew this was her charge.

Jasmine could feel the strain she was putting on her parents, so she eventually moved out into an apartment between BU and her parents' home. They were close enough to help her, but she always told her mom, when Holly tried to coax her into not moving out and staying, "I put myself in this situation, so I'm going to fight through it and work my way out."

She juggled nursing school, making multiple doctor appointments a week for Peyton's various ailments, and working part-time at BU's on-campus clinic because she didn't want to just depend on her parents, who were living on a mostly fixed income, now that they were retired.

It was a late night; Jasmine was studying at her kitchen table and feeding Peyton at the same time. No words were spoken, but she took a break from studying, and smiled at Peyton as he was cooing in his baby chair.

Even though things were tough, whenever she felt overwhelmed, she'd look down at Peyton, and his smile alone would give her the strength to continue pushing forward.

Special Needs

Life over the next few years seemed to fly by. With every struggle faced, both Peyton and Jasmine became stronger, closer, and more in love with each other. As much as Peyton needed his mom, Jasmine needed him.

Peyton was five years old now. With each day that passed, he was proving to be very smart. Doctors diagnosed Peyton early on with one of the rarest types of Down syndrome, mosaic Down syndrome.

This type of Down syndrome only accounted for about one

to two percent of all cases, and patients usually exhibited fewer symptoms than the two more common types of the syndrome.

Peyton had a real shot at developing and accomplishing many things, barring, of course, Jasmine being able to get him the early assistance he needed in order to hone certain language, motor, and social skills.

At one of Peyton's doctor's appointments, the doctor said, "Ms. Hopkins, I want to be very clear. All of Peyton's test results are very positive that he will, in fact, be a high-functioning Down's child. That said, you both have a very long road ahead, and it won't be easy to maneuver. He's progressing well, but these next few years will be critical to his overall cognitive development. Can you tell me a bit about your support system?"

Jasmine shared her support system, as the doctor also reassured her that there were programs that could also assist with Peyton and his cognitive development. Jasmine was hopeful, but the rollercoaster of difficulties she and Peyton would face was just beginning.

As their journey together continued, Peyton and Jasmine were often in and out of the emergency room for fever, constipation, constant crying, and even impacted bowel. There were numerous times Jasmine had to stop studying or leave work to take Peyton to the emergency room, for one reason or another.

She never complained or even blamed Peyton. She had resolved that she could be a great mother to him and still accomplish her dreams. With each appointment, each sleepless night, and every tear she dropped as Peyton was in pain, she became stronger and more determined.

Throughout the years, Jasmine did it all: cooking, cleaning, playing with Peyton, bathing Peyton, putting Peyton to bed, and then while exhausted, studying late at night to complete her dream of saving one life at a time as a nurse. Little did Jasmine know she was saving her own life as well! She was slowly becoming a self-sustaining, independent, brave, and courageous woman.

She was writing her own story of greatness.

Peyton was eventually fitted for glasses and underwent his ear tube surgery, and Jasmine was able to balance all of this with nursing school with the help of her parents. They were in their groove, Peyton and Jasmine. Things weren't easy, but with the help of her parents, Jasmine was making it work.

Wanting to ensure that Peyton had what he needed, Jasmine decided to attend nursing school part-time. That way she could make all of his doctor's appointments, scheduled therapy sessions, and work on the side to supplement her financial aid scholarships. She was just about ready to graduate from nursing school and take on the challenge of becoming a registered nurse as Peyton entered first grade.

Because of Jasmine's scholarship with BU Nursing, Peyton had a paid part-time nanny/nurse, a speech therapist, and a physical therapist named James Wellington, whom everyone called James. James and Peyton had been working together since before Peyton could even talk. The two grew to have a very special relationship. James had worked with several Down syndrome children before, but for some reason, he and Peyton just clicked, and he became somewhat of a mentor for young Peyton.

To learn some of James's methods, Jasmine often attended the sessions since the curriculum James taught, in the beginning, was critical for her to continue with Peyton throughout normal everyday life.

First Day of School

On the morning of young Peyton's first day of school, Jasmine awoke early and made her way to his room.

Peyton's room door was partially open, so Jasmine stood there silently, watching him sleep.

She took a moment to contemplate their journey together thus far, as the love of her heart was preparing to embark upon this new feat. She had gone from days she didn't know how they would survive together to being at the moment where her beloved son was starting his journey into the real world: first grade.

She opened the door slowly and walked over to his bed. Standing there, watching him sleep for a bit, she felt a sense of pride, a moment of extreme love... Love at which she had arrived at the point of finding some sense of normalcy with her and Peyton's life demands. Her baby was starting a new chapter of his life, and the two of them were both ready.

As she slowly sat on the bed, Jasmine traced the outline of a heart on his forehead, as she had done nearly every night and every morning since his birth.

Peyton began to stir. As he opened his eyes, the two of them exchanged smiles. Excited for the day to come, he threw the covers back, jumped out of bed, and sat on his mom's lap.

She sat there for several minutes hugging him before she grabbed his head, looked him in the eyes, and said, "I just want you to know that Mommy's proud of you. You've come so far, and you've worked so hard, baby. Mommy is proud of you. You are going to love school."

She kissed him and held him tight. "Oh, baby," she said with a smile.

"Annnd I'm going to meet so many new *fwends*, right Ma?" he asked with enthusiasm.

"That's right Pey Pey. You are going to meet so many wonderful people, but none of them will love you liiike..."

Peyton knew what was coming. She had woken him up like this before.

"Oh no," he yelled as he began to wiggle out of his mom's arms.

"Liiike your *moootherrr*," Jasmine said as she chased him across the bed and tickled him. "Oh boy, I'm getting too old to be chasing you down all over the room," she joked.

"Well, you just have to get younger or faster, like me," Peyton replied, now halfway hiding behind the open closet door.

"OK, I laid out your clothes, Pey. Let's take a bath, brush our teeth, and then—"

He cut her off. "We go to *schoool*!"

Jasmine smiled because Peyton was so excited for school, and she loved seeing his joy.

As happy as she was for his first-day excitement, there were still moments that her happiness was tainted by the thoughts in the back of her head, wishing Peyton had his father as well.

After brushing his teeth, Peyton put on the clothes his mother had laid out for him, while his mother was packing his lunch in the kitchen. Just before he made his way downstairs, he walked past his mother's room and noticed the closet door was open, and the light was on. He walked over to turn off the light and close the door, and as he grabbed the door handle, something caught his eye. It was an old suitcase lying in the back of the closet.

Peyton opened the door all the way out of curiosity, pulled out the suitcase, and laid it on the bed. The suitcase was closed and had a Polaroid picture of his mom taped to the top of it. Rubbing his hands over the old leather, he opened the suitcase to see what was inside.

"Pey, come downstairs. I want you to have breakfast before school," Jasmine yelled.

"Coming, Mama," Peyton yelled back. He liked the suitcase, and really liked the picture of his mother taped to the top. He kissed the photo of his mother, removed the clothes from within the suitcase, and placed them neatly on the bed before heading downstairs.

When he turned the corner, Jasmine saw the suitcase in Peyton's hand, "Where did you get that, son?"

"I found it in the closet upstairs, and I found this picture of you on the top of it. Can I use this for school, Mama? Pleeease," he begged.

Jasmine didn't have the strength to tell young Peyton that it was the very suitcase his father left behind years ago when he had walked out of their lives.

"Why is your picture taped to the top of it, Mama?" Peyton asked innocently as he looked over the suitcase, admiring its stitching and metal buttons.

"That suitcase belonged to your father, Peyton. He would always take random pictures of me, and I guess he just kept that one taped to his suitcase."

"Oh wow, so this was my father's." Peyton was excited. "OK, so I can keep it and use it for school, right?"

"Baby, I already bought you a backpack for your school stuff. I got you the Spiderman one you wanted! Remember?" Jasmine asked, holding back her thoughts. "But if you want to use it, I mean… you can."

Peyton was two years behind most first graders, but his test scores came back high enough for him to enter classes with students that were not mentally challenged. He'd be starting first grade as an eight-year-old, but he didn't know the difference. He was just excited to be joining kids his age in school.

Peyton walked to the kitchen's junk cabinet and grabbed the scotch tape. He tore off a clean piece of tape, took the picture of his mother, and taped it to the underside of the suitcase top.

"I don't want it to fall off during the day," he said with a smile, looking at his mother.

He was quite independent, so he placed his lunch, school supplies, blanket, and certificate of graduation from his speech therapy all inside the suitcase. For some reason, his speech therapy graduation meant so much to him. Maybe it was because he and James had become so close. James had become like a father figure to young Peyton.

"Why are you putting that in there, baby?" Jasmine asked.

"In case my dad comes back, I want to show him what I did and *all* my awards, Mama."

Jasmine's heart broke when she heard this, but she knew she had to be strong for Peyton. She smiled and shook her head. "He's going to love it, son. I'm sure he's going to love it!"

They got in the car and drove to school. Peyton was so excited that he didn't say one word to his mother the entire drive.

As they got closer to Pearl Washington Elementary School, Peyton lowered the window and began to scream, "I'm *going to schooool!*" He yelled out of excitement.

Jasmine smiled because she was so excited to see him so filled with joy for this day.

When they parked, Peyton hopped out of the car, ran to the back seat door, and pulled his father's suitcase out. Holding his suitcase tightly with his right hand, Peyton looked up at his mother, smiled, and reached his left hand out to her.

Hand in hand, Jasmine obliged and proudly walked her beautiful son inside for his first day of school. After finally finding their way to his classroom, Jasmine checked him in, hugged him one last time, and watched him walk away to talk to the other kids.

Just as she was preparing to leave, she noticed Peyton place the suitcase on the ground. She flashed back to the moment Mark had placed the suitcase down, walked out of the house, and out of their lives forever.

She watched as Peyton told the kids around him, "This was my father's. It's his suitcase, but I get to use it for school. Isn't it cool?" he added.

Kids being kids, "Ewww, it looks funny. Why is it old like that?"

Peyton just continued to explain why it was cool and showed

the kids the stitching and all the cool buttons... He was so into details and the artwork of the antique suitcase.

Jasmine gathered herself. "Goodbye, Pey. Have fun at school. I'll see you after," she yelled from the entry of the classroom.

Either Peyton didn't hear her, or he was so involved with his new classmates that her words were drowned out by his excitement to meet new friends and his friends asking about his father's old suitcase.

Either way, Peyton was practically in first-grade heaven!

Elementary Graduation

Young Peyton continued to grow through elementary school. Being high functioning and extremely focused, he worked hard to accomplish award after award. Grade after grade, Peyton received awards for perfect attendance, most improved, science projects, spelling bee champion, and reading alike.

During Peyton's fifth-grade reading exam, all the parents gathered in the back of the class while the students read passages from books. As Jasmine sat with the parents talking in the back, she could barely hear audible words from the students presenting at the front of the class.

The students continued to read passages aloud, which were being graded by Mrs. Delphin. Jasmine became annoyed because she quickly realized that although she was there to hear her child present, the other parents were there for a social hour. The talkative parents clapped as each student finished, but Jasmine was the only one paying attention.

After the readings, all of the students received a certificate from Mrs. Delphin. Little did the children know that Mrs. Delphin planned to award the student who read the best without looking at the text.

Peyton had studied for days for this presentation, so it was no surprise that he won the reading award. When Mrs. Delphin announced his name as the victor, he grabbed his trophy and immediately ran to his mother and jumped into her arms.

"I'm so proud of these young ones and their commitment to reading. Parents, give them all a big handclap. They are the top readers in our grade," Mrs. Delphin said with pride.

The parents began to clap and cheer for their children. Most of the students took their certificates to their parents with pure joy on their faces, yet no regard for their awards. Not Peyton. After hugging his mother, he walked over to his cubby where his things were.

Jasmine began talking to one of the parents while she nonchalantly watched Peyton walking toward the cubby. He grabbed his suitcase, opened it, placed his hard-earned award inside, and then closed the suitcase. Before he placed it back in his little cubby, Jasmine saw him rub his hands over the top of the suitcase. He'd now had this suitcase for years, and as much as his mother tried to get him a newer backpack or suitcase, he always refused. "Why get another one, when I have this one from my father?" he'd always question.

Peyton then turned his attention to his mother, smiled hugely, ran to her from across the room, and jumped in her arms again.

She was so proud of him, and her tight bear hug let him know just that. She kissed his cheek and whispered, "I am so proud of you son! Great job up there. We are going to get ice cream today because of the great job you did, baby."

"Mama, I'm not a baby. I'm a young man, right?" Peyton asked with a frown on his face. He was slightly embarrassed for the other kids to hear his mother call him a baby.

"Riiiight, you're a young man. My strong little young man,"

Jasmine said with a smile.

The two of them left the school and went to Peyton's favorite ice cream shop, Scoops & Scoops, which was right next to the park. Jasmine and Peyton enjoyed many days at this park as he would play with the kids while she studied for upcoming exams.

Jasmine and Peyton had finished their ice cream cones and were enjoying each other in the park—sliding down the slide together, Jasmine pushing young Peyton on the swing, and building sandcastles in the sandbox.

"I'm going to go sit with the other parents for a second, OK, Pey?" Jasmine said.

"OK, Mama," Peyton replied as he went back to join the other kids on the playground.

Jasmine smiled and watched him from afar. She really had no intention of actually sitting and talking with the other parents. She was tired and wanted to rest on the bench as Peyton played and enjoyed the park.

So there, in the beautiful early summer day, she pulled out her books and began studying for her upcoming continuing education exam. She didn't get much studying in since Peyton was calling to her every thirty seconds to watch him master the winding slide.

Jasmine became bored with studying, so she placed her anatomy book back in her bag and pulled out her favorite self-help book, *The Flight of the Phoenix: Living Forward*, and continued where she had left off. Though she had read and completed the book several times before, she always promised to pass it on to someone, yet she always found herself starting it over.

She loved this book because it spoke to the essence of what she had to focus on while raising Peyton alone. The book was full of messages centered around transferring one's time, energy, and focus from the things that couldn't be controlled, *the what ifs*, and transitioning those key life variables to the things that Jasmine could control, *the what is*, in order to course-correct the past, live in the present, and forge a better future.

Jasmine and Peyton's life continued like this, with the two of them in their groove, and Jasmine being a single parent, ensuring that her beloved Peyton was happy and progressing in life.

Jasmine would put Peyton to bed, read him a story, and rub his head until he fell asleep. Every night she'd trace a heart on his forehead as he would drift away into a happy slumber. Peyton, despite his ailments, always woke and fell asleep happy because he knew he was loved. Though Peyton felt the love of his mother, Jasmine longed for the love of his father.

She had arrived at the point where she no longer wanted Mark's love to comfort her, but rather his love to be ever-present in Peyton's life. She knew Peyton deserved that!

CHAPTER 9

A GLANCE BACK, A LOOK FORWARD

The Thursday night before graduation, Peyton was snoozing comfortably with his mother by his side. Jasmine studied, as she'd done many nights before, with a cup of green tea, and two slices of lemon. Out of the corner of her eye, she caught a flash of Peyton's coveted suitcase, and she couldn't take her eyes away.

She hadn't opened that suitcase in years, but she walked over, bent down, and knelt beside the ancient relic that had once held such a special place in her heart. Jasmine tried to remain as quiet as possible, so she wouldn't wake Peyton.

As she pulled the two suitcase buttons apart, the two golden latches popped open.

For some reason, Jasmine was nervous. Though Peyton had used this suitcase now for years, she had never really gazed upon it or even had the courage to look within, mostly out of fear that doing so would bring back past pains of Mark packing up and walking out of her life forever.

After slowly opening the suitcase, she reviewed the contents. On top, there was the reading trophy that Peyton had just received from Mrs. Delphin, but it was the remaining contents that broke

Jasmine's heart and gave her pause.

Inside, Peyton had all his books, notebooks for school, and his speech therapy study book. Jasmine moved those things out of the way, and she saw that Peyton had been collecting all of his awards and certificates for years.

In the past, whenever Jasmine would ask Peyton why he never wanted his certificates or awards displayed throughout the house, he always replied, "I'm saving them for later, for something more important."

On the underside of the top of the suitcase, two pictures were taped: a picture that Mark had taken of her sleeping from so long ago, and to her surprise, a picture of her and Mark.

How Peyton had managed to find that photo, she had no clue. Just before Jasmine was going to close the suitcase, she noticed a small sliver of paper peeking out from behind the old photo of her and Mark.

She slowly removed the piece of paper that she could now see was a small, one-sentence note in Peyton's handwriting. It was simple, short, and to the point, yet the six words nearly brought her to tears. "I will find you one day!"

Jasmine closed the suitcase, and their lives continued…

Peyton graduated from Pearl Washington Elementary School with excellence, and his mother was overjoyed as he crossed the stage in his droopy cap and gown. Though she was excited for the progress she and Peyton had made, she knew there was more ahead.

In that time, Jasmine and Peyton appeared as though they were finding their way.

Life continued…

Though it took her longer, Jasmine graduated from nursing school while Peyton was in elementary school and continued part-time nurse practitioner schooling. She took a year off between the two, to ensure that Peyton was developing well, and she didn't want her grades to suffer due to her exhaustion.

During this year off, Jasmine continued to volunteer with the Boston University clinic in hopes that her dream to nurse there would still be achievable someday. After her year hiatus, Jasmine picked back up in the program exactly where she had left off. She was even more invigorated and motivated to conclude the program because volunteering had shown her how many communities were underserved.

Time ticked on, and Jasmine was in her final rotation of nurse practitioner school, nearing graduation.

Because she maintained a perfect GPA in both nursing school and her nurse practitioner program, Jasmine was offered positions at Presbyterian Hospital and St. John's Outpatient Clinic, both affiliates of Boston University.

She was ecstatic, as life seemed to all be falling into place. After all the hard work, sleepless nights, and cheeks wet with endless tears, she was finally getting to a place where her hard work and perseverance were paying off.

Even though Presbyterian and St. John's offers were contingent upon her passing her NP exam, she had been offered two of the most coveted and well-paying positions for a new NP.

Upon receiving the offers, Jasmine immediately called her parents to share her great news. It was hard to tell who was more excited; Jasmine screaming into the phone, Peyton dancing in the background, her mother Holly crying on the other end of the phone, or her dad, Peyton Sr., doing his weird happy salsa dance as he listened in on the speakerphone.

She was there, happy, present, and in the moment!

Jasmine and Peyton's life continued… After elementary school graduation, the next challenge Peyton faced was middle school.

He began playing sports, and he really enjoyed wrestling. This would also be the first time Peyton competed in the Special Olympics. He was hesitant at first because although he knew he had Down syndrome, his mother never allowed him to think he was any different or less than any other child.

He wanted to know why he was competing in the Special Olympics and not the "Regular Olympics," as he put it.

"Babe, it's because you're my special son, and when you grow up, you'll prove to everyone that you'll be in the big Olympics and win gold medals for our country. This is just your tryout."

Jasmine always had a way of comforting Peyton without making him feel inferior to any other child.

Though he didn't place in any event his first time out, he got his first taste of competition, and he ran with it. He loved competing so much. It was as if it gave him a sense of accomplishment to be out there with people who were like him.

Peyton competed in the Special Olympics every year of middle school and wrestled for Oak Park Middle School, the feeder school for Stockbridge High School. His first victory in the Special Olympics came his seventh-grade year, where he won both the 200-meter dash and the 100-meter dash. He placed first in both and placed second in both the long jump and triple jump. As one could imagine, Peyton was over the moon with excitement.

Upon crossing the finish line after the 200-meter dash, Peyton continued running, running toward the stands to find his mother as he'd realized that he had just won first place. He was running toward Jasmine, screaming and arms flailing with excitement. She ran to him just as fast toward the end of the bleachers to meet and embrace her newly crowned champion.

Taming their excitement upon embrace, Jasmine kissed Peyton on the cheek and told him to scurry back to the winner's circle so he could receive his first-place award.

Peyton ran even faster back to the winner's circle as it was his first first-place award, and he was excited to stand on the podium and wave as he had seen in all of the movies he'd watched of athletes winning awards. It was a beautiful moment.

With each medal, certificate, ribbon, and award achieved throughout middle school, Jasmine and her parents were there to support Peyton. After each victory, Peyton would take his award, place it in his suitcase, and prepare for his next competition. It was as if filling this suitcase full of awards and trophies was getting him mentally closer to accomplishing a goal, a goal to find his father one day and to prove to him that he was, in fact, worthy of his love.

During middle school, Peyton continued working with James Wellington, his therapist, and they remained quite close.

James was married with kids of his own, but Peyton quickly became like one of his own children, since James had lost his younger brother, who was special needs, in a car accident when he was young. Apparently, Peyton was much-needed therapy for James as well.

Throughout their years together, James ensured he attended as many of Peyton's events as he could, as he quickly became a friend of the family. Often James and Jasmine would discuss Peyton's insatiable need to acquire and store treasured accolades. From what began as a "cute little thing," both Jasmine and James could tell that Peyton had transitioned the fairytale of this suitcase into his hoped reality.

As Peyton entered high school, his drive for competition continued. He collected awards for the chess club championship, and the Lincoln Douglas debate team after winning State, all while taking part in the Special Olympics and winning medal after medal, ribbon after ribbon.

Peyton also became a standout on the wrestling team. In his eleventh-grade year, he placed third in the state. He was the first Down syndrome wrestler in the state of Massachusetts to ever place in the state tournament.

Placing third in the tournament, Peyton was just two points

away from wrestling for the State Championship.

Peyton graduated from advanced speech therapy in his junior year at Stockbridge High School. Prior to the ceremony, Peyton was honored as James asked him to give the commencement speech.

At the conclusion of his speech, James, the lead therapist, came to the podium. "I want to take a moment to award Peyton Timothy Love with the award of leadership and bravery. Peyton came to me some fourteen years ago, and he was afraid to learn, afraid to try, and fearful of not knowing how he'd overcome certain challenges life threw at him.

"I look at him today. He is a star student, an amazing athlete, a cheerful volunteer, and a true example of what we should all strive to be—brave within leadership, relentless in adversity, and most of all, caring. Peyton, you are most deserving of this award. Please join me back on stage and receive this great honor for your bravery and continued leadership."

The crowd cheered.

Peyton cried because although they'd given this award out every year to the graduating class, he never thought he would win the award. As Jasmine ran to the stage to take pictures of him receiving his award, Peyton looked at her, leaned into the microphone, and said with a smile on his face, "I'm only here because of you!"

This stopped Jasmine in her tracks, and she began to shed tears of joy. Peyton put his index finger up toward the ceiling and traced a heart mid-air. Jasmine smiled, took a picture of Peyton receiving his award, and walked back to her seat. She was there... happy... and in the moment.

Peyton continued growing and finding his way throughout life.

High school graduation was finally upon him, yet another accomplishment he couldn't wait to place within his suitcase of hope. At this point, the suitcase was so full he had to choose which awards to leave in and which to remove for display around their home.

After his graduation, Peyton went to the Golden Gliders roller rink with a few of his friends while his mother was preparing dinner.

As she took his jacket upstairs to hang it, she saw the suitcase Peyton had kept for over eighteen years, proudly carrying it around almost every day. She bent down and opened the beat-up old suitcase. It had been years since she'd looked within.

Inside, Peyton had trophies, awards, medals, certificates, pictures of his track meets, and his entire history of competition and accomplishments all within this one suitcase.

Jasmine's attention was drawn to a folded note propped between the photo of her and the other photo of her and Mark. The photos had clearly been taped and re-taped several times over the years, and this note was much longer than the single sentence she'd read years ago.

Jasmine took the note, opened it, and it read:

> Dad, you don't know me yet, but I have always hoped that one day you would. My name is Peyton Timothy Love, and I have so many things I want to tell you. I don't understand why you left my mother and I, and she barely talks about you.
>
> I am in high school now, and I have done many things. I am the captain of the debate team, I am pretty good at wrestling, and I even have won several events at the Special Olympics this past year. Those are just a few of the things I've done. I

don't know why you left, but I still do hope you come back someday soon because I've done so much that I hope you will be proud of one day.

I've often heard people say that it's difficult dealing with a Down syndrome person like I am. For that, I am sorry. If you had to leave because of my condition, then please forgive me.

I am writing this to you today in hopes that one day, you will read it, and we can start over. The truth is, I've seen so many of my friends throughout my life, and they are happy with their fathers. I have always wanted you to be at my events with me, but hopefully if I collect enough awards and show you what I am capable of, you will come back.

Well, until we meet...Peyton Love, With Hope!

The letter had been signed and dated during Peyton's junior year of high school. Jasmine realized that Peyton had been carrying the weight of his father leaving for so many years, which is why this suitcase and filling it meant so much to him.

She'd never had the strength to tell him the truth, that his father never wanted him after knowing he'd potentially be born with Down syndrome. Was it the right time to tell him the truth, or should she just continue to harbor those truths in order to preserve Peyton's idea of his father on a pedestal?

The note broke Jasmine's heart because she now realized why Peyton always wanted to keep and collect things. At each stage of Peyton's life, he'd worked hard to accumulate trophies, awards, ribbons, certificates, and anything that proved his accomplishments, and more importantly, his perception of his self-worth.

CHAPTER 10
COLLEGE AND THE NP'S SPIRAL

Peyton worked hard throughout high school, and because of his efforts and SAT score, he was offered a partial scholarship to attend Boston University. College came fairly easy to Peyton because his entire life until that point was all about discipline and hard work to overcome challenges. So, freshman and sophomore years came and went before Peyton even made his first B in a course. It was Dr. Bott's Chemistry II class, where Peyton made an 89.8, and "There will be no rounding," Dr. Bott had professed all year long.

Jasmine had been working at St. Johns hospital in multiple specialties as a nurse practitioner for several years and worked her way up the ranks to become the head of the nursing program, managing staff and residents, and in charge of the intern curriculum.

Because she enjoyed working with the nursing students so much, she also maintained an associate professor role within Boston University's nursing program. Due to her demanding work schedule, she only taught a few online courses, but seeing young students' zeal for nursing as they followed in her footsteps was clearly her passion.

Jasmine and Peyton both seemed to be excelling at life and growing together. Throughout this time, the one thing that remained constant was that Peyton always managed to keep his estranged yet cherished father's suitcase close by his side.

Whether he was going to school, doctors' appointments, joining his mother at BU for her classes, or just simply having lunch at the park, Peyton's suitcase was never too far from his grasp.

Having chosen civil engineering as his major, Peyton had gone through his core curriculum at BU and was now deep within his specialty courses. To beef up his résumé in hopes of landing an excellent internship, Peyton joined the National Association of Engineers at BU and later ran and became the chapter's first president with special needs.

He was so proud of this accomplishment because it was yet another he could reveal to his father one day.

Seemingly flying through college, Peyton graduated with honors, and signed an internship offer to move to Atlanta and join Wholverton Associates, one of the leading civil engineering firms in the nation. He hoped to receive a full-time offer after his year with the firm.

"Let's do something special for your internship offer, Pey," Jasmine yelled upstairs.

The Beginning of the End

One winter morning, Jasmine was taking a normal blood test with all of the nurses at work, something they did routinely prior to donating blood at a "for cause" blood drive. She was supervising the interns this week, so she was excited to teach them the process of drawing blood and the protocol for getting it tested. Additionally, she taught the students how to do certain scans for markers and submit the scans for results.

It was a normal day. Jasmine had fulfilled her purpose to which she'd spoken to so many years before. *Changing medicine, and saving lives, one life at a time.* She was happy. She laughed with her coworkers and often showed them pictures of Peyton that he'd occasionally send her from Atlanta. She was so proud to see how far he had come.

Jasmine had visited Atlanta a few times over his intern year to surprise him, cook for him, and just visit with her much-loved son. On March 20th, her father's birthday, she planned a surprise trip to Atlanta for her parents and her to go down, surprise Peyton, and all enjoy each other. Little did she know, this would be her final trip to Atlanta.

When they arrived in Atlanta, they checked into the hotel and immediately went to Peyton's job to surprise him. Jason Dickersen, lead engineer and Peyton's mentor at the firm, informed them that Peyton was on-site for one of their projects in Towne Brookhaven, but offered to drive them all out to be a part of the surprise.

"Peyton is doing a wonderful job down here with us. I have to admit, I was a little worried about how he'd handle the workload with all of the projects we have going on at the time, but that kid is truly driven," Jason said.

Sitting in the backseat with pride, Jasmine's dad just smiled and looked outside the window as Holly held his hand and leaned on his shoulder.

"That's our boy," Peyton Sr. whispered to himself as he turned and smiled at Holly.

When they arrived on-site, they all got out of the truck, Jason handed them each hard hats, and they followed him inside the building.

Jasmine was so nervous walking inside because although she

had been to visit Peyton in Atlanta before, she'd never actually seen him at work, in his element.

In pure Peyton fashion, as they walked up, he was barking orders and asking questions to perfect his craft.

"Hey Peyton, I found some people at the office who wanted to see you," Jason joked.

Peyton turned around, looked at Jason, and then he saw his mother and grandparents standing there with big smiles on their faces. He dropped his schematics, yelled at the top of his lungs out of excitement, and ran to his family.

"Oh my God, like... like, what are y'all... how did y'all get... what in the world are y'all doing here?" he exclaimed out of excitement and pure joy. "I had no clue y'all were coming."

"Yeaaah, well, your mom surprised us as well. All she said was for us to pack a bag for the weekend and not to ask any questions," his grandfather said with laughter.

"Oh, Mom!" Peyton hugged his mother tightly. "I love you so much."

He was so excited he went back and forth between his mom and his grandparents, hugging them in utter disbelief and joy.

"I'm so happy to see y'all. I wish I would've known y'all were coming. I could have requested off work today—"

Jason cut him off. "Hey, man, how often does it happen where you get surprised by your mom and your awesome grandparents? Get outta here and go show them the city. But you'd better not be late Monday morning," Jason and Peyton laughed.

Peyton embraced Jason, thanked him, and walked out with his family. He was in utter bliss. It was a perfect moment!

He took his family on an entire tour of Atlanta. They went to Stone Mountain, Atlantic Station, the MLK memorial, as well as many other sights around the metro Atlanta area. They laughed and enjoyed each other's company, all while not wanting the trip to conclude.

Sunday morning, Jasmine woke early to go and get everyone coffee. When she came back to the hotel, her mom had ordered breakfast for them all, and Peyton and his grandfather were sitting on the bed reminiscing about the weekend.

"I'm so glad y'all came out to see me. Everything was perfect, and it was just the break from work I needed," Peyton said as he leaned on his mother's shoulder. Jasmine doled out the coffees and joined her dad and son on the bed.

It was a wonderful weekend that was ending all too soon, but the family spent the remainder of the morning listening to Peyton tell them about his time as an intern for Wholverton Associates.

When it was time to go to the airport, Jasmine became teary-eyed. Her dad grabbed her and hugged her tight. "Don't cry, baby," he said.

"I know. I'm just going to miss my baby boy," she replied.

"Aww, Mom. Don't cry. I'll be back in Boston in no time," Peyton reassured her.

They hugged, said their final goodbyes, and got in the taxi headed for the airport.

As Peyton watched them drive away, he looked into the sky and just smiled because, at that moment, he wasn't thinking about the suitcase. Not one thought of proving that he deserved to be loved crossed his mind. He was loved by those who meant the most to him, and he knew it. He was there, in the moment, and happy!

CHAPTER 11
JASMINE'S PATH

Days had gone by, and Jasmine was back in Boston, working. She received a call from the lab that her results from the blood test and scans were ready. The doctor wanted her to come in to discuss her results, which slightly shocked Jasmine because in the past, they'd read her results over the phone since she was an employee of the hospital.

Either way, Jasmine thought she would capitalize on this potential teaching opportunity by bringing the interns with her to receive her results. While there, she could continue teaching them protocols around receiving and even what to expect when doctors were delivering results.

Jasmine walked into the office with a few of her interns to receive her test results. Her facial expression quickly changed as the doctor entered the room, saw the three eager interns, and asked with a straight face, "Would you mind if they waited outside, Ms. Hopkins?"

As the interns began to leave the room, Jasmine asked, "Do you mind if they stay? This is a part of the job they also need to understand... delivering bad news and how to empathize with patients."

Jasmine as always looking for a way to positively influence the "next generation of healers," as she would often call the young nursing students.

The doctor agreed to let them stay as he began to share the findings of her bloodwork and scans. She had practically zoned out, hearing the results.

The doctor continued, "There's no way of knowing. It could be benign or malignant. We'll just need to do more tests to confirm."

In disbelief, Jasmine lowered her head as her eyes began to tear up. Though she was distraught over the news, her heart broke, not for herself, but for the future of her beloved son.

After six weeks of additional tests, scans, and multiple opinions, Jasmine was diagnosed with pancreatic cancer. As she arrived home that day, she sat outside in the parked car, and called her parents to share the news she'd received, since it was now confirmed.

They were hysterical yet trying to be strong for Jasmine. The entire family was stymied because cancer didn't run in the family, and Jasmine was by all means very healthy. She drank very little, had never smoked, and lived a rather fit life. It didn't make sense.

Jasmine had spent most of her life giving back to the world and caring for others. Now she was staring one of the most aggressive cancers in the face, with no promise of pulling through.

As her parents began to cry, all Jasmine could think was, *How am I going to tell Peyton? How will my son continue in this world without me?*

Jasmine stayed the night at her parents' home, snuggled up next to her mom in her childhood bed as her mind raced. Being in healthcare, she knew the signs and symptoms of something wrong with the human body's biology. She was very aware of the signs and symptoms of cancer, yet for years she had been so involved with Peyton, helping others, and making a life for herself and her son, that she asked herself, *Did I miss the signs? Did I miss opportunities to get checked more regularly?*

She thought back to times when she had been exhausted or even had mild abdominal pains yet was too consumed with life to stop for a moment. She blamed herself because all of her time in medicine had taught her that pancreatic cancer is one of the silent cancers as the organ is one of the deepest in the body, often not producing symptoms until the cancer has spread.

"How could I have missed this?" she whispered to herself in disappointment. "Stupid. So stupid."

Her mother, hearing Jasmine's whispers and feeling the occasional tear stream down her cheek, stroked her daughter's hair until they both finally fell asleep.

Waking the next morning was like one of those moments you wake, hoping that what happened the day before was all a dream, and that you were coming back to reality... a reality where things actually made sense.

Jasmine opened her eyes slowly, mentally hoping that it was all just a nightmare, but as she felt her mother's warmth, she knew that this was her new reality. It was all real.

Jasmine and Peyton usually FaceTimed two to three times a week while he was in Atlanta. So even with all of the doctors' appointments and treatments, she made sure their tradition continued, as it made Peyton happy, and kept her mind off of her diagnosis and everything else.

Months had passed, and the doctors, even with treatment, had given Jasmine at most nine months to a year to live. She had waited as long as she could to give Peyton the news, but she knew it was time to tell him so he could begin to mentally prepare for the inevitable while she still had the strength to help him through the process.

She called him.

"Hey, Mom," he said.

As Jasmine broke the news to Peyton about her diagnosis, he began to cry hysterically. She'd waited four months to tell him because he was doing so well in his job, and she didn't want to give him bad news just yet. Also, a part of her hoped for a miracle, that she wouldn't have to ruin his world. She was so happy and so proud of him. She just wanted him to be happy a little while longer.

After learning of his mother's news, Peyton left Wholverton Associates on long-term leave to return to Boston and take care of his mother. When he landed in Boston, he went straight to the hospital, left his luggage at the front desk, and ran to the elevator.

Panting and pacing, Peyton was becoming more anxious. The elevator was taking too long. He looked left, looked right, and eventually saw the sign for the stairs. Running toward the sign and nearly slipping on the floor, Peyton grabbed the handle, just as a nurse yelled, "Umm, sir, no running, please!"

Peyton flung the door open, sprinted up the stairs to the fourth floor, and opened the fourth floor's door, looking left and right. He'd known what floor his mother was on but didn't know her exact room number.

Running to the nursing station, panting, he asked the first nurse he saw, "Ma'am, can you... can you help me... find, find my mother's..."

"Well, sir... I can help you. Why don't you take a breath and tell me your mother's name?" the nurse said.

Before Peyton could respond, he stood straight up and saw his grandfather leaning against the glass door of a room just behind the nursing station, and his grandmother sat in a chair by the bed.

"Never mind, I found it," he said, out of breath.

He could tell by the looks on their faces that it was more serious than his mother had let on. He slowly walked to the room, and his grandmother stood up and embraced him, then his grandfather hugged them both as well.

"Is she awake?" Peyton asked as he crossed into the room, seeing his mother lying there.

Peyton stayed with his mother for the remaining months of her life, only leaving the hospital to go to his grandparents' home to eat, shower, and rest. He rarely went to his mother's home because he felt as though it was empty and cold without her warm presence.

His mother was his entire world, so the thought of losing her was nearly unbearable for him. Each visit, his mother downplayed her prognosis because she wanted to protect Peyton. But he could tell that her frail body was getting weaker and weaker.

Carried to the End

"Peyton, come here," Jasmine whispered.

Peyton walked slowly to the bed. "I'm here. What's wrong, Mama?"

He knew her condition was serious, but he didn't understand fully the scope of what was going on. Jasmine had shielded him from most of her ailments because she didn't want him to worry. She knew Peyton couldn't fathom living in this world without her, the woman who had sacrificed all for him.

Although he didn't understand the gravity of what was going

on with his mom, he knew he had to be strong for her, just as she was being strong for him.

As Peyton looked at all the tubes and machines hooked up to his mother, he could only imagine how much pain she was going through.

She did her best to put on a brave face for him, but he knew that she wasn't the same. Her voice was softer, she wasn't nearly as vibrant as he'd known her to be, and she slept most days due to the sedating medications. With every wince and moan she allowed to escape her lips, Peyton became more and more broken.

As he sat at her beside one evening, Peyton's fingers crawled up the hospital blanket to meet with his mother's fingertips. He grabbed her hand, held it firm, and rubbed her forehead with a cool, wet towel.

"Mmm," Jasmine sighed.

"Mama... The... the doctors said... well I overheard them saying that at this point, there is nothing more that they can do for you, but make you comfortable. You still believe in miracles, right?" Peyton asked, squinting his eyebrows in concern.

Jasmine smiled. "Of course I believe in miracles, Peyton. You were my first miracle, son." She rubbed his hand. "Peyton, I have always tried to be there for you, and you have made me prouder than any other mother in the world can be of their son. I have watched you grow from being a baby to a boy and into a phenomenal man. I know it hasn't always been easy on you, but I've done the best that I could to teach you that you're just as much of a man as the next. You are the gift that the Lord put here to change the world. You are going to do great things, and I want you to know that I'll always be with you."

"Mama, don't talk like this. Why are you talking like this is the end? I heard the doctors explaining to Grandpa and Grandma that everything is internal, so that means you're going to be just fine."

"Baby, I will be fine because this is just life sometimes. Even if now is my time and I have to go home to be with God, I will still always be with you!"

"Well, tell God that I want you here with me, like here, on earth, in Boston with me, so he's going to have to wait!" Peyton said sarcastically.

The two just chuckled and laughed together…

"Come here, son," she said.

Peyton laid his head on his mom's chest, and she pulled him closer because she wanted her baby to climb into the bed.

"I want you to listen to me, OK. Son, this is just my time. There's nothing more the doctors can do for me, but that's not important.

"What I want you to know is that you're the most important thing to me. I want you to know that the greatest gift that God ever gave me was you. I could not have been the person I am today without you. You're the reason I am at peace! You're the reason I've been able to help so many people in my life."

Peyton began to weep. He reached his shaky hand up and rubbed her face. "Mama, I love you. Please don't talk like this. I love you, and I need you."

"I love you too, son. Life is amazing, and we just have to live the journey that is—"

He cut her off. "Mama, you're talking like you are saying goodbye."

"Peyton, quiet now, baby, because I have to share something with you that has taken me a lifetime to learn."

With tears in his eyes, "K, Mama. What is it?"

"Baby, you have to find it in your heart to forgive your father because if you don't, you'll find yourself living in a world of regret. You can't become who the world needs you to be, demands you be, if you can't find it in your heart to find your father and forgive him."

She continued, "Your greatest gift is your ability to love

unconditionally, and you can't let your dad take that away from you. You can't let anyone take that away from you. Remember, love covers everything, son. It's not just your last name; it's your legacy."

"Pure forgiveness is in its truest form when the person is undeserving. This is the last thing I want you to do for me. The truth is, son, none of us deserves forgiveness, but grace covers our mistakes. I want you to always remember that. I watched you, all your life, carry that suitcase around, filling it with trophies and awards to show your father and prove to him you are worthy of his love. But Peyton, I want you to know, you have been worthy of all the love in the world from the moment you were born, son."

Peyton was trying to listen to her life lessons, but all he could think about was the fact that his mother was saying her final goodbyes. "Mama, please don't go. Where will I be if you leave me now? How am I supposed to learn how to forgive without you here? What will I do now? He didn't even want me because of who I am, and he left you. I don't know how to forgive him. I need you here to teach me. Please don't say goodbyes, Mama." Peyton leaned on her shoulder with tears in his eyes.

She turned on her side, pulled his head up, and looked him in the eyes. "Peyton, you'll live on carrying on the love and the bond that we share. Remember—"

She grabbed his hands and rubbed his face. "Promise me, Pey, promise me," she whispered. "Promise me you'll find your father and forgive him!"

"I promise, Mama, I promise. I won't let you down. But how do I forgive someone that didn't want me, that didn't want us? He should be here now, taking care of you, and he's not. I've worked my entire life trying to prove to him that I was worthy of being his son."

Peyton began to cry more. "Like... why do I have to forgive someone who never wanted me? Why do I have to forgive someone who didn't want the angel of my life? Mama, I'm not that strong," he said while wiping the tears from his face.

As Peyton was talking, his mother clenched his hand and face, kissed him on the forehead and whispered, "Know who you are, and know that you are the love that the world needs. Give that and be that!"

Seconds later, the monitor began to beep faster and faster until it flatlined...

The nurses and the on-call doctor rushed in. "Sir, we need you to move back and let us work. Nurse, push five of epi..." the on-call doctor yelled.

"Doctor, doctor, she's *do not resuscitate*."

"Is she? When did she change her directive? She didn't have a DNR when she checked in. I need you all updating charts sooner!"

"She changed it last night. She said she wanted to change it after she spoke to her son one last time." The nurse looked at Peyton, crying in the corner.

"Son, do you have anyone here? Is there anyone we can call for you?" the doctor asked.

Peyton didn't answer. He just slid down the wall, yelling, "Help her. Help my mom. Why aren't y'all doing anything? Help her. She's a good person. Help my mom. *Pleeease*? Don't just stand there. Why isn't anyone doing anything? Help her. *Help her!*" he pleaded.

Peyton couldn't understand why they weren't trying to revive his mom. He jumped up and ran to the bed. "Mom, don't go. Don't leave me!" he screamed as tears ran down his cheeks.

He started doing chest compressions. Looking frantically back at the nurse behind him, "Is this right? Is it? Am I doing it right?" he asked desperately.

"Somebody help me. This is a hospital, right? Help me!" he yelled as he looked back at the staff all standing in the entrance to the room.

As he continued with chest compressions, the nurse tried to stop him, but the doctor grabbed the nurse's arm and whispered, "Leave him be... leave him be."

"Doc, please help me. Am I doing it right? Mama, come back to me. Mama, don't go. You said you'd always be here with me. You promised!"

Peyton's chest compressions were futile, yet he persisted. He continued for nearly six minutes until exhaustion took over him. Sweat dripped from his forehead and tears ran down his face. Peyton was torn inside. The staff just waited with him, watched him to ensure he didn't hurt himself, and even occasionally wiped the sweat from his forehead, as his compressions slowed.

They eventually tried to move Peyton out of the way so the doctor could confirm time of death. Peyton fought and begged them to let him continue to revive his mom. "Pleeease. She's coming back," he begged.

He fought the staff so he could stay close to his mother. As he became more and more agitated, the doctor had to call for additional staff in the room just to restrain him. "It's time, son. It's time to let her go."

"Nooo, I can't, I won't," Peyton yelled.

They managed to restrain Peyton, and he stopped fighting. As the security officer pulled him back, he began to cry harder, and the guard just hugged him. "It's OK, son. It's OK. She's going to a better place. And you carried her to the very end. She'll always be with you. I'm sorry. I'm so so sorry, Mr. Love. She loves you, and you love her. That will never end. That love will never die, son."

Peyton hugged the security officer and cried in his arms as he looked at his mom just lying there, lifeless and still. He was broken. He was there, then, in the moment... at the end.

As the doctor was preparing to call time of death, the silence in the room was deafening besides Peyton's sobs. Now that he was calm, Peyton walked slowly to his mom's side. The doctor nodded to the staff that it was OK.

As he got closer to the bed, the doctor placed his hand on Peyton's back. He rubbed Peyton to provide some level of comfort. Since Jasmine was basically family and well-liked at the hospital, her passing was different. All the nurses on staff were now lined up outside of the room to say their final goodbyes.

Peyton kissed his mother's forehead and whispered softly, "I love you, Mom, and I promise." He reached his hand toward her forehead and traced a heart upon her.

The heartfelt moment ended with their hands interlocked, tears on Peyton's cheeks, and his final heart on the crest of his mother's head.

Peyton was broken, but he was there, then, in the moment. He was at his lowest point, but he was there at the end with his mother. He carried his mother to the very end.

Jasmine died at 2:23 a.m.

PART III

CHAPTER 12
RAIN AND THE FORGOTTEN LIGHTS

290 Beach Street, San Francisco, California.

Peyton stepped on the tram on a brisk, cloudy San Francisco morning, determined, driven, and full of hope. He had such hope because he had come to the moment in his life where he would finally find his estranged father, forgive him, and fulfill his mother's dying wish. Though his grandparents were skeptical of what Peyton would uncover, or the type of person he would find, they supported his passion to find his father.

After waiting a year after Jasmine's passing, Peyton began his quest. Searching for months and working up the courage to confront the man who had abandoned him so many years prior, Peyton had his mind set and took the leap of faith.

This leap, however, would prove to be the largest of his life, with no promise of reward or resolution.

So many thoughts clouded his mind as he read the map and knew he'd exit the tram on Fillmore Street. *Will my father recognize me? What will I say to him after all these years? Will he invite me inside, and the two of us just pick up life from that point on?* All these thoughts ran through Peyton's head, but he didn't allow the fear of the unknown to avert the mental journey ahead.

As he rode the tram to the stop closest to his father's address, the questions that loomed the most and circled the coils of his mind were: *Why did you leave me? Why didn't you want me?*

Seemingly simple and normal questions to ask, but after twenty-nine years, he wrestled with how he would approach these questions and ensure that they didn't come out jumbled and confused. *Where will I even begin?* Though he didn't know how or where he would start his questions, he pressed forward with determination.

Peyton got off the tram at the Fillmore and Chestnut Street exit, and walked nearly four blocks uphill, following his phone's GPS and walking instructions. With each intersection he passed, he became more and more nervous, stomach churning with each step, yet he pressed on.

Questions of doubt filled his head, but his hope for the future trumped his doubt with each step uphill.

As he crossed Pierce Street, he saw a park bench and noticed several people playing with dogs, families having picnics, and kids frolicking through the tall grass. He walked over, sat down, laid his suitcase on the ground, and opened it up.

Peyton had carried this suitcase with him for decades. It was the only piece of his father that remained.

He decided to take a break on the park bench after walking for nearly thirty minutes through the hills of San Francisco's lovely marina district. He reached down into the suitcase, and pulled out a brown paper bag that held his sandwich and a water bottle.

Though it was likely that Peyton was in fact hungry and thirsty from his travels, it was more likely that he was either extremely nervous, killing time, or simply trying to work up the mental courage to face the very person he'd wanted in his life for years.

The fact remained that he'd come too far to turn around now.

He was there, present, in the moment in his life for which he'd waited. He had no choice but to continue his journey to find and reunite with his father.

As he sat and ate, consistently doubting his purpose in San Francisco, he found solace and peace in thinking about his lovely mother and in knowing that he was fulfilling her dying wish.

He whispered softly under his breath as he watched the dogs fetch frisbees and tennis balls. "You've come too far, Pey. Everything will work out as it should. There's absolutely no chance that he won't want me after he sees all that I have accomplished," he whispered between bites.

He finished his sandwich and water, threw away his trash, and continued his journey of hope.

As he walked closer to the address, he saw a man of tall stature, full beard, and brown hair standing outside his home watering his flowers. Peyton's heart nearly jumped out of his chest. He walked slower, not knowing what the first words to his father would be.

As he moved closer, the man looked up and greeted him cordially. "Hello there, how are you, sir?"

"I'm... I'm... fine... and you sir?" Peyton replied nervously.

"Well, it's a beautiful day, so I am just out enjoying this weather and taking care of these flowers. Couldn't ask for a better day, am I right? Though I did hear it was about to rain soon," the bearded stranger said while tending to his flowers.

"Yeah, it's definitely a beautiful..." Peyton looked up and noticed he was at 270 Beach Street, "...day. Those are beautiful flowers, by the way, sir." He was a bit relieved. A piece of him wasn't ready to actually meet his father yet, but he took the next step regardless.

"Oh, thank you. Well, you have a great day. Love the vintage suitcase, by the way," the stranger replied.

Peyton looked down at the suitcase he had clenched tight within his hands, his palms sweaty from thinking as he'd approached that the man watering the flowers was his father. He thanked the gentleman and continued walking down the street.

As he walked further and further down the path to discovery, his thoughts ran rampant. With every step forward, he took mental steps backward. Though he became more excited, he also became increasingly afraid of the potential of not being accepted. How could so few steps host so many thoughts?

There he stood, 290 Beach Street. It was a simple yet beautiful Victorian-style home. The home was painted sky blue, trimmed with white paneling, and surrounded by roses of all colors. Peyton liked roses a lot. His mother had kept them around the house for years while he was growing up.

Peyton was always observant. As he stood at the bottom of the steps, he admired the architecture. Though the home was connected to other homes, his attention was drawn to the "Welcome, All Are Welcome" sign posted above the crest of the door. Fortuitous, he might even say...

He took a step upward...

It seemed like an eternity as he climbed the stairs. *What will I say? How will I feel? How will I be received?*

With each measured step, Peyton became more apprehensive, but he continued upward.

Standing at the door of destiny, the door of wonder, the door of questions, Peyton was at his eternal mental crossroads. He placed the suitcase down, gathered his courage, and rang the doorbell. His heart was so loud he could nearly hear it beating from within his chest.

He could hear a dog barking, someone running to the door, and the usual, "I'll get it."

As the door began to open, his life moved in slow motion. It was the moment he'd waited on, but what would greet him? What would be on the other side of this door of eternity?

A young lady answered the door, and she looked at Peyton

confused, as though she was waiting on a delivery. He was not what she'd expected.

"Hi, can I help you?" she asked.

"Umm, yes, I'm looking for Mr. Love, Mark Love."

"Yeah, that's my dad... what do you need?" the girl asked.

"I... I just..." Peyton could barely get the words out because he'd waited nearly thirty years to meet his father only to take steps to meet him and find out he also had a sibling.

For the first time, Peyton not only realized that his father had started an entire new family, but he began to consider that might be why he'd never come back for Peyton.

"I'm Peyton, and I just need to speak with Mr. Mark Love," he said.

She looked back. "Daaaddy, someone's at the door for you," she yelled.

Waiting in anticipation, Peyton heard, "I'm coming, I'm coming." It was the first time Peyton had even heard his father's voice. His heart nearly fell through his stomach. Being as observant as he was, his attention was drawn away from his father's voice.

Looking past the girl, Peyton could see a painting that read, "Live simply, Love Generously & Learn Constantly." Although he was more nervous than he'd ever been, for some reason, reading that quote gave him a sense of calm.

He looked down at the suitcase, awaiting the confrontation... awaiting the moment he'd finally meet his father. He had photos and a few stories from his mom but had never met the man he'd worked all of his life to prove his worthiness to.

Behind the young lady, he could see two males sitting on the couch watching what seemed to be the English Premier League. "Who's playing?" Peyton asked.

One of the guys looked at the door and replied, "It's a replay of Man United and Chelsea."

"Oh, I love Man United," Peyton replied.

One of the guys laughed and said, "Ohhh no, not another Man U fan. Our father is delusional and loves them as well."

"Who's delusional?" a man said jokingly, his voice coming down the stairs and headed toward the door.

Though this moment had been building in Peyton's mind for years, he took comfort in the fact that he and his father already had something in common; their love for Manchester United's football club.

Peyton stood bewildered because he realized he not only had a sister, but he also had two brothers.

The weather had been threatening to rain all day, and it just so happened that at that very moment, the threat became a reality.

"Ooo, it's raining," the girl said. "Would you like to step inside, out of the rain?"

"No, thank you, I'm OK," Peyton replied.

She gave way as she opened the door a bit more.

Peyton's heart beat fast, his sweat masked by the drizzle that was upon his face. Just then, a man of medium height, with a full head of gray hair and a huge smile, came around the corner, grabbed the door, and opened it fully.

"Hey, man, what's going on? Did I hear I have a true Man United fan at my door?" his dad joked.

"Yes sir, umm, yes sir," Peyton answered. Although his lips were answering the question about soccer, his heart and mind were investigating the man who stood before him, his father.

"Good, because these clowns don't truly know soccer. They just like who's winning at the moment," his father said as he looked back and joked with what Peyton assumed were his sons, Peyton's brothers.

"A Manchester United fan is always welcome in my home, so what can I do for you, sir?"

Peyton just stood there for a moment. He didn't respond.

He stood there, looking at his father for the first time. He had so many questions. Where would he begin his inquiries? What would he say? How would this meeting go? These thoughts clouded his mind.

"Sir... sir, how can I help you?" Mark asked.

"I'm... sir, I'm Peyton," Peyton stuttered.

"OK, nice to meet you, Peyton. What can I do for you?" his dad asked nonchalantly.

"No. No, I mean... I'm Peyton..." he said awkwardly, with his brow furrowed and his hand over his mouth.

"No, I heard you. What can I do for—"

"Love... I'm Peyton Love."

He watched as his father's countenance slowly transitioned from happy, to confused, to disbelief.

Everything started to slow down. It even seemed as though the rain had slowed. There Peyton was meeting his father for the first time, and there were no words he could form besides, "I'm Peyton, Peyton Love." He needed to say it. "I'm your..."

His father looked down, saw the suitcase, his old suitcase, and quickly stepped outside on the porch with Peyton, drawing the door closed behind them.

"Dad, where are you going?" the girl asked.

"Nowhere, I'll be back. I'll be right back," Mark replied to her as he latched the door.

Standing in the steady rain, Peyton looked at him and said, "I'm Peyton Love, I'm your... I'm your son."

His father just stood there for a moment. Then the two of them looked each other up and down, his father looking at the suitcase, then back at Peyton.

"I'm your son," Peyton said again.

What Peyton heard from his father next cut through his soul like a sharp Ginsu knife through hot margarine.

"How did you find me?" Mark asked.

Peyton had waited years to find his father. He'd lost all he had in his mother's death, he was so excited to meet the man who'd fathered him, yet these were the first true words his father had for him.

Peyton was immediately broken. Raindrops hitting his face, he reached down and grabbed the suitcase.

"Is that... Is that mine? I haven't seen that in..." his father stuttered.

"Yes, it's the one you left behind. I've kept it all this time," Peyton replied.

"But why? It's so old."

"I kept it because it was all I had of you. All my life, I worked hard to fill this suitcase with things that would make you proud, in hopes of one day finding you and showing you—"

Mark cut him off. "Wait. You can't just come here, drop this on me, in front of my family, and expect—"

Now it was Peyton's turn to cut him off. "Am I not your family? You're my *father*. At least let me show you all that I've done... all I've accomplished!"

"Listen, you cannot just show up here after all these years, on my doorstep with my family inside, and drop this bomb on me," Mark said forcefully, though whispering, so his children inside wouldn't hear the ruckus.

Peyton, taking the cue from his father, leaned closer to Mark. "Look, it wasn't my intention to drop a bomb. I just wanted to find my father. Imagine, if one of them," Peyton pointed toward the glass door and the living room, "who I assume are my brothers and sister, imagine if you didn't know them, didn't know where in the world they were... would you not move heaven and earth to find them?" Peyton's voice began to escalate.

Trying to deescalate the conversation, Mark placed one hand on Peyton's shoulder. "Peyton, is it? Peyton, I understand what you're saying, but like I said, I have a family now, and they don't know my entire past."

"So because I'm your *past*, does that mean I don't exist?" Peyton asked rhetorically, shaking his head.

"No...No, I'm not saying..." Mark stuttered, trying to manage his discussion with Peyton without alarming his children inside.

"OK. OK. I understand. Just let me show you some things first, please?" Peyton begged as the rain hit his face. His emotions were heightened because here he finally was meeting his father, and it wasn't going anything like he'd dreamed it would. He believed in the impossible, in the occasional fairy tale ending, even though his life had been anything but a storied fairy tale.

Peyton kneeled and started to open the suitcase. "I've collected all these things to show you one day." When he opened the suitcase, the first thing he pulled out was the photo of his mother and father. "See? Look, I've kept this photo for all of these years because I knew it had meaning to you. Look how happy you and my mom were. Look—"

His father cut him off. "Peyton, I'm sorry, but I can't do this right now. You have to go. We can't do this on my porch with my family inside."

"Go? Where will I go? Where *can* I go? I came this far to find you!" Peyton exclaimed as he began to cry. "My mother died, and you weren't there. I needed you for years, and you weren't there. I struggled all my life and wanted my father, and you weren't there. We struggled and my mother gave me all that she could, and you weren't there. All I had were a few stories of you, and you weren't there... And after all of that, all you have to say is, 'I can't do this right now?' Really... really?" Peyton took a small step back and looked at his father in disgust. "That's all you have to say to me? You're more afraid of what your children, my siblings, will have to say instead of being worried about what your very own child whom you've never seen in nearly thirty years has to say?"

Mark nonchalantly leaned back on the front door, shrugging and shaking his head. "Peyton, you have to go. I'm sorry," he said, whispering so Peyton's siblings inside wouldn't hear.

"My last name is *Love*. That's your last name. It's me. It's me, your son, your Peyton Love. I know I'm mentally challenged, but I'm smart enough to have found you. I'm smart enough to know how to forgive. I'm smart enough to know that even though you left us, we can start from today and move forward."

"I'm sorry, Peyton. You have to leave," Mark said with little care or concern for how Peyton was feeling. Though Mark apologized several times, his words were empty.

Peyton looked up from trying to show his father all his awards and realized that his father still didn't want him after all this time.

The rain hit his face, masking the tears that began to flow. Drop after drop, Peyton's heart was breaking as his worst nightmare was becoming a reality right before his eyes. "If I'm not wanted here with my father, where do I go? What is there left for me?" he pleaded in pain.

His father simply said, "I'm sorry. I have to go inside with my family."

As Mark turned and began to walk into the house, Peyton grabbed his arm. His father pulled away in disgust.

"Please … please don't go again. I feel so useless saying this, but I need you right now. I need you, Dad. Please don't go."

His father walked into the house and closed the door in his face.

Brokenhearted, Peyton grabbed his suitcase, closed it without latching it, walked to the bottom of the step, and spoke softly to himself, "How did it come to this? How did I get here?"

The rain pouring harder, Peyton, broken and alone, walked across the street and sat on the curb. He clutched his suitcase on his chest, held the photo of his father and mother, and just cried.

The photo slipped from his hands, and he watched it lie on the ground in the rain. The collecting water quickly washed the photo and began to take it away.

Peyton watched the photo slide down the curb. It flipped multiple times, and for the last time, from afar, he caught a glimpse of his father and mother smiling, as though they were smiling back at him.

The photo made its way to the gutter. Just before it would be lost forever to him, he considered grabbing it and saving it. Instead, he watched it fall out of sight.

"What's the point?" he whispered, resting his head on the suitcase, broken.

Peyton set the suitcase on the ground, opened the top, and looked at all the trophies, awards, certificates, and accommodations he had amassed. He had nothing left in the world. He was angry, crying, and sitting in the rain all alone, while the father he'd wanted to meet for nearly three decades was no more than a hundred feet away, discarding him yet again.

For the first time, Peyton wasn't calculated. Reason and rationale escaped him. Angrily, he flung the top of the suitcase open, kneeled down next to it, and grabbed the first medal he'd won in the Special Olympics in the fifth grade.

Grasping it tightly in his hands and looking at his father's home, the home where his father lived without him, the home where his father had started a new family, the home where his father had cast him out yet again, Peyton held the trophy tightly.

Passion and anger overcame him, and he threw the medal at his father's home. Once the trophy hit and broke the glass of the front door, he became even more enraged. He pulled medal after medal from the suitcase his father had left so many years ago and hurled them toward the house. In anger, and with tears in his eyes, he grabbed and threw... and threw. With every medal, with each trophy he threw, he became even more distraught.

Balling up certificates, he launched them toward the house, even though they didn't stand a chance of reaching the home from across the street.

But that didn't stop Peyton from grabbing the next award and letting out his rage and frustration on the innocent Victorian home.

The neighbor that he'd seen earlier tending to his flowers was witnessing the chaos, perched upon his porch, admiring his flowers receiving fresh rain. He was worried because he was good friends with Mark, and he'd only caught very little of Mark's exchange with Peyton.

The concerned neighbor took out his cell phone and called the cops.

Meanwhile, a distraught Peyton continued to throw his trophies, medals, and awards toward the home.

"The thought of you meant the world to me. Finding you was my everything; it was my last hope," Peyton yelled with tears in his eyes. "I worked hard all my life to find you… For what? To be denied? To be discarded yet again?"

Peyton was humiliated and in pain as he hurled the contents from the suitcase toward the house he'd thought would become his home.

Inside, his brothers and his sister screamed at their father. "Dad, who is this guy that wanted to see you? Why is he throwing shit at the house? He's already broken the glass door, and he's not stopping."

"Everything will be fine," Mark answered with frustration. "Y'all just go upstairs."

Meanwhile, Peyton had nearly exhausted the contents of his suitcase. All that remained were his graduation certificate from speech therapy, a few medals from the special Olympics, a photo of his mother taped to the underside of the suitcase, and her note that he'd kept.

You are meant for greatness. In times of turmoil, remember that you have gone to hell and back.

Don't stop now. Continue to press forward. The world demands the LOVE you can give. Forgive, love like crazy, and be the man the world needs you to be. Be PEYTON LOVE.

Peyton fell back on the curb. As he sat there, contemplating life and his father not wanting him, his eyes watered over. Red and blue lights caught his attention. Hazy from the rain and his tears, Peyton looked up to see two SFPD squad cars pulling up.

"Son, please place the suitcase on the ground, stand up, place your hands in the air, and turn around." They'd seen the last trophy he'd thrown toward the home as they were arriving on the scene.

"Sir, can you hear me?" the officer yelled. "Stand up, get on your feet *now*, place the suitcase on the ground, turn around, and place your hands in the air. You can't just go around destroying property in this neighborhood."

The second officer, on seeing Peyton's face, said, "Aww shit, he's retarded."

"I don't give a shit. He can't destroy private property," the first officer said.

"Sir, I say again, *stand up, place the suitcase on the ground, turn around, and place your hands in the air. Do not make us tase your ass.*"

Peyton complied with the officers. He placed the suitcase on the ground, stood up wet from the rain, crying, and raised his hands as instructed.

As the officers arrested him and walked him to the car, Peyton said, "This is my dad's home. My father is inside. Ask him. He will tell you."

"Sir, please don't resist. Just keep walking. We can talk and figure this out once we get you in the car. Are you carrying any weapons we need to know about?"

"Weapons? What?" Peyton asked, confused, as he stumbled to the squad car.

The officer read him his Miranda rights and walked him to the police car. Just before Peyton was placed in the car, he looked at the house and saw his father standing outside on the porch, watching.

"Daaad, Daaad, tell them I'm your son. I'm your son. Don't let this happen. Please ... please help me. Pleeease," Peyton begged his father.

After they placed Peyton in the car, Peyton leaned against the window and sobbed.

The officers went to Mark, who was now standing at the bottom of the porch, spoke with him briefly, then walked back to the car.

"Son, you're going downtown. You can't destroy property without consequences."

His father just let them take Peyton. As the car slowly drove away, Peyton made eye contact with his father. No words were yelled from the back of the patrol car, there were just tears, and Peyton watching his father turn away slowly to return to his new life. Peyton was destroyed, weeping in the back of the car with his knees pulled up to his chest.

The ride to the police station was silent yet contained the loudest mental moments Peyton had ever had in his life. Thoughts, sorrows, and regrets encompassed his mind.

After he was booked into the station, the second officer said, "You'll get a phone call, son. Do you have anyone you can call?"

Because he was ashamed to call his grandparents and inform them that he'd been arrested, there was only one person Peyton wanted to call. His mentor, his friend, and the only other person he had left in the world.

"You have a collect call from the San Francisco Police department. Press one if you want to accept."

James accepted the call. "Hello?"

Speaking into the phone, barely understandable, Peyton sobbed, "He didn't want me. I have nothing!" His eyes were red from hours of crying, his clothes dirty from the rain and sitting on the curb. He'd never been so low. He poured his heart out to James, who comforted him, letting him know that he wasn't alone in this world.

Peyton sat quietly for the next few minutes, listening to James. He had no more words to give. He just listened. Peyton hung up the phone, leaned against the wall, and the officer helped him back to his cell. He walked into the holding cell, kneeled down, and placed his face in his hands. He was there, in the moment, and broken.

The next morning, James was at the police station to bail Peyton out. Peyton initially didn't have many words for James as he finally got into the car, buckled his seatbelt, and laid his head against the window.

Barely a mile from the jail, James could see the mental anguish on Peyton's face, so he decided to pull the car over into an empty downtown parking lot. Pulling Peyton close, and hugging him, he began to whisper into Peyton's ear. "You will get through this moment, Peyton. This, like many moments before, is just a stepping stone toward greatness."

Peyton responded, "I just can't believe it. I have nothing. Why me? What am I on this earth for? I don't want to live anymore, James. I have no purpose here. Why did God make me like this? I did everything right, James. He clearly didn't want me because of how I am. Why did God make me like this, James?"

James had very few uplifting words, but he sat with Peyton in the car for nearly an hour and provided a shoulder for him to lean on and a listening ear. James had always been against Peyton going to find his father because he felt like Peyton had come so far, and he feared this potential setback. But in normal James fashion, he supported Peyton's decision and vowed to stand behind him regardless of the outcome.

Darkness

Peyton walked to the door of his hotel room, which James had booked for him prior to searching for his father.

They had adjoining rooms, but even though James had already entered his room, Peyton, being in a weird state of mind, just stood there, holding the room key.

Leaning against the door, Peyton contemplated how he had gotten to where he was. All his life, he'd waited to meet his father... Waited to prove that he was worthy of his father's love, yet this day, this moment, this time had come and gone, and he didn't find it.

He placed the key into the door, walked in, closed it, and stood at the entrance in silence. All he had was the hurt that still loomed within his heart... the hurt and the suitcase in hand.

It was mostly empty now. Along with his mother's note and photo, all that remained were a few medals that didn't have the pleasure of being tossed.

Peyton appeared unbothered and seemingly numb from the entire ordeal. Or maybe it was that he was emotionally drained. He turned on his music from his phone and sat on the bed, staring at the ceiling, with his back against the headboard.

After some time, he walked to the kitchenette, opened a pack of ramen noodles, and filled the cup with water. James knew

Peyton's routine of ramen noodles before bed, so he'd ensured the room was fully stocked with all Peyton's favorite flavors. Peyton loved mixing chicken and shrimp.

He opened his suitcase and began packing up his things while the noodles were cooking in the microwave. He wanted to leave and return to Boston as soon as possible, but James had convinced him to stay a few days in case his father came to his senses and wanted to see him.

The microwave buzzed, so Peyton retrieved the bowl of mixed noodles and tried to open the seasoning packets. As he struggled with them, it was evident that his heart was weighing heavy, as he occasionally stopped, looked toward the ceiling, and shook his head.

He wasn't hungry but knew he needed to eat. Yet all he could think about was finding and losing his father all over again.

His frustration at not being able to open the packets transferred to his frustration at how his life had spiraled downhill. For the first time since he was released from jail, Peyton broke down. He cried and yelled as he took his frustrations out on the entire room. He threw the TV to the ground, flipped the mattress on the ground, and threw his beloved suitcase toward the door.

As he launched the suitcase toward the door, Peyton fell back onto the floored mattress. He stopped and looked toward the kitchenette. His eyes caught something. He saw the knife he'd set atop the counter that he'd planned to use to open the seasoning packets.

James heard all of the commotion and ran to Peyton's door. Knocking on the door frantically, James yelled, "Peyton... Peyton, let me in!"

Ignoring James's knocking, Peyton slowly walked toward the kitchenette and stared at the knives on the countertop. There he stood as the moment unfolded. Broken and feeling alone, scarred with the continued pain of not being wanted, and feeling at fault, he considered ending his life alone, in his room, without anyone to care for him. He had reached his lowest of lows. He was ready to end it all.

James continued to knock, and Peyton continued to ignore him.

He pulled the paring knife out of the set, walked to the corner where he'd thrown the suitcase, and slowly fell to the floor with the wall supporting his back.

A silent moment ensued with only knocks and begging from James at the door, as Peyton sat in the corner crying, holding the knife.

He placed the knife up to his wrist and just stared at the blade as he gently ran the sharp edge against his skin.

By this time, James had gone down to the front desk, got a key for Peyton's room, and was running back up the stairs since the elevator was taking too long.

Peyton was still sitting in the corner with the knife, next to his suitcase. He had a flashback of his mother in the hospital, explaining the moment she had first connected with him, and the words of affirmation that she'd recited to him, before he had even been born.

> You are going to be strong. You are going to face all adversity and push right through it. I will always believe in you, and though things will get tough, I'll always be here with you. There is nothing that you can't survive, nothing you can't fight through.
>
> In the inevitable moment where you feel like this is your end, just know that you were created for greatness, and greatness demands sacrifice. Not sacrifice of the known, but rather, the sacrifice of facing the unknown... The sacrifice of facing the

end. The sacrifice of giving your all and not knowing how you will survive through any moment. The sacrifice of believing that your love will surpass and overcome ALL!

His life with his mother always being by his side, with their moments of pure happiness, flashed through his mind. Jasmine was no longer physically with Peyton, but the words of strength she'd recited to little Peyton when he was yet inside of her gave him strength.

Peyton dropped the knife and began to sob. Just then, the door opened, and his mentor James ran in and saw the state of the room with Peyton on the floor in the corner, crying, knife near his leg. James, as always, was right on time for Peyton. He ran to him, fell to the floor, and held him in his arms. "All will be OK, Peyton. We'll get through this, son."

Peyton looked up at James, and the two just embraced each other as the night slipped away. Peyton fell asleep right there on the floor, and James covered him with a blanket.

Knowing that Peyton had met his threshold, James cleaned the room, packed their things, and booked them a mid-morning flight back to Boston for the following day. He took the photo of Peyton's mother out of his suitcase, and placed it in Peyton's hand.

Peyton woke the next morning with his mother's photo in his hand to find James sitting by his side, drinking coffee. He looked up at James and whispered, "I want to thank you. I'm sorry for—"

James cut him off. "We're going home. This city doesn't deserve you. I have you now."

Peyton stood up to see his bags packed and the room organized. He thanked James, apologized for his behavior, and the two of them headed for the airport.

CHAPTER 13
VOICEMAILS

While in college, Peyton had secured an internship with Wholverton Associates, one of the largest and most respected civil engineering firms in the nation. He did such an amazing job that after he finished his internship, they offered him a full-time position in their Boston satellite office. Peyton had now been working for Wholverton Associates for six years, and he was a senior civil engineer in charge of the North Charleston District bridges and traffic commuting division.

Meeting his father after so many years, only to find him and realize that he was still not wanted, had changed Peyton. In the five years since Peyton had met his father, his life had become rather bleak. Going through life feeling alone, Peyton went home day after day, with feelings of no purpose.

His few moments of happiness during these years were mainly derived from the love he received from his grandparents and his relationship with James. However, these fleeting moments of happiness were often met with memories of what he deemed defeat. Defeat at not being enough. The defeat of losing his mother. The defeat of finding his father only to be turned away yet again.

On an ordinary Tuesday night, Peyton said his goodbyes at work, clocked out, and walked to his car.

Before his mother had passed, he'd usually spent his rides home FaceTiming her and telling her all about his day. But now, he just drove home, day after day, in silence.

Arriving home, Peyton walked to the back of the car, opened the trunk, looked at the suitcase, and paused a moment before picking it up. He walked into the house, placed the suitcase down next to his couch, walked to his kitchen, and made his usual cup of noodles.

This was his routine, nothing special, just going through the motions. Every night, he made his dinner, sat down, and watched Netflix before preparing for bed and starting all over the next day.

Peyton was showering for bed when he heard his phone ringing. Figuring it was either James or someone calling from work, Peyton ignored the call and let it go to voicemail.

When he got out of the shower, he kneeled down beside his bed to say his nightly prayers. "God, thank you for everything you have provided me. Thank you for showing me the beauty that exists in the world. I only ask three things: help me to be a better person tomorrow than I was today, help me to give love to the world, and take care of my mother. Mama, I love you, and thank you for taking care of me from above. I miss you, and I hope to see you soon!"

As Peyton climbed into bed, he remembered he had a missed call. He leaned over, grabbed his phone, and saw a number he didn't recognize, with a 415 area code. He saw that he had a voice mail, but since he didn't recognize the number, he cleared the missed call, turned over, and went to bed.

The next morning, Peyton woke up and said his prayers like

every morning, then went to the bathroom to complete his morning routine.

Walking around his home in tighty-whities, Peyton made his breakfast and packed his lunch for the day.

For years, like clockwork, James had sent Peyton inspirational messages in the mornings. When Peyton finished packing his lunch and making his breakfast, he grabbed his phone, and there was his morning inspirational quote from James.

> Life is what you make it today. Yesterday is gone. You have two choices: take today and own it; or focus on yesterday, which you will never see again. Which choice will you make?

Peyton smiled as he read the message. He replied,

> You already know which one I'm going to choose. The only choice she would have wanted me to make!

As he watched the three dots while James responded, he noticed the notification of a voice mail from last night.

James replied with two simple emojis, the strong-arm emoji and the angel emoji. A very simple response, but James always had a way of speaking volumes to Peyton.

He closed the thread and decided to listen to the voice mail.

"Hello Mr. Peyton, my name is Penelope. We met a few years ago in San Francisco. I'm... well, I think I'm your sister. We met briefly, and I'm so sorry how things turned out. I don't really know what to say, and honestly, I don't know why I'm calling. I guess I just want to speak with you.

"I'm so angry that we never got a chance to know each other, and so many years have passed, although I guess we can't focus on the past. In that moment you stood on the porch, I can't believe that I was face to face with my own flesh and blood and didn't even know. Anyway, if you want to talk, I'd love to speak with you. My number is 415-555-8004. Call me anytime. I'd love to just talk. I hope you have a great day, and I hope to hear from you soon!"

Peyton's heart dropped as he listened to the message. Even though he was preparing to leave for work, he set his suitcase down, fell onto the couch, and listened to the message repeatedly. He wanted to call back but didn't know what he'd say to his sister. Sitting and thinking for a while, he went to his missed calls, and stared at the number for what seemed like hours.

He pressed the red missed call number... it rang as he sat in nervous anticipation.

"Hello... Peyton...?"

"Hi, yes, it's me, Peyton."

"Oh gosh, it's really you. Thank you so much for calling me back. Hold on, let me go somewhere where I can talk."

"Oh gosh, I forgot you're on the West Coast. Did I call too early?" Peyton asked.

"Nooo, not at all," his sister replied. "I'm at this silly hot yoga class. Who takes hot yoga at 6 a.m., right?" She laughed. "Hold on, let me step outside."

"OK, no worries." Peyton sat there with his heart beating out of his chest. He was so nervous but so excited at the same time. He was speaking to his family for the first time in years.

"OK, sorry about that, I'm back," she said.

"No, no, you're fine."

"Oh gosh, I'm so glad you called me back. How are you? Like I can't believe it's actually you!"

"I know, right? It's you. I'm good. Thank you for reaching out to me. I'm good, though. I'm just actually getting ready for work."

"Oh nice, is now a good time to chat, or do you need to go?" she asked.

Both were very nervous and not really knowing where to take the conversation.

"No, I'm good. I was just walking out the door, but I'm always super early to the office because I like to set the temperature before anyone gets there," he joked.

"Hahaha, makes sense. You're like me, then. I like to control the temperature at work too. My brothers… Oh gosh, our brothers always tell me that I'm a control freak."

They both laughed.

"So, I don't really even know where to start," Penelope said. "Honestly, I didn't think you would call me back. I figured you'd hate us because of how things turned out when we initially met."

"No, I could never hate you. Our last name is *Love*, right? Hate could never be between us, right!?" Peyton replied.

"Oh my gosh, you're so right. Love is our last name and our mantra, right!?"

An awkward silence followed as they both felt the same for each other, yet neither knew exactly how to say it.

Penelope continued, "So you said 'get to the office.' What do you do? Like I still can't even believe it's you."

"Well, I'm a civil engineer here in Boston. I basically work with traffic and bridges in our commuter division. It's a fancy way of saying that I make sure the traffic lights, specific to the bridges, are operating efficiently, so we don't have traffic jams."

"Ha, well, we probably need you here in the Bay Area, because all we have is major traffic on the 101." Penelope laughed.

Peyton sat back and talked with his sister for an hour, each of them getting to know the other.

As the call reached its end, Penelope asked, "Hey, Peyton, so the real reason why I was calling was, I have taken a leave of absence from work, and once I tracked you down, I just wanted to know if it would be OK if I came out to Boston to officially meet you, and spend some time with you?

"You don't have to answer now, but after I found out about you a few years ago, it tore my heart up that we had no clue that each other existed. It's taken me a long time to forgive my father, but now I'm here and I want, or better yet, need to meet you."

Peyton remained silent and didn't respond.

"Peyton, are you there? Did I lose you?" Penelope asked.

"No... No... I'm here. I'm just in shock, honestly. I never thought that I'd hear from you or my father. How, how is he?"

"He's OK, well as can be expected. You don't have to answer now, Peyton. You can think about it, but I totally understand if you don't want to see or meet me. I just worked up the courage to call you. I mean, you're like my family. You're my brother, and I've wanted to meet you and get to know you. Just think about it. You have my number, and you can—"

Peyton cut her off. "There's nothing to think about. Of course, I'd love to meet you. I can show you around Boston and take you to all of my favorite eateries," he joked.

"Oh my gosh, I would love that," Penelope smiled with excitement. "Like I said, I took a leave of absence from work, so I can literally come out whenever. You just let me know what time works for you!"

Peyton could hear the excitement in her voice, and though he was just as excited, a part of him didn't want to get his hopes up just to be, let down again. He corralled his excitement and answered calmly. "OK, you can come this weekend or next, whatever works with your schedule. Right now, work is slow so I can take some time off and show you Beantown. By the way, do you know why they call it Beantown?" he asked.

"No, I don't actually." She laughed.

"Good, neither do I, but maybe we can find out together." Peyton snickered. "I've lived here all my life and still have no idea why we call it Beantown, but the thing I do know is, the Red Sox would smash the Giants in any series. Go Sox."

"Haha, you're probably right. We haven't won in years." Penelope chuckled. "OK, well, I'll come next weekend, so I can get some things in order first. Does that work with you? I'd like to spend a week getting to know you and seeing Beantown from your vantage point," she said.

"That would be perfect. Though I have no clue why we call it Beantown, I do know *all* the amazing spots that you *must* see!"

"OK, then it's a deal. I'll send you my itinerary after I book today. Just text me your email address, OK?"

"OK, that sounds great, Penelope. I'm excited to meet you. I knew the day I saw you that you were my sister. I was just sad that we didn't get a chance to officially meet," he said.

"Water under the bridge Peyton. We have now, and we'll focus on today and our future!" Penelope reassured him.

Peyton snuffed. "Hmph, wow, just wow," as he correlated what Penelope was saying with what he had just read from James's morning inspirational text.

"What?" Penelope asked cautiously. She didn't want to say the wrong thing and ruin their potential reuniting prior to it happening.

"It's nothing. It's just amazing how life works at times. I'm really excited to see you. I'll send you my email address. Send me your itinerary. I'm so excited to meet you!"

"OK, big brother, I will. I'm so glad you called back. You literally made my day. Now let me get back in here and sweat until I can't breathe. I'll see you soon."

They said their goodbyes, hung up, and both of them just sat on their sides of the US, smiling in excitement to meet each other.

Penelope sent him a text, a picture of her smiling, with the caption,

> I found my big brother, and today is AMAZING!!! Looking forward to meeting you again. With LOVE!

Peyton smiled as his eyes began to water reading that message. He felt wanted and loved by family for the first time since his mother had passed and his father had discarded him.

He took a photo of his suitcase at his feet and sent her the picture, saying,

> One day really soon, I'm excited to show my sister my city, as well as this most treasured relic of a suitcase.

After getting dressed for work, Peyton smiled, picked up his suitcase, and walked out of his door, looking to the sky and whispering, "Thank you, Mama. I love you, and I know you had something to do with this from above!"

He locked the door and went to work with a new smile and love for life. He was there, present, in the moment, and happy!

CHAPTER 14

BEANTOWN: TWO LOVES

As promised, Penelope sent her itinerary over to Peyton. He received it and put a calendar reminder in his Outlook. He sent her a text:

Peyton: I received your itinerary. I'm looking forward to hosting you! :)

Penelope: OK good, just send me your address. I'll just take an Uber to meet you.

Peyton: Not a chance.
There's no chance I'm going to let my sister come into town, and not meet her at the airport with the full red-carpet service LOL.

Penelope: You're so sweet to me, and we haven't even met yet. But seriously, you really don't have to. I don't want to take you away from anything you have going on. I don't mind taking an Uber at all.

Peyton: It's settled already. It's no trouble at all. From the moment you told me that you took a leave of absence, I mentally took time off as well, so we could spend time together exploring the city and getting to know each other.

Penelope: Oh Peyton, you didn't have to do that at all for me.

Peyton: I know, but I wanted to. I want to spend uninterrupted time with you. There's so much I want to show you, plus I want to introduce you to someone that's really important to me.

Penelope: Ooh, is there a future Mrs. Love I'll be meeting?

Peyton: No, not yet. LOL

Peyton: But my mentor, that I have known since I was a child, is dying to meet you and spend time with you as well. Is that OK?

Penelope: Of course, I'd absolutely love to meet anyone that's important to you.

Peyton: OK, perfect. I'm looking forward to meeting you, Penelope.

Penelope: Likewise, Peyton. See you soon brother.

    The entire week, Peyton had a new pep in his step. The world seemed different, brighter, and full of hope. He could smile again. He could smell smells again. Colors were more vibrant, and the world made sense again.

    With each passing morning, he counted down the days, and since he was a Capricorn and needed the sense of accomplishment, he marked each day off on the calendar. "One day closer until she's here," he said to himself.

    All week Peyton told all of his coworkers that his sister was coming into town, and they were all excited for him. He wanted to create an entire itinerary for her visit, so Peyton reached out to several tourism companies to get some ideas on top of his own.

The night before Penelope was supposed to arrive, Peyton double-checked the exhaustive list he'd compiled of about forty sites they could visit. He was clearly excited.

It was nearing midnight, and he hadn't slept a wink. Little did he know, neither had Penelope.

They were more similar than Peyton could have known.

Penelope spent the entire week looking at his Instagram, researching Boston, and telling her brothers about her upcoming visit. She didn't tell her father where she was going, just that she was taking a trip to get away for a bit, swearing her brothers to secrecy, of course.

Penelope and her father spoke multiple times a week. They were very close, but she played this trip very close to the chest. Honestly, she was afraid to tell her father that she was going to visit Peyton because she didn't know how he would react.

Would he be happy for her, or would he discourage her? That and the fact that her father was dealing with something very serious in his life made Penelope decide to keep this from him. But it didn't matter to her. She was headstrong and excited to finally meet her brother. She sent Peyton a text:

> Hey, I don't know if you're awake, but I just wanted to say for the millionth time, that I'm so excited to meet you tomorrow.

As she packed her bags, she continued to check her phone to see if Peyton would text back. He was three hours ahead of her, but her excitement didn't allow her to respect time zones. And then she saw it, three dots…

> Excitement is an understatement. I haven't been able to sleep for an entire week. Get here safe, and I'll see you at baggage claim.
>
> Hugs & Kisses. See you soon!

Peyton replied with the hug and smile emoji:

See you tomorrow...

Five a.m. and Peyton's alarm went off. He had only slept a few hours, but he felt more rested than he had in years. It was likely the adrenaline rushing through his veins or his heart pounding out of his chest; either way, it was a big day for him.

Penelope's flight was landing at 2:43 p.m., so Peyton started his morning routine as early as possible; he wanted to be ready.

In the past, his prayers were rather long, as he sat and spent quite a bit of time thinking about his mom after prayer. But today, as he kneeled down, he did so with anticipation. "God, and Mom, I just want to say thank you for today. Thank you for always being there for me. Please give me the words to say to Penelope. Most importantly, help me be a better person today than I was yesterday."

When Peyton concluded his morning prayers, his phone buzzed, and he knew it was James checking in.

> Peyton, I have no words of inspiration today. Today, you are the inspiration. You inspire me. You inspire me to hope. You inspire me to press forward through any situation that affects my life. You, yes you, are the inspiration for today.

Peyton smiled and responded:

> I'm not here without you James. Thank you.

He placed his phone on the bed and began getting dressed for the day. He made and finished his breakfast, then cleaned the entire house in preparation for Penelope's arrival.

Walking with haste to the car with the largest smile on his face, Peyton put his hybrid in reverse and started a journey that would alter his life forever.

When he arrived at Boston Logan, he parked and grabbed a sign from the trunk that he'd made for his sister's arrival.

He received the notification through the flight tracker that her flight had landed, so he went inside and waited patiently at baggage claim. Passenger after passenger came down the escalator. Peyton became more and more excited. Excited for what the future held and ecstatic to meet a member of his family.

And then, just like that, there she was... He saw Penelope halfway up the escalator, but since there was a TSA agent at the bottom prohibiting people from entering via the opposite direction, Peyton just ran to the bottom of the escalator with sign, and yelled, "*PENELOOOPPPPPEEEEE!!!!*"

She looked a tad older than what he remembered, but he knew right away she was the girl he'd met so many years ago.

Those in baggage claim looked at him with caution initially. A man randomly screaming in the baggage claim was unusual.

As Penelope heard his screams and saw his sign, she yelled, "*PEYYYYTOOONNN!*"

Penelope began running down the escalator as soon as she saw his sign. Others saw his sign and quickly understood why they both were so excited.

SISTER, I FOUND YOU!
YOU FOUND ME!
WELCOME TO BOSTON!"

As they ran to each other in what felt like slow motion, Peyton dropped the sign and embraced his sister for the very first time. The surrounding crowd began to clap and cheer—their positivity was infectious to all those viewing this apparent reuniting.

As they embraced, it was like the entire baggage claim had disappeared. The two of them just hugged each other, pausing only to see each other's faces and then quickly returning to their embraces of joy, crying tears of happiness.

"I'm so glad you're here," Peyton said.

"I'm so happy to meet you. My heart is so full right now, Peyton," replied Penelope.

Peyton just stared at Penelope as she spoke. "Let's get your bags and get out of here. I'm sooo glad you're here," he said while nodding.

"Oh my gosh, I love your sign you made for me... you made for us!"

Peyton and Penelope gathered her bags and walked to Peyton's car.

"Here, let me get that for you." Peyton grabbed her suitcase. "I hope it's OK, but I made up my guest room for you. I didn't know what you liked to eat, so I went to the store and got as much as I could think of." He laughed.

"I'm easy peasy, Peyton. I'm just happy to be here," she said.

The two of them drove to Peyton's home, and the entire ride, they caught up on so much lost time—so many questions, so many conversations that they'd never had the opportunity to have.

Arriving at Peyton's home, he smiled and said, "This is my home. It's not much, but it's mine, and it's cozy."

"Peyton, stop... it's beautiful. It's exactly what I imagined. I'm just happy to be here with you. I know this might sound weird, Peyton, but I love you. I mean, you're my actual brother! Like *wow!*"

Peyton listened to Penelope, looked her in the eyes, and responded, "I love you more than you will ever know."

The two of them walked inside and began to live their new lives *together*.

Port Before the Calm

The entire week, Peyton and Penelope toured the city of Boston. Since Peyton lived so close to the train, getting around town was not only easy, but was an adventure in its own right.

Peyton hadn't used public transportation much, and Penelope was from San Francisco, so they were figuring this out together and having a blast doing so.

The two newfound family members enjoyed a mid-day Red Sox game together, walked the Freedom Trail, and saw all that Boston had to offer. They were in pure bliss.

On the fourth morning, Peyton yelled from the kitchen, "Hey, Penel, you want coffee?"

"Oh, you read my mind, if I don't have coffee, I won't make it today." She laughed.

"OK, I'm making breakfast as well. How do you like your eggs? I like mine scrambled... it's the bessst."

"Yeah, scrambled is fine," she replied as she was walking into the kitchen.

Penelope sat on the barstool and swiveled around as Peyton poured her a fresh cup of Pike Place roast coffee. "Mmm, that smells good, Pey. Thank you."

"Mm-hmm." Peyton looked over his shoulder with a smirk. "My mom used to call me Pey," he said with a grin.

The two of them sipped their coffees as Peyton made Penelope's plate of breakfast, and placed it in front of her. He toasted two slices of wheat bread for them both. "Do you like jelly on your toast? I have grape and strawberry," he said proudly.

"Yeah, either is fine with me," she replied.

Wanting to see if they had a favorite flavor in common, "OK, say which one's your favorite on the count of three," Peyton said.

"One, twooo, threee..." They counted in unison.

"Strawberry," Peyton screamed with a big smile on his face.

"Grape," Penelope yelled.

"Whaaat?" They each spent the next few moments jokingly making their cases as to why the other was wrong about the best jelly flavor.

Peyton said, "Here, let me spread this for you." He spread Penelope's grape jelly on her toast in the shape of a smiley face.

Penelope smiled, and they both just sat and ate their breakfast, talking about the plans for the day and enjoying their time with each other.

Peyton was exhausted, as was Penelope, but neither wanted to tell the other. They didn't want to be a party pooper.

"Sooo, Peyton, how do you feel today?"

"What do you mean?" Peyton asked.

"Well, I'm really excited to hop on the double-decker bus today because I've never been on one, even though they're very popular in San Francisco, but I have to be honest—"

Peyton cut her off. "I am *exhauuusted*."

Penelope laughed hysterically. "Oh my gosh, I am too! I didn't want to say anything because I didn't want to spoil our time together."

"No no no, you have no idea how tired I am. I haven't walked this many steps through the city in years. Trust me, we're on the same page." Peyton nodded in confirmation.

The two of them laughed at the other not wanting to ruin the day of tourism, and that they both were feeling the exact same way.

"So, I have an idea. What if we just spent the entire day watching Netflix, ordering takeout, desserts, and shoving popcorn in our mouths?" Peyton suggested with a huge smile on his face.

"That sounds sublime, Pey! Let's do it," Penelope agreed.

They spent the entire day hanging out on the couch, enjoying each other, laughing hysterically at *The Office*, and gorging themselves on every type of takeout Peyton could fathom to order.

As day turned to night, Peyton got up and went to the bathroom. When he came back, he saw that Penelope was looking at his suitcase.

"Peyton, this suitcase is freaking awesome. It has that old-school feel, you know, like vintage. Where did you get it? How have you kept it in such great condition?"

"Well, it's funny you should ask. That suitcase has so much meaning to me, and actually, it has so much meaning to you as well."

"Huh, how does it have meaning for me? Do you mind if I open it?"

"No, not at all, go ahead," Peyton responded.

As Penelope opened the suitcase, Peyton walked around the corner and sat on the couch beside her. She marveled at the inner lining of the vintage suitcase. "Wooow, Peyton, this is absolutely amazing. Wait, who are these people in this photo?"

She'd seen two photos that Peyton had taped to the underside of the suitcase. She rubbed the photos and smiled. "Who are these people, Peyton?" She asked.

Peyton had reprinted the old photo of his mother and father, which had washed away into the San Francisco gutter many years before. Next to it, he also had his mother's college photo taped to the underside of the suitcase.

A part of Peyton wanted to let the photo of his mother and father be lost forever, but the other part of him still felt connected to his father, even after he had been discarded.

"Well, that's my mom, and that's... that's my... our father. This was a photo they took before I was born. I converted it to a digital copy several years ago, so I could reprint it, if something ever happened to it; and thank God I did," he said sarcastically.

"Why's that?" she asked.

"Ohhh, I guess you could say, I 'lost' the original."

"Oh, OK. Well, yes, in that case, smart thinking on converting it to digital. But *wow*, you've had this photo of them for so long. That's *amazing*!"

"Yeah, I've kept it for so long because it's the last remaining photo that I've got of our father and my mother."

"Would you mind if I took the photo out?" she asked kind of hesitantly.

Peyton paused because the photo meant a lot to him. The photo had only been removed from the underside of the suitcase when he met his father for the first time years ago on that rainy San Francisco day. Until that day, Peyton had placed new strips of tape on the photo to hold its integrity, but also to mark the year that had passed since he'd searched for his father.

"Sure, no problem. Just handle with care." He smiled.

Penelope removed the photo and sat back on the couch next to Peyton.

As they looked at the photo together, Penelope leaned over and rested her head on Peyton's shoulder. He put his arm around her, and they just stared at the photo.

"Peyton, your mother is beautiful…"

"Was… she passed away a few years ago. She's my angel now," Peyton whispered softly.

"Oh Peyton, I'm sorry. I didn't know. I didn't mean to…"

"No, stop it; you're fine, you didn't know. She was an amazing person and now forever my angel. I mean, look how angelic and happy she looks in that photo." He smiled.

"Did she ever tell you what happened between our father and her?"

"Well, she didn't speak much about our father, but she told me that they were happy at one point. They were high school sweethearts, they went to college together, and then I basically ruined everything."

"Don't say that. I'm sure she never felt like you ruined anything."

"Nah, I'm joking, they ended because she wanted to keep me, but our father didn't because of my, well, you know, my condition." He lowered his head a bit.

"I'm sorry, Peyton. You're literally perfect. My perfect big brother."

"Don't be. Life happens, and how we deal with life determines what our legacies will be for ages to come, right?" Peyton always had a way of quoting his mom when he needed strength, even if he was quoting it to himself.

"You're right, and thank you," Penelope replied. "Wow, she was really gorgeous. And look how happy they were. I'd love to know their story one day."

"The truth is, Penel, I don't really know their story… I never had a chance to really speak to my mother about Mark, and she rarely opened up about him. I think it was always too hard and painful for her to talk about."

Penelope didn't press further on the issue as she could see that even though Peyton was keeping a smile on his face, the thoughts of his mother and father's past still haunted him.

As she was about to place the photo back to the underside of the suitcase, Peyton reached out his hand. "Wait, let me see them," he said softly.

Penelope smiled as she handed him the photo. It was rare that he actually pulled this photo out of the suitcase to look and reminisce on times with his mom, as he usually only removed the photo to provide fresh tape.

But there he was, looking at his father and mother, thinking about all the happy times he'd had with his mother, mixed with the pain that still existed from his father… and all with his sister. It was a surreal moment for Peyton.

"Here, I'm going to go and get some fresh tape." He handed the photo back to Penelope, went to the kitchen, and returned with a freshly opened roll of scotch tape.

As he reached out for the photo, Penelope smiled and said, "Let me help you, if you don't mind."

"Mind? I've always wanted family, and now I have it. I have you." Peyton kissed his sister on the cheek.

She held the photo up against the underside of the suitcase, and Peyton began to tear off strips of tape. Penelope looked at him tearing the strips of tape, stretched out her arm, and said, "Hey, stick them here."

As he placed the first strip of tape, Peyton looked at Penelope, "I used to have to do this alone for so many years. It's not a super-difficult task, but it's good to be able to do this with family. Thank you."

"I'm happy to be a part, Peyton. We're family."

The Calm Before the Storm

It was Penelope's final day with Peyton, and they were going to a Red Sox game with James, walking the city after, and then finishing the night with James at one of Peyton's favorite restaurants.

They'd had the opportunity to spend so much quality time all week. Penelope went to Peyton's job and met his boss and all his colleagues. He showed her around as if it were show and tell in grade school again, and she was a pretty, shiny 1914 Buffalo nickel. He was so proud and ecstatic to introduce Penelope to all those who held value to him. His grandparents were on vacation, but he still found time to FaceTime them, and introduce his lovely sister.

Penelope had met James upon her first day in Boston, but the Red Sox game was the first time the three of them would actually get to spend quite a bit of time together. Penelope was excited about this because she'd heard so much about James, and she wanted to know more about the kind of man he was since he'd taken Peyton under his wing many years prior.

Walking into the stadium for the day game, James and Peyton began to place their friendly wagers on who would win today. It was a big game, Red Sox vs. the Yankees.

Though James had been born and raised in Boston, his father was a longtime Yankee fan, so his allegiances and loyalties to the Yankees ran deep. But Peyton had no problem still calling him a fraud since he was, in fact, from Boston.

Penelope witnessed first-hand how important James was to Peyton. At the game, they yelled chants at each other as Peyton cheered his Red Sox on to a hopeful victory. They had a great little tradition. Whichever team lost during these big games, the other had to purchase and wear the opposing team's jersey or paraphernalia all the way home.

Upon entering Fenway Park, James purchased popcorn and drinks for everyone, so Peyton insisted on buying the seventh inning stretch snacks. Inning after inning, the two of them were like two peas in a pod. Talking trash, yelling at the umpires when calls didn't advantage their respective teams, all while laughing and enjoying each other's company.

They made sure to include Penelope. "Penel, we have to get you a proper Sox jersey, and I know just the vendor. He's a good friend of mine," Peyton said. Growing up, going to Red Sox games, Peyton had become good friends with several of the vendors, staff, and even a few of the assistant coaches.

Before the three of them found their seats again, Peyton took Penelope to his favorite vendor, a Down syndrome man by the name of Dirk Jacobs, and purchased his sister a top-notch Red Sox jersey as well as a jumbo Sox Number-1 finger.

"Thank you, Peyton. I absolutely love it." She grinned.

"Hey, this isn't fair, you're making new Red Sox fans, and she just got here," James joked.

"She's family. She had no choice but to be a Red Sox fan," Peyton replied.

The two, Peyton and James, seemed to be in their own little world. Penelope enjoyed the game, but she was more excited to know that, if nothing else, Peyton had a strong male figure in his life who cared for him. She watched the two interact but eventually looked away as her facial expression changed and she became sad.

Her mind flashed back to that moment, looking outside of her window and watching a man being taken away in handcuffs. She thought back to the moment her own father, whom she loved dearly, had watched without doing anything as the police officers took away her very own brother, his own son.

How could my father have allowed something so terrible to happen to such a pure soul? she thought.

As Peyton looked her way and saw that her countenance had changed, he said, "Are you OK? What's wrong?"

She lied so she wouldn't ruin their day. "Oh yeah. I'm fine. I think it's just the pollen in the air that's getting to my eyes. I'll be fine!"

"Oh, OK. Yeah, we have really terrible ragweed here. The pollen counts are high right now too."

"Do you need some eye drops?" James asked.

"No, I think I'll be fine. It's not that bad. Thank you, though," she replied.

Penelope realized that she couldn't change what had happened all those years ago, so she decided to live in the moment and enjoy her brother and her newfound friend James.

She stood and joined in on heckling the Yankees. "Yankees suck. Yankees suck..." She and Peyton heckled and taunted James, even though the Red Sox were losing handsomely.

Peyton looked to his right and put his arm around her with so much joy in his eyes. He looked her in the eyes and joined in on her chants, but even louder. Practically yelling at each other, "*YANKEES SUCK! YANKEES SUCK!*" They were absolutely happy, and it was a perfect day.

The Red Sox went on to mount an amazing come-from-behind victory, and per their tradition, James purchased a Boston Red Sox hat and wore it all the way home.

Peyton and Penelope hopped in a cab after the game and said their goodbyes to James. "OK, we'll see you later at Tico's?" Peyton said.

Tico's was a little Italian restaurant that Peyton and James had eaten at many times. The restaurant was a staple in Boston and had been around for nearly fifty-three years. Family-owned, authentic Italian cuisine, and the best live music in the city, according to Peyton, Tico's was truly amazing.

But Tico's always held more meaning for Peyton, because Tico's is where his parents had taken the beloved photo that he'd kept in mint condition all these years. The photo had been taken the night Mark and Jasmine went out to celebrate Mark's completion of the LSAT.

Peyton and Penelope had gotten home from the game fully exhausted and drained from the heat, so they both decided to take much-needed naps.

When Penelope woke to the sounds of Bobby Womack, she got up with a smile on her face and began getting dressed for their dinner with James.

"*I was the thiiird brother of fiiive…*" Peyton had always loved Bobby Womack, and he belted out the words. "Is that too loud?" he asked.

"Oh no, I love Bobby Womack. Turn it up. Great music to get the night started with," Penelope said.

"I'll be ready in ten minutes," Peyton said. "But no rush. Our reservation isn't for another hour and a half."

"OK, great. I'm going to shower, and then I should be ready in about thirty minutes," Penelope replied.

Peyton got dressed to impress, slicked his hair back, and even put on his class ring from Boston University. As Penelope walked around the corner, he was sitting on the couch watching ESPN and the highlights from the game. He looked up and saw Penelope. "Wow, you look absolutely stunning, Penelope."

"Thank you, Peyton, and don't you just look drop-dead handsome," she said as she walked up and straightened his jacket for him.

"I called an Uber already and it will be here in four minutes, so we can actually walk out now."

"Oh, OK. I didn't mind driving if you were tired of driving," Penelope said.

"Oh, no, that's not it. I just want to have a couple glasses of wine tonight in celebration. Celebration of you being here, of us being able to finally spend time together, and just life. Plus, Tico's literally has the best selection of Italian wines."

"Perfect, then let's go celebrate and get some vino in our systems," she said.

The two of them walked out of the house, got in the Uber, and Peyton texted James:

> We're en route.

James replied:

> OK good, me too, see y'all soon.

They all met, coincidentally, at the same exact time in front of Tico's. Peyton and James performed their ritual handshake, which always ended in a hug.

Standing back and marveling at Peyton and James's relationship,

Penelope smiled and pushed them closer and closer to the door until the three were finally inside.

"Mr. Love, we have your reservation ready. It's good to see you again, sir." It was Peyton's favorite host, Nicole, at the front. Since Peyton was a regular, they always sat him and James up at the exact same table; it was the table Mark and Jasmine had sat at during their celebration, which made Peyton feel closer to his parents.

"I see we have three tonight," Nicole said with a smile.

"Yes! Nicole, I'd like you to meet my sister, Penelope. She'll be joining us tonight."

"*Your sister!* Oh my gosh, Mr. Love, I had no idea you had a sister."

Peyton just smiled and kept his thoughts to himself, yet his facial expression said it all: *Neither did I.*

Penelope reached out her hand and greeted Nicole. "Nice to meet you. Peyton has told me all about this place. I hear it's amazing."

"Well, we try our best here at Tico's. We hope you enjoy it. Y'all follow me. We have you all set up."

When they arrived at the table, Peyton (being the gentleman that he was) and James (being the one who'd taught him to be a gentleman) both reached out to pull out Penelope's chair.

Nearly bumping heads since they went for the chair at the same time, the two laughed, and James ceded chair control to Peyton.

The three of them sat and enjoyed quite a bit of wine before they even ordered their meals for the night. Unbeknownst to them, Nicole had told the manager, a second-generation Italian owner of Tico's, that Peyton was there for the first time with his sister. The owner then told the chef that he would be comping the meal, and that he'd be ordering for the table.

As they were laughing and enjoying each other, Chef Cathleen came to the table. *"Peyyyton, welcome back, and I hear we have a new guest, your sister."*

"Yes, ma'am. This is my sister. Penelope, meet Chef Cathleen," Peyton said with pride, looking at his beloved sister.

"It's very nice to meet you." Penelope reached out her hand to shake the chef's hand.

"Well, I wanted you all to know that tonight, if it's OK, I'd like to prepare for you all some of my signature dishes. Peyton, I know you have tried the entire menu, but I still have a few tricks up my sleeve."

Peyton's eyes got bigger. "That would be awesome. James, what do you think?"

"I'm all for trying new things. Let's do it," James replied.

"And don't y'all worry, Francesco will be comping tonight's meal. It's on us!"

"Whoooaaa, this just keeps getting better," Peyton replied with a massive smile on his face.

"Wow, Pey, you were right. This place is amazing," Penelope said.

"Yes, it is, Penelope," replied Chef Cathleen. "You just wait and see."

Dish after dish, the staff brought out several small plates from Chef Cathleen's creations. Every succulent bite, the three of them enjoyed together. From wine to dessert, it was an absolutely amazing night. Per usual, the lights were dimmed as the live band began to set up.

"Oh, Penelope, you're going to love these guys. They're a traditional French band named En Masse, and they can all literally play every instrument on the stage."

"I already love this. This is the greatest night I've had in a very long time, and I'm absolutely stuffed." Penelope sighed.

James looked at Penelope and agreed, "I'm fuller than a tick on the hide of a water buffalo."

"James has the best dad jokes, doesn't he?" Peyton laughed.

The three of them sat there enjoying their wine, enjoying each other, and the vibrant tunes of En Masse.

As they were preparing to leave, Francesco came to the table. "So did y'all enjoy everything? Is there anything else we can get y'all?"

"Oh, sir, it was absolutely phenomenal," Penelope replied.

"Yes, Fra. Can we please pay for something? Please!?" Peyton begged.

"I won't allow it, Peyton. You've been coming here since you were a kid, and tonight is very special. We had the pleasure of taking care of you and James, annnd your sister. It's our pleasure."

"Well, thank you, Fra. It was absolutely amazing," Peyton said.

"Yes, it truly was. Please give my compliments to Chef Cathleen. Everything was just perfect," Penelope agreed.

"Well, you just make sure to come back to visit us, OK?"

"Oh, I will. I definitely will!" Penelope replied with a smile.

They thanked Francesco one more time, stood up, and walked outside to get some fresh air. It was a clear, brisk night, and nearly every star was out.

"I'll call the Uber. James, do you want to come over for a bit? We're just going to go home and watch some Netflix. Right, Penel?"

"Yeah, you should join, James."

"Oh, I wish I could, but I have to be up early in the morning. I have new kids coming in tomorrow," James said with regret.

They all hugged and said their goodbyes. Peyton and Penelope hopped in their Uber, and nearly fell asleep on the way home. They were so tired after their weeklong visit together.

The Storm

Upon arrival, they walked into the house, "So what is it going to be tonight?" Penelope asked.

"I don't care. I'll let you decide. I'll likely be passed out before the movie gets halfway through," he replied.

Penelope put on one of her favorite childhood movies, *Toy Story*.

"Ooo, I love this movie," Peyton said. "OK, pause it., I'm going to shower and then we can watch it. I hate that you have to leave tomorrow."

"Me too, but I've also had an absolutely amazing time."

Penelope's face and words didn't match, so Peyton thought something was wrong. He could tell something was on her mind. "Don't worry, Penel. We're definitely going to see each other again," He tried to console her without knowing why her countenance had changed.

"No, I know. It's not that, I just, I just… I guess I just really enjoyed our time together, and I hate that it has to end tomorrow."

Peyton hugged her. "But it's not ending tomorrow. It's just beginning."

Penelope began to cry.

"Don't cry, Penel. I promise this isn't the end for us. We're family now."

She cheered up a bit with a half-smile on her face as she hugged her brother, "I know. I love you, Peyton."

"I love you too. Now pop us some popcorn. I'll be right back, and then we can watch the greatest movie ever."

Penelope smiled, "OK, I'll get us some popcorn and juice ready. Oh, and I'll go ahead and pack too, since we have to leave early in the morning."

"Deal, I'll be right back," Peyton replied. Peyton was on an all-time high, but as he turned, he saw Penelope sitting back on the couch, placing her head in her hands, as she began to cry. It had to be something more than just the end to a great week. Something was clearly bothering Penelope.

Minutes later, "Here I come, TO INFINITY ANNNNND BEYOND," Peyton yelled from the back room.

Penelope tried to wipe her face so Peyton wouldn't know she had been crying, but as he ran out of the back room with his Buzz Lightyear shirt on, Penelope looked up at him, and he saw her face. He rushed over to her and sat next to his sister. He hugged her and said, "Penel, don't cry. What's wrong."

"Peyton, I need to talk to you."

"OK, I'm listening. What's wrong, Penel?" Now Peyton was concerned.

"Well, I came to Boston for two reasons. First, I came to meet you and really get to know my brother. I've had the absolute best time anybody could ever have with a family member. You have been so gracious despite all that has happened to you...You've—"

Peyton cut her off. "Penelope, you don't have to—"

It was her turn to cut him off. "Let me finish. Seeing your life and so much that you've accomplished despite the challenges you've faced in your life is truly inspiring. I sat back and watched how you and James interacted, and it truly warmed my heart. You and James are both amazing men. I just truly one day hope to be the type of person you are!"

"Oh, Penelope, but you are already. Your heart is so pure. You have no idea how much your coming here has meant to me. It's literally been a dream come true. I will always cherish this time we have spent together."

"I've just had a great time. But there's another reason I wanted to come out and meet you."

"OK, what is it?" Peyton could tell that something was really bothering her. "You can tell me anything, Penelope." Peyton sat back and grabbed his sister's hand.

"Well, well... it's our father..."

Peyton's heart sank because this entire week, he hadn't thought about his father that much. He was too busy enjoying Penelope. "Yeah, what about our father?" he whispered.

"Peyton... he's dying..."

Penelope continued talking, but Peyton could barely pay attention. Peyton could see her lips moving, but he couldn't process anything that she was saying. Even after all he'd experienced the first time he'd met his father, immediately upon hearing those words, he wanted nothing but to be there for his father.

"Peyton, Peyton, are you OK?" Penelope asked.

"Yeah, yeah, sorry. I'm listening. It's just a lot to take in right now."

"I know. I truly wanted to come and meet you and spend time with you, and I've loved every moment we've spent together, but I also wanted you to know. You deserved to know. I mean, he's your father too."

"What's wrong with him?" Peyton asked.

"It's all quite complicated, and I'm definitely not the doctor of the family, like Tim, but he entered liver failure some months ago, and he also has issues with his left ventricle. He's on the transplant list, but with his rare blood type and basically needing a multi-organ transplant, his prognosis isn't great. That's really the reason I took a leave of absence from work. I wanted to be there with him for as long as I could. I know it's a lot to drop at your feet, but I wanted you to know."

"No, I'm glad you let me know, Penel."

The two of them sat up practically all night discussing their father, and all the health issues he was having. Eventually, Peyton turned off the TV, and he and Penelope held hands and talked about their father's situation.

Peyton stroked her hand to comfort her, and Penelope cried

on her brother's shoulder, until they both eventually passed out... They were both there, then, present in the moment. They had each other.

The next morning, Penelope woke first and began making coffee since she knew Peyton always loved his coffee in the morning. She poured him a cup as he began to stir.

"Wow, we passed out on the couch. Are you OK?" he asked.

"Yeah, I'm fine, how are you? I made you some coffee."

"Aww, thanks, Penel. What time is it?"

"It's 7:42. I'm going to finish packing."

They were both quiet. Looking at each other with assuring smiles, Penelope finished packing her bags, and Peyton finished his coffee.

"I'm going to brush my teeth, and then I'll take you to the airport, OK?"

"OK, sounds good, Pey."

They didn't talk much on the ride to the airport. Penelope just looked out the window, admiring her last moments in Boston. When they arrived, Peyton parked and went around the back of the car to get Penelope's luggage.

"Thanks, Pey. Listen, I had a great visit, and I truly look forward to seeing you again. I'll call you when I land in San Francisco, OK?"

"OK. I've enjoyed you being here as well, and I'm so glad you came to see me, though I hate to see you go."

Penelope smiled. "Yeah, but like you said last night, we're just starting. We're family now!"

They hugged, and Peyton watched as Penelope turned, grabbed her bags, and walked into Boston Logan International Airport.

CHAPTER 15
FORGIVENESS BEGINS

Peyton hadn't allowed his emotions to show because he wanted to be strong for his sister, but when he got back to his car, he sat in the front seat, and the flood of his emotions all rushed upon him at once.

He sat in the garage of short-term parking for nearly an hour and just cried. His phone buzzed, and per usual, it was James with an inspirational message.

> Look how far you've come from the point you thought was the end.
> Keep moving forward through all.

Timely as ever, Peyton unlocked his phone, called James, and told him the news about his father. He spent the next few minutes talking to James and weeping over the potential that he would be losing his father all over again.

"Peyton, why don't you go home, and I'll come over later," James said.

"No, it's OK, James, you don't have to come. I think I'll just go home and rest for a bit. Thank you, though. I'll be fine."

Peyton walked through his front door, sat on the couch, and could still smell Penelope's lavender body wash. He picked up the pillow she'd slept with on the couch, held it to his chest, and took a nap.

When he woke, he'd a missed call from Penelope, and a text, saying:

> It was really good to hang with you, Peyton. Thank you again for your amazing hospitality as well as showing me all around Beantown. Greatest vacation ever, and I look forward to seeing you again.

Just then, Peyton realized where he needed to be. He whispered aloud, "I have to be there for him. I have to be there for her, for them."

He texted back:

> Sorry Penel, I got home and absolutely passed out on the couch. I could still smell your lavender body wash lol. It made me miss our Netflix nights and popcorn. I'm glad you made it back safely and I look forward to seeing you again as well.

Peyton texted James shortly after:

> I know you might not approve, but I have to go out to San Francisco to see my father. I know he might not want me, but I can't just sit and do nothing, I have to see him.

James responded:

> Peyton, you were raised to be bigger than any situation. The situation with your father and how he treated you is no different. I always knew that you were larger than that hurt. I fully support you going to see him in his time of need. Just promise to keep me posted, and let me know if you need anything OK? How long are you planning to visit?

Peyton sent a final text:

> I definitely will keep you posted and thank you for your support. No

clue how long I'll stay. I guess I'll play it by ear. Talk to you soon.

Then he placed his phone down on the couch, went to his room, and started taking clothes out of the dresser. He collected enough for a week, for at the very least, he'd have enough for several days. He figured he could always wash clothes and recycle his outfits.

As Peyton was packing, he was in a determined state of mind, as if he had to get to San Francisco in order to be there for someone who had always loved him. This was just the type of person Peyton had been taught to be by his mother.

Walking back to the living room with his hands full of folded clothes, Peyton saw his father's suitcase on the floor next to the front door. He placed his clothes on the couch, opened the suitcase, and began packing his clothes within.

After packing, he got online to book a flight to San Francisco for the following morning. He found an early-morning flight that would get him into SFO at 8:40 a.m., and another indirect flight that wouldn't get him into SFO until 7 p.m. He chose the early flight.

That entire night dragged on as he sat in his home, thinking about the last time he'd met his father. Peyton didn't text Penelope to tell her that he was coming because he wasn't sure that she'd approve. He figured he'd show up and deal with the consequences of showing up unannounced.

With so many thoughts going through his head, and wanting to speed up the time, Peyton went to sleep really early, setting multiple alarms to ensure he didn't miss his flight.

When morning came, he woke, had his coffee, said his prayers, said goodbye to James, and called an Uber. The entire ride to the airport and while going through security, he was so nervous that his hands were sweating and shaking.

What would his brothers think of him? Would Penelope want

him there? What would happen to his father? All these thoughts raced in and out of Peyton's mind, but the one thought that remained was, what would his father say, and would his father want him there?

Peyton sat at the gate, listening to music, and trying to calm his nerves, but nothing worked. He opened his suitcase, which he was carrying on, pulled out the photo of his mother and father at TICO's, and smiled. At that moment, Peyton mustered the mental strength for this journey into the unknown.

As they began to board the plane, Peyton stood up, gathered his suitcase and the bag of snacks he'd purchased and made his way down the Jetway. With his head held high, and hope in his heart, he walked with purpose as he boarded the plane and set off on a journey that would alter his life forever.

Round Two Goes to Love

Peyton touched down in SFO, a place that he hadn't been in nearly five years. The last time he was in San Francisco, he'd met his father for the first time, been discarded by the man he'd wanted to find and know all of his life, and even got arrested. Surely, things couldn't get worse. Or so he thought.

Peyton got off the plane and decided to stop at the IHOP inside the terminal for breakfast. He had time to kill, and he always had to have his coffee in the morning. When he turned his phone on, he'd had a message from James:

> Love you buddy, make the most out of this trip, and take it hour by hour, minute by minute, second by second. All will be as it should.

Peyton replied.

> I landed, grabbing a quick bite before heading to the hospital. I'll talk to you later today, James.

The waitress brought Peyton a fresh cup of coffee, "We just took this pot off the burner. It's really fresh. I hope you like it hot."

"Oh, piping hot coffee is the only coffee, am I right?" Peyton replied.

"I like your style, sir. Are you having breakfast with us, or just grabbing a coffee? My name is Chaya, by the way."

"Well, Chaya, I'd absolutely love an egg white omelet with chicken sausage and spinach, if that's possible."

"Not a problem. Coming right up, sweetheart," Chaya responded.

Peyton spent the time waiting on his breakfast flipping through the myriad of pictures he and Penelope had taken while they were in Boston. He'd already created an album, and he smiled as he flipped through the photos.

When he finished his meal, he paid, grabbed his suitcase, and called an Uber to Palo Alto Medical Foundation. Peyton knew that Penelope worked at PAMF, plus she'd mentioned while she was in Boston that their father was being taken care of by her friends and those she trusted.

The Uber pulled up, and Peyton got inside.

"Cool suitcase, bro." Ronny, the Uber driver, looked back and said, "So we're headed to Palo Alto Medical Foundation? Going to surprise someone?"

"Yup, PAMF. And thanks, this suitcase was my father's suitcase."

"Cool, OK. I'll get you there, brother."

During the ride, as much as Peyton tried to drown out his doubt with music, he couldn't help but think about how and if he would be accepted. He finally gave up and turned off his music. He looked out the window and thought about the last time he'd seen his father. It had been nearly five years ago, and here he was, rushing to the side of the very man who didn't want him after nearly thirty years.

Just then, he thought of his mom's final words, "Give love to the world, and forgive your father." For some reason, those words always gave Peyton comfort. Here was his mom in her final moments, and all she could think of was ensuring he became the man the universe demanded of him.

"We're here. Is this entrance good?"

"This will work perfect. Thank you, sir."

Peyton got out of the Uber and stood in front of the building, clutching his suitcase to his chest. After a few minutes, he worked up his courage and went inside.

Becoming: Against Odds

Peyton walked in and immediately found a staff member who could help him find his father's room.

"Sir, it's not visiting hours yet if you're not family. We don't open up visiting hours until ten a.m. Mr. Love doesn't have you listed as family, sir, and I'm sorry, sir, but we have a strict policy here."

"Ma'am, I understand what you're saying, but I'm his son. Mark Love is my father. I just need to see him. I'll text my sister Penelope, and she will confirm that I'm family."

"Penelope Love? She's been here all night. She's here now."

"She is?" Peyton asked.

"Yes, sir," the staff member replied.

"Well, she's been here all night with her father—our father,"

Peyton replied, annoyed and sarcastic.

"He came in very depleted of electrolytes and with shortness of breath, but we pretty much have him stabilized," said the woman.

"Stabilized, what does all that mean?" Peyton asked.

"Sir, I'm sorry, but we can't discuss confidential patient information with you unless you're listed as family."

Peyton pleaded with the nurse. "Rachel, is it? I know you're just doing your job, but it's 9:42 right now, and that's only eighteen minutes from normal visiting hours. I'm his son. My name is Peyton Love. That's my father, and based on what my sister explained to me, I don't know how long my father has left on this earth. Please don't make me wait another minute to see him."

"Be that as it may, sir, we can't verify that until he's awake; however, friends of the patient are allowed to see him once official visiting hours begin."

Peyton put his elbows on the desk and placed his head in his hands. "I only need a minute to see him, ma'am. I just need to see him," he begged.

Nurse Rachel could see his eyes tearing up, and she knew he was sincere, so she decided to bend the rules. "OK, I can give you a visitor sticker, but you must wear it the entire time, and I'm going to need your ID left here, sir."

"OK, that's not a problem, and thank you so much," Peyton replied.

She gave Peyton a visitor sticker and said, "I'll walk you to his room."

"Thank you so much," Peyton replied.

"Now, Mr. Love, your father is going to be a little out of it, OK? He was sedated for his pulmonary procedure to help his breathing, so he might be still slightly sedated."

Meanwhile, Mark had undergone a minor procedure to help him breathe, and he was just starting to wake up as the drugs were starting to wear off. He began to open his eyes, but everything was blurry. He looked toward his door, and he could see figures near the room but couldn't quite make out all that was going on.

Mark looked down and saw Penelope asleep next to his bedside, her head leaning on his arm as her hand held his. He reached his other hand up to rub her head, but the IV constricted his movement.

Penelope began to wake up as she could feel his movements. "Dad, how are you feeling? Are you OK?"

Mark whispered with a scratchy voice, "I'm OK, baby. I'm OK. I can't believe you're here. I thought you were away on your trip."

"I was, but I flew back and came straight here."

"Oh, Penelope, my baby girl, you should have gone home and gotten some rest."

"I rested just fine here, Daddy. I wanted to be with you." She grabbed his hand. "I needed to be here with you. Dad… there's something I need to tell you…"

As she was preparing to tell him that she had gone to see Peyton, Peyton and Nurse Rachel were walking up to the glass door.

Mark was listening to Penelope, but noticed people walking towards his door.

With each blink, his vision became clearer. He noticed a silhouette of a man standing next to what appeared to be a staff member.

"Penelope, what time is it?" Mark asked.

"Wait, Dad, I have to tell you where I went," Penelope said with tears in her eyes, holding his hand.

Mark was halfway listening to Penelope, while also trying to see who was at his door. He couldn't quite make out what was being said by the blurry man and the staff member, yet he knew they were talking about him.

Rachel's voice outside the room was faint, yet Mark was trying to make out what they were discussing.

"Don't get your hopes up. He'll be out of it for a couple more hours, so if you want to come back…"

Peyton cut her off, "I don't have anywhere else in the world that I need to be right now."

She smiled and said, "OK, go on in, sir…"

"Dad, I went to see… I, I went to see…" Penelope was still trying to share with her father where she'd been.

Mark looked over at his daughter. "Huh?"

Just then, the glass door to Mark's room slid open, and Penelope and her father looked back at the door.

There stood Peyton.

Penelope looked up in utter surprise. "You, You, You're here!" She was in shock. "I can't believe you came."

"You think I'd let you face this alone? Never!" Peyton answered with tears in his eyes as he walked to his sister's side.

Mark's vision cleared as Penelope released his hand and ran to Peyton. She grabbed him and hugged his neck, kissing him on the cheek. "Oh Peyton, thank you so much for coming. I wanted you here with me above anyone else. How, how… I mean, like wow, I can't believe you are here." She could barely formulate clear sentences out of shock and excitement.

"Penel, there's no other place I could be right now." Peyton leaned closer to her ear and whispered, "We're family."

Mark watched all of this unfold, finally realizing what Penelope had been trying to tell him about her trip and where she'd actually gone.

Penelope released Peyton. "Peyton, this is… well, you know who this is. This is our father."

The two of them, Mark and Peyton, just looked at each other.

Peyton placed the suitcase down and walked slowly and cautiously to his father.

Mark's eyes began to tear up. "You… It's you. Peyton Love."

"Yes, sir, it's me. It's me," he replied with caution. Peyton walked to his father's bedside and looked him up and down, noticing all the tubes, cords, and machines hooked up to his dad. His mind flashed back to his mother's final moments in the hospital. It was all too familiar, too close to his heart.

"You came to see me? I mean, why? After all the hurt and pain I put you through? Why in God's name would you come to be here for me now? I don't deserve you being here," his father said with regret.

Penelope began to cry as she sat back in the chair and watched her father commune with his firstborn for the first time.

"Dad… Dad, there's absolutely nowhere else in the world I want to be than right here, right now, in the moment with you, by your side."

Mark began to cry, and he reached his hand up to touch Peyton. Peyton began to cry too, as he leaned down to embrace his father for the first time in over thirty years. He'd waited for what seemed an eternity to feel love from his father.

As the two embraced, Mark began to cry hysterically. "I'm so sorry for what happened when we first met, and I'm sorry you have to see me like—"

Peyton cut him off and looked him in the eyes. "Stop it. We're here now, we have now, and that is literally the only thing that's important to me." He would not allow his emotions and feelings of abandonment to rob them of this moment.

"How did you find me? How did you know?" Mark asked.

Penelope got up out of the chair. "That's what I was trying to tell you, Dad." She looked at Peyton. "I found Peyton and spent the last week with him in Boston. He's an amazing man. I told him about your condition, not knowing he would…" Penelope couldn't speak because she was both extremely sad and extremely happy at the exact same moment.

"You see, Penelope came out to see me, and we had the most beautiful time in Boston. Before she left, she opened up and told me everything you were facing, and I couldn't just stay in Boston. I needed to see you. You're my father," Peyton said with sincerity.

Mark was overcome with emotions as Peyton and Penelope told him all about their time together in Boston. They began to tell him all the sights they'd seen and all that they'd done during her visit.

The three of them spent the next few hours just laughing and talking about Penelope's trip to Boston. Peyton stood up, went to the suitcase he'd set by the door, kneeled down, and opened it up.

"And you still have that old suitcase, I see," his dad said.

"It was the only thing that I've had of you. Well, one of the only things," Peyton replied. He took out the two photos that were taped to the underside of the suitcase and walked back over to his father and Penelope.

He handed his dad the old Polaroid of his father and mother. "This was you and my mother at—"

"At Tico's," his father cut him off. Mark placed his hand over his mouth as he became emotional.

"Yes, sir. That was you and my mother at Tico's. And this, this is me and Penelope, at the exact same table at Tico's." Peyton showed him a picture from his phone.

Mark grabbed the phone, looked at the picture, and shed another tear. "My two children... My two beautiful children," he said with both pride and regret in his voice. Mark pulled Peyton close and whispered, "Peyton, you can't understand how much you being here means to me. I'm not worthy of you being here for me. The fact that you kept the suitcase, and kept this photo, I... I... I just don't know what to say."

"Don't say anything. We're all here now. We have now," Peyton replied, standing back up.

Mark was quite tired from the procedure, and after hours of talking, he said, "I'm kind of tired, y'all. I'm going to rest a bit."

"OK, Dad. I'm going to stay with you," Penelope said.

"No, Penel. You go home and get cleaned up. I'll stay…" Peyton looked at his dad for confirmation. "If that's OK, of course," Peyton said, looking back at his father.

"Of course it's OK."

Penelope kissed her dad, "OK, I'm going to go home, shower up, catch a nap in a real bed, and I'll be back up here later, OK?"

"OK, baby. I love you," Mark whispered in her ear as he kissed her cheek.

Penelope left, and Peyton pulled up a chair and sat by his dad's bedside. The two just talked, and Peyton told him all about his trip to San Francisco.

"So, how's your mom, Peyton?" Mark asked.

Peyton looked down. "I'm sorry, D—Dad," Peyton stuttered, not really knowing what to call his father… "She passed away some years ago. Before she passed, one of her last wishes was for me to find you. That's why I came to find you five years ago. Though I apologize for just showing up, her passing was heavy on my heart, and I knew I wanted to fulfill her final wishes."

"Peyton, I'm so sorry," Mark said. "I can't express to you how sorry I am for how I treated you. Knowing now that you were likely in your lowest of low places at that time, I literally have no words to express how regretful I am at the way things turned out. I hope you will find it in your heart one day to forgive me."

"Stop it. It's not important right now. We're here now. You get some rest. I'm not going anywhere. I'm here now. You're here now. You're my father."

"And you're my son." Those were the final words Mark said to Peyton before dozing off to sleep.

Peyton pulled the blanket up to his father's chest to cover him up. As his father slept, Peyton sat there watching him breathe. He had finally met his father in a way that he had always imagined it; *WANTED*.

He was there, in the moment, happy, and loved.

CHAPTER 16
TIME'S GIFT

It had been a week that Mark was stable. Since he was waiting on both a blood match and a multi-organ transplant, there was nothing the doctors could do for him but wait... wait for the right donor.

"Mr. Love, I'm very pleased with your stats and how you've progressed. How are you feeling?"

"Yeah, I feel really good, Dr. Orengo. So, what happens next?" he asked her.

Dr. Orengo was the general surgeon who coordinated with the transplant group on Mark's team of doctors.

"Well, next we send you home to be with your family. We wait, and we hope for a donor. But for now, you're stable, and you might as well wait at home, surrounded by both your family and some decent food," Dr. Orengo joked.

"Yeah, I didn't want to say it, Doc, but the food isn't that great here." Mark and Peyton looked at each other and laughed.

"You know, I've never heard anyone say that they loved the food here, so I believe you, but we'll work on that," Dr. Orengo replied.

While Mark had been hospitalized, trying to stabilize, the

entire family came to visit sporadically. Peyton stayed the longest and most nights. He went to Penelope's home to shower and clean up when he needed to, but he rarely wanted to leave his father's side.

During this time, they caught up and exchanged stories. Peyton finally met his two brothers, and Mark shared stories of Jasmine from their past. They enjoyed their time with each other, but there was still so much left unsaid.

Most conversations were kept high-level because Peyton didn't want to ruin what time they had left with past pains or old hurts... He wanted so badly for his father to survive so they could be a family for once.

During that week of getting to know each other, Mark tried several times to bring up the hurtful past and apologize to Peyton, but Peyton always found a way to cut him off and divert the conversation.

Why is Peyton so afraid to face those emotions? To face that pain...? What's waiting on the other side of that emotional mountain? Mark wondered.

Since Penelope had gone back to work, Peyton's brothers, Timothy and Jay Paul, came to the hospital to check their father out since he was being discharged. Timothy stayed outside the room with Dr. Orengo to discuss expectations and at-home care since Mark was going home.

"Well, your father's stable, but he desperately needs a liver donation as well as the left ventricular vessel repair and/or donation, as we discussed."

"How long does he have, Doc? Seriously, shoot me straight!" Timothy asked.

"It's not a matter of how long, honestly I couldn't say really. We're surprised he made it this far and that he actually stabilized. We'd usually keep patients like your father in the hospital, but since his blood type is so rare, there's not much we can do for him here. Just make sure he gets a ton of rest. I'm giving each of you a pager in the event that we get a donor. We've alerted UNOS of his condition and he is status-one, which means he's at the top of the list. The difficulty here is finding a match with his rare blood type. But listen, son, keep your head up and keep believing. These things will work out as they should."

Timothy thanked Dr. Orengo for all of her efforts, and he and Jay Paul gathered their father's things and prepared to leave the hospital.

"Hey, guys, I'm going to pack up my stuff and meet you all at the house, OK?" Peyton said.

"Are you sure? We can wait for you," Timothy replied.

"Yeah, I'm sure. Get Dad home so he can rest. I'll be there shortly."

Peyton had other thoughts, though...

When Mark, Timothy, and Jay Paul left, Peyton asked the nurse to page Dr. Orengo.

"Oh, hey, Peyton. I thought y'all left," Dr. Orengo said.

"Yes, ma'am. My brothers took my father home. I just wanted to talk to you for a minute, if that's OK."

"Of course, Peyton. How can I help?"

"Well... well... Dr. Orengo, I wanted to possibly get tested to see if I'm a match to donate."

"Wow, Peyton. That's a huge step. Are you sure? The recovery can be quite grueling, and it's quite an extensive procedure. That, plus you must be a match for your father, and his blood type is very rare. All of your siblings have been tested, and none of them were a match."

"Yes, ma'am, I'm sure. I don't know if I'll be a match, and I don't even know if he'll allow it, but I have to try, right?"

"Well, Peyton, that's very admirable. I don't mean to pry, but are you and your father close?" Dr. Orengo asked.

Peyton nodded yes, but his body language said no.

Dr. Orengo continued, "I just want to make sure you're doing this for the right reasons. If you two aren't close, I need to know that you aren't thinking about this life-altering decision in an effort to bring you all closer."

"To be truthful, Dr. Orengo. No, we aren't close, but in a way, we are. I've always felt connected to my father, and I've waited so many years to find him, and now that I have, I just can't imagine losing him—not yet, not now, not again."

"I understand, Peyton, and I'm not trying to talk you out of it, but your father's body is very diseased. Even with the surgery, I want to set the right expectations; there's no guarantee that he will even make it off the table."

"Make it off the table? What do you mean, Dr. Orengo?" Peyton asked.

"I'm sorry, I mean that he might not make it out of the surgery. He may actually pass away during surgery because of the condition of his body. Since we would have to harvest your organs first, I just want to set the right expectation prior to you undergoing such a serious set of procedures."

"Yes, ma'am, I understand that, but I have to try. Wouldn't you, if it were your father?"

"Well, Peyton, it *was* my father. I donated a kidney to my father, so I completely understand your thinking; I just want to give you the full picture. However, if you're sure you want to go through with this, then we can at least test you to see if you are a match. I'll call Rachel back, and we'll get you started with the test. It may take a day or two to get your results back, but I promise to rush them, OK?"

"Thank you, Dr. Orengo. I really appreciate you spending this time with me to explain the full situation."

"That's not a problem, it's not only my job, but I also enjoy ensuring that families have both hope and the right expectations," Dr. Orengo reassured Peyton.

Nurse Rachel returned and took Peyton for testing per Dr. Orengo's orders. The entire time, all he could think about was finding his father and praying that he wouldn't lose him again so soon.

When the testing was complete, he thanked the staff and caught an Uber to meet his brothers and his father, as promised.

By the time he arrived, Penelope was there, and she ran to her brother and embraced him. She whispered in his ear, "Thank you again for being here through all of this. It would not be the same without you."

Timothy, Jay Paul, and their father were sitting on the couch, watching soccer. Mark was wrapped in a blanket with his oxygen tank beside him. As Peyton walked to the couch, Mark hit Timothy on the leg, and pointed to the other couch, signaling for him to make way for Peyton. Timothy obliged, and Peyton sat next to his father. The five of them sat there, watching a Manchester United playback of Chelsea, enjoying spending time with each other. They were all there, in the moment, happy.

Hey Batta, Batta

Peyton spent the entire week with his father and his siblings. Every day, he woke early to make breakfast, and Penelope would wake with him and make coffee by his side.

They often reminisced about their time in Boston, while Mark, Timothy, and Jay Paul were asleep. The two of them had formed an amazing bond so quickly. They were so alike. All they both wanted was for their father to live and be loved by their family.

Mark's wife had passed years earlier before meeting Peyton.

Though her brothers had gotten past their mother's passing, Penelope, being the only girl, had been very close to her mom, and she was still dealing with the pain of losing her.

Perhaps this was a common thread that enhanced Peyton and Penelope's bond.

Throughout the week, it appeared as though Mark was regaining more of his strength with each day. He no longer required his cane and only used the oxygen when he needed it. The hospital had sent him a lightweight backpack armed with an internal oxygen device to ensure he could get around with ease.

It was a Friday morning, and the weather forecast was great. Peyton and Penelope finished breakfast and took their coffees outside to the porch to watch the remaining sunrise.

They didn't say much, but the two sat on the porch together, Peyton on the second step, and Penelope above him on the top step.

"Wow, this is so beautiful. Why can't every morning look like this?" Peyton asked rhetorically.

They finished their coffees and decided to go back inside. "I think the oatmeal should be ready now," Penelope said.

"Yeah, you're right. Let's get the gang up," Peyton agreed. "Breakfast is ready," he yelled from the front door after walking in.

Being the gluttonous one of the family, Jay Paul was always the first one downstairs and sitting at the table. "Peyton, I'm so glad you're here because Penelope can't cook for shit, so we've had to order breakfast almost every morning for the last few months," Jay Paul said.

"Oh, yeah, right. You eat everything in the house. That's why we always have to order breakfast. You're a hog that literally eats everything." Penelope laughed.

"Well, I'm a growing young man." Jay Paul shrugged.

"Growing? You're nearly twenty-five. You're not young anymore," Penelope joked.

Mark and Timothy joined the crew downstairs. "It's nice to have everyone in the house again. I really appreciate you all coming to stay with me," Mark said, looking at Timothy as he helped his dad down the stairs.

"Dad, we are happy to be here with you, plus it beats driving into the city every day anyway," Tim replied.

Although Jay Paul still lived with his father, Timothy and Penelope lived about forty-five minutes away in San Jose. Timothy had a medical practice there while Penelope worked in Mountain View, about fifteen minutes from San Jose.

"Hey, I was thinking, what do y'all think about going to catch a Giants game today?" Mark asked.

"Ahh, Dad, I can't. I have to be back at the office," Penelope said.

"Well, I guess it's just the guys today then," Timothy teased.

"Oh yeah, and before we go, they have the carnival in city center. Let's stop by there first," Jay Paul said, rubbing it in Penelope's face.

They all looked at Jay Paul with a side-eye.

"What are you, six years old?" Mark laughed.

"What a kid," Penelope teased.

"Nooo, that sounds fun. I haven't been to a carnival since I was a kid. Let's do it," Peyton said.

"Well, it's set. We're going to the carnival and then the game. But you all know how long those games drag out. Dad, you sure you can handle a full game?" Jay Paul asked.

"Well, I feel a lot better, Jay, and I have my oxygen pack. If I feel like I'm getting tired, we can always leave early. That way, we'll beat the traffic and get home to watch the highlights and the spot game."

They all laughed. "You mean the game that I always win?" Timothy replied.

"No, you mean the game that I'm now going to win," Peyton said.

"Ohh, Tim, I think you might've met your match," Penelope said jokingly.

They sat there and finished their breakfast. Penelope kissed her father and hugged her brothers, and the boys all got dressed for their day of fun.

They set out for the carnival first. Mark didn't ride any of the rides, but he enjoyed watching his boys embrace Peyton and seeing all of his sons together for the first time. They shot basketball and missed every shot, played games yet rarely won, and ate as much cotton candy as they each could stomach. Though they won very few tickets, they all were having an amazing time.

Over the years, Peyton had gotten used to ignorant people making fun of him because he had Down syndrome, but having it happen with his brothers and father was the last place he wanted to experience it.

An ignorant man laughed when Peyton could barely swing the hammer as he and Jay Paul were playing the sledgehammer carnival slam game.

"Duuur, look at me. I've got a hamma," the drunken man said, making fun of Peyton.

This saddened Peyton, not because his appearance was being made fun of, but rather because he wondered if his father had thought of him in the same way as this drunken idiot, all those years ago, causing him to abandon him and his mother.

Jay Paul was the hothead of the group, and he immediately went to Peyton's defense.

Just before a scuffle erupted between Jay Paul and the drunken idiot, Mark and Timothy pulled them back and decided it was time to leave the festivities.

"Oh shoot, we have to get going to the game. It's a one p.m. start," Timothy said. So, the four of them hustled out of the carnival grounds and set off for the game on the tram.

Upon arrival, they stopped by the gift shop, and Mark bought them each matching SF Giants jerseys. Since they were going all-out, they purchased the #1 fingers, hats, and even game-day books.

"OK, since you bought all this, I demand that you allow me to get the hotdogs," Peyton said.

"OK, well, if you're getting the franks, I'll get the popcorn," Jay Paul kicked in.

"Fine, I guess I'm stuck with the beer," Timothy said, laughing.

"Of course, you lush." Mark swatted at his ball cap.

After getting all of their food and beverages, the four made their way to their seats to enjoy the game.

They cheered, laughed, and watched as Timothy yelled at the umpire for every poorly called strike.

At about the fifth inning, Mark said, "Hey guys, I'm getting a little tired."

"OK, we can leave," Peyton replied.

"No, it's OK. We can leave at the seventh-inning stretch. This game is far too close, and I don't want to miss it," Mark replied.

"OK, well, let us know if you want to leave before then," Peyton said.

They laughed, they cheered, they joked, but mostly they were all there, present in the moment, having a blast, and happy.

When the seventh-inning stretch came, Timothy and Jay Paul were joking with each other, but Peyton looked over at their father and could tell that he was struggling but trying to be strong for the boys. He had put his oxygen on without them knowing, so Peyton thought it was time to go.

Peyton turned to his brothers. "Hey guys, I think he's ready to go. He seems tired."

"Hey Dad, let's get you home. We had a long day. Let's head home, so we don't miss the highlights," Timothy said.

"OK, are y'all sure? I think I could make it two more innings," Mark said.

"Oh yeah, we are good. I'm tired anyway," Jay Paul said.

They all went home on the tram, just talking about the great day they'd had. They laughed about Peyton's terrible shooting at the carnival, and Timothy's awful dart-throwing, where he'd won a four-leaf clover key chain for hitting one balloon.

Timothy and Jay Paul walked ahead of Peyton and Mark. "Today was a good day. I had all of my sons with me, and it was perfect. Plus, the way you shot the basketball was both funny and amazing." Mark and Peyton laughed together.

Nearly home, the crew walked past the neighborhood corner store.

"Hey, we're going to stop in and grab a case of beer for SPOT and highlights tonight," Timothy said. "Dad, you want anything?"

"Nah, I'm good, Tim, y'all go ahead." Mark held on to the side of the wall as he watched the boys go inside the store. He was beginning to feel weak.

"Hey, we are right around the corner. I'm going to get Dad home so he can sit down and rest, OK," Peyton said.

"OK, yeah, we won't be long. We'll pick up some beer and go next door to grab some Chinese food. You want anything specific, Peyton?"

"Nah, I'm not that hungry. Just bring me a few eggrolls," he replied.

Carrying bags full of SF Giants souvenirs and carnival paraphernalia, Peyton and Mark said goodbye to the brothers and continued home. As they got closer to the house, Mark began to walk slower, and his breaths were getting shorter and shorter.

Peyton was walking slightly ahead of his father, so he didn't notice Mark's steps getting shorter and that he was starting to stagger.

As Peyton looked back, Mark stood up straight and smiled. He didn't want Peyton to see him hurting and struggling to walk.

Peyton was super excited to have his father back in his life, so much so that he couldn't realize what was happening behind him, yet metaphorically right in front of his eyes.

Mark was close to the end...

Every time Peyton would start to look back, Mark stood up straight to put on a good face, so Peyton didn't see him struggling. A part of Mark wanted to protect Peyton's newfound joy, as well as preserve the lovely week they were having together.

They arrived at the steps of the home. "Wow, what a day, huh?" Peyton looked back and said.

As Mark was climbing the steps, he slipped on the bottom and grabbed the rail for balance.

Peyton rushed to him. "Are you OK?"

"Yeah, son. I'm good, just not as young as I used to be." The two chuckled. "Go ahead and get the door. I'm good."

Broken Damn

Mark and Peyton walked into the house. All the lights were off except for the one above the microwave, so it was quite dark. Mark tripped on a pair of shoes as the two entered.

"Are you OK, Dad?" Peyton asked.

"Oh yeah, I'm fine. You wouldn't believe that I've told Jay Paul to stop taking his shoes off right in front of the door, and just leaving them there practically a million times... that boy." Mark placed his right hand on his forehead, smiled, and shook his head. "That boy will literally be the death of me."

Peyton just smiled as his father moved the shoes out of the way.

"Hey, I'm going to turn on ESPN so we can watch the highlights. Who knows, we may even see ourselves on TV. You were pretty close to that guy who caught the foul ball," Mark said.

"Oh, now that would be awesome," Peyton replied.

"Yeah, anytime we go to Giants games, we always hurry home to see if we can catch ourselves on TV. A silly game, I suppose, but whoever spots us first gets the coldest beer. I guess it's a weird tradition since all the beers are cold." Mark chuckled.

Peyton turned on the living room lights as Mark grabbed the remote and turned the channel to Sports Center.

Peyton had spent two weeks with his new family. He was so happy to have finally found his father again, even though it was in extreme circumstances. The entire time, Penelope was still out on leave and his two brothers spent quite a bit of time after work over at the house as well. The five of them had spent nearly every day together.

"Hey, Peyton, I'd like to show you something," Mark said.

Peyton had never had the chance to show his father all his awards, because years before, he'd emptied his suitcase, throwing all the contents at the house in frustration. He sat on the couch and watched as his father walked to the closet in the hallway, opened it, and came out with a box.

"I kept something because I think a part of me knew or hoped we'd have the opportunity to meet again."

He wanted to show Peyton a trophy of one of his proudest accomplishments. Years ago, Mark grabbed it out of the street as he'd known it was important to Peyton.

"Whoa, what do you have there?" Peyton asked.

Mark sat next to Peyton on the couch, "I've been keeping this for quite some time. I guess I just never wanted to get rid of it, and I'm so glad I didn't."

Peyton was even more curious now.

As Mark opened the box, he reached inside and pulled out a trophy. Turning the trophy around to face Peyton, Peyton's eyes lit up!

"Oh my God! How? When? How in the world…?"

"I kept it since that day. I went outside and picked it up, cleaned it, glued it back together and..."

"Oh my gosh, I haven't seen this thing in years."

It was Peyton's Special Olympics trophy, the final item that he'd pulled out of the suitcase and thrown at his father's home. And now, there they were, five years later, looking at it together. Peyton reached over, grabbed the trophy, smiled at it, and wrapped his arms around his father and embraced him.

Mark hugged him back, though his face changed, as if he were growing sadder as Peyton became more excited.

Peyton continued in shock, completely overjoyed that his father had seen at least one of his accomplishments. He began telling Mark all about seventh grade, when he won three events in the Special Olympics. "Do you have all the others?" he asked.

"I don't. I just—"

Peyton cut him off. "It's OK. I'm just glad you have this one. I'm just like 'wow' right now."

Mark was trying to stop Peyton. "Peyton, I need to tell you something."

Peyton was too excited to see or hear that Mark was being sincere. He just continued rambling on, so his dad just smiled and shed a tear.

"Dad, why are you crying?"

"I should have been there to see this and say that... that, I'm so proud of you. It's one of my only regrets in life." Mark lowered his eyes.

Peyton shook his head with resolve. "We can't go back in the past. You're here now. You're here now." He struggled to hold back his tears. "My beautiful mother taught me forgiveness and that everything works out in good time—God's time, not ours. You're here, Dad, and I'm not going to hold on to the past, or I'll lose the present." Still fighting back tears, he said, "Let's stay focused on the *now*." He looked up at his father and said, between sobs, "I have my dad back, and we are going to sit and sip beer and try to spot us at the game tonight. What can be better than that?"

Mark smiled. He wiped away his streaming tears and replied, "Yes, we sure are, son!"

"Hey, while we wait on Tim and Jay to come back, I'm going to shower up and get ready to kick y'alls' asses in this spotting game y'all play."

"*We play*... we play, son. You're a part of this now, too," Mark corrected him.

Peyton smiled and went toward the bathroom. "Before I go, do you need me to get you anything from the kitchen? Are you good? You feel OK?"

"Yeah, son, I'm OK. Thank you. But..."

Peyton smiled and turned away, so he didn't see that his father was both in pain and trying to stop him, reaching out for him. It was like something was wrong, and he just wanted Peyton next to him at that moment. Peyton couldn't see his father's outstretched hand.

Peyton yelled from the bathroom, "Hey, I have an album on my phone of all my trophies and awards I've been waiting to show you. Just unlock my phone. The code is 0509. Look under the album ONE DAY!"

"Hey, Peyton. Shower later. I really want to talk to you, son," Mark called back.

Peyton joked, "I'm not going anywhere. Not another word out of you. I insist, take a look through that album. You're going to love it."

Peyton turned on the water as he was preparing to shower. His father was still on the couch, looking at all the pictures of the trophies, certificates, plaques, and awards Peyton had amassed over the years.

Picture after picture, Mark swiped through, seeing how awesome his son was and how much he had missed. With each slide of his finger, Mark became more and more heartbroken.

Peyton didn't know, but his father's time with him was quickly coming to an end. Mark was looking at the photos and looking up at the restroom, hoping that Peyton would come back out soon.

He stood up to try to go knock on the door. He felt like he really needed to apologize to Peyton. He had to tell him that he was truly sorry and that he recognized how awesome a man Peyton had become, despite his absence.

He stood up, but his body was too weak due to his ailments and being out all day at the game. He should have been home resting per the doctor's orders, but he had wanted to spend as much time that he had left with Peyton.

As Mark tried to walk toward the restroom, he stumbled a bit and grabbed the wall for balance. When he couldn't take another step, he fell back to the couch in slow motion, his breathing becoming slower and sporadic.

Simultaneously, Peyton was in the bathroom, looking into the mirror, preparing for his shower while trying to hold back his emotions. Since he'd arrived in San Francisco on this second trip, he hadn't allowed himself to be overcome with feelings. He'd held everything back and pushed all his thoughts of abandonment away because he wanted to cherish and live as much time with his father as he had left.

However, this attempt to *dam up* his emotions was quickly becoming futile.

Standing there, looking into the mirror, he became really emotional because he had so many questions. He needed to get them off his chest, but he struggled with balancing seeking answers from his father while not destroying what they had now.

He turned the water up higher so his father couldn't hear him sobbing through the door as he stared into the mirror.

Peyton couldn't pull himself together because, at that moment, he couldn't stop thinking about the mother whom he'd lost and the father whom he'd initially found but who still hadn't wanted him.

Knowing that his father had kept the one trophy brought him some happiness, but it was a double-edged sword because it also reminded him of that day his father had allowed him to be taken away in handcuffs instead of being there for him.

He flashed back to that day—begging his father not to allow the officers to take him away, imploring his father to help him, and watching his father stand on the stoop and do absolutely nothing. He was broken.

Not thinking rationally, Peyton got into the shower fully clothed and just let the water beat against his face. Masking his tears, the water soaked his clothes and his heavy heart.

Drop after drop hit Peyton's face. He flashed back to his childhood, and the several times he'd cried, asking his mother where his father was. The time he fell off the swing set, when his mother died, when kids teased him for not having a father during "bring your father to school" day, or when he'd won trophy after trophy, only to watch other athletes stand proudly with their fathers…

For the first time, everything was hitting Peyton at once. The damn of emotions had broken, and his heart was pouring out through his tear ducts. Going in and out of different flashbacks, Peyton was now crying hysterically and heartbroken. Not thinking clearly, he ran out of the shower and into the living room in anger…

Peyton held his face in his hands and asked, "Why? Why? Just tell me why? Where were you? Why didn't you want me? I needed you. I wanted you. I had no one. Why did you leave me? Why wasn't I good enough for you? What scared you about me sooo much that you let me go thirty years without you? Why did you let them take me away like I was a petty thief or something? I'm your son. I'm your son," he repeated, yelling.

"My mother died, and you were nowhere to be found to

comfort me. You just left and started a new family. What did I ever do to you?" Peyton was livid, tears streaming down his furious face.

After receiving no answer, he finally looked up and saw his father barely breathing and reaching for him on the sofa...His father was reaching out his hand, whispering very softly, "I'm sorry, I'm sorry Peyton, I'm sorry son, I should have been there..."

Peyton ran to his father. "Dad, nooo. Wait, I'm sorry. Wait, I'm sorry I said all those things!"

Mark whispered, "I'm sorry, Peyton. I should have been there for you that entire time. I shouldn't have let them take you away. Your mother passed, and I wasn't there. I was a coward. I'm so sorry, son. I love you, and you have made me so proud, Peyton." He was fading.

Peyton dropped to his knees, pulled his father closer to him, and held him to his chest.

Peyton was crying and yelling, "I just got you back. I just got you back. You can't go now... God, no... God, no!" he yelled, teary-eyed.

Pulling his dad closer, looking toward the ceiling, he said, "If you take him now, I'll have nobody. Don't do this to me. Not again."

Mark grabbed Peyton's hand and locked their fingers. He whispered, "Peyton, you know what to do. Your mother taught you well and raised you perfectly. You love. You love better than I did. Love with all your heart. The world needs your love!"

These were the same words Peyton's mom had told him at her end.

Mark softly continued, "I wasn't there for you then, but now I'll never leave you. I'll always be a part of your life."

Peyton was crying hysterically. Soaking wet, he held his father's body close as his voice faded...

Just then, Timothy and Jay Paul walked back into the house,

arguing about who would win the upcoming spotting game.

"When was the last time you won?" Timothy laughed.

"*Man*, it's because you just point at random locations on the TV, without even looking, and it just so happens to be somewhat near where we are."

As they entered the house, they both saw Peyton kneeling with their father. Peyton looked up with tears in his eyes. He screamed to his brothers, "Helllppp meee! Helllppp!"

Timothy and Jay Paul ran over to their father. Timothy immediately called 911 and then called Penelope. Jay Paul was talking to Peyton, trying to understand what had happened.

Minutes later, the commotion concluded with red lights flashing outside and the EMS team rushing inside. They placed Mark in the ambulance and hurried him to the hospital.

As Peyton, Jay Paul, and Timothy followed the ambulance in Tim's car, Jay Paul picked up his phone and called Penelope again. She didn't answer.

"I'll text her," Peyton said.

> Penel, come to the hospital quick. Dad fainted and he's not doing well.

Peyton saw the three dots of Penelope texting back, but he didn't check the message because he and his brothers were all frantic.

"Guys, I need to tell you both something," Peyton said.

Timothy turned around and looked at Peyton. "What is it?"

"I got tested to see if I was a match for Dad. I got the results back a week ago... Dr. Orengo called me personally, and confirmed... I'm... I'm a match."

Jay Paul slammed on the brakes and pulled off the side of the road. "Peyton, we can't ask you to..."

Peyton cut him off. "You're not asking. I'm telling you both. I'm going through with it. I must. I need to be there for him."

The three brothers all met in the middle of the car and hugged. "Jay, drive...*drive!* Let's get there," Timothy said.

The brothers arrived at the hospital, parked the car, and rushed inside. They met Dr. Orengo, who was already waiting. "Calm down, guys. Calm down. We've stabilized your father, but, Peyton, if we're going to do this, we have to do it ASAP."

"I'm ready, Dr. Orengo. I'm ready. I just need to speak to my father first," Peyton said.

"I'm assuming you haven't fasted today, so we need to wait until tomorrow morning for the procedure. We still have time," Dr. Orengo reassured him.

The brothers waited outside the room as Peyton went in to speak with their father.

"Dad, are you awake? It's me, Peyton. I need to talk to you."

Mark woke up and slowly turned to Peyton. He could tell that his father was fading.

"Listen, I need you to hold on a little while longer," Peyton said. "I just found you, and I refuse to leave you now. I did something. I got tested a week ago, and I'm a perfect match for you, and I'm going to donate the liver portion for you. Dr. Orengo said we'd have to wait until tomorrow since I've eaten today, but she said we should still have time."

Mark could barely speak, "Son, I can't ask you to do that, and I won't let you. You have your whole life ahead of you to live, and I was never there for you. I don't deserve this from you."

"Dad, stop. My mom taught me to forgive, and that true forgiveness only comes when someone doesn't deserve it, yet you make the decision to forgive, like God does for us."

Mark had tears streaming down the left side of his face.

"I want you to know—"

Mark cut him off. "Peyton, son, my beloved son. I need to say something to you. Please allow me. I want you to know that I'm truly sorry that I wasn't there for you. I'm sorry that I wasn't at your games. Sorry that I wasn't there to see you grow. I'm sorry that you struggled without me. I'm sorry that your mother had to struggle, and I wasn't there to comfort her. I should have been more of a man. I should have been the man that I see standing before me now. You are the pride of your mother, and I'm honored to have played even a small part in you coming into this world.

"Please forgive me. I need you to know that you are enough. You've always been enough. Down syndrome has made you the best man I know. I'm just sorry it took me over thirty years to figure that out. You've given me a lifetime of joy in a matter of two weeks. Please forgive me," Mark poured his heart out.

Peyton began to cry. He grabbed his father's hand as Mark spoke.

"Come closer, son," Mark said.

The two hugged each other, and Mark whispered into Peyton's ear, "If this doesn't go well, I want you to take care of your siblings. They need you. You need them. But more importantly, be a better man than me, son. Be better than I was to the world. Give *love* to the world. You are the epitome of our last name."

Peyton kissed his father on the cheek. "I forgive you, Dad, and I'm going to save you."

Peyton stayed the entire night by his father's side, as did his siblings.

The next morning, the door to the room opened, and it was Dr. Orengo and her team. "It's time Peyton, we need to get you and your father prepped for surgery ASAP."

As the nurses rushed in to prep Mark, Peyton's hand slid away from his father's, but the two never broke eye contact. Penelope and her brothers all hugged their father and kissed him.

As they rolled the bed toward the operating room, one of the nurses said, "This is as far you all can go. We're prepping Peyton and your father now, and we'll come out as often as possible and provide y'all with updates." The kids said their goodbyes as they took Mark away.

"Don't worry, guys. I'll be fine. I'm proud of each of you. Penel, take care of your brothers until I return. And take care of Peyton when he wakes up. He'll need you. I love you, baby. My sweet baby girl."

"I love you too, Dad." Penelope kissed her father's forehead. "I'll keep the boys out of trouble until you're strong enough again to choke-slam both of them for getting out of line."

While they wheeled Mark back, Peyton was being prepped. Timothy, Jay, and Penelope all sat in the waiting room. They were there, present, and waiting with hope.

CHAPTER 17
LOVE'S HOPE: GOD'S PLAN

Bright lights, indiscernible conversation, and a foggy view from opening eyes. As Peyton was waking up, still groggy from the procedure, he looked around briefly, unaware of what was happening around him. He was in and out of consciousness several times in the recovery room.

His sister walked over to him. "Peyton, Peyton, can you hear me?" She rubbed his forehead.

Doctor Orengo asked, "Peyton, can you hear me, son?"

Peyton was still fading in and out from the aftereffects of the anesthesia, so his responses were muffled and incoherent.

"It's going to take him a while. The surgery put a lot of stress on his body," Dr. Orengo replied.

His sister pulled up her chair, sat by his side, and held his hand. As a tear rolled down her cheek, she grabbed his hand and held it tight. "You just take your time, big brother. We aren't going anywhere," she said. "We're here for you. We'll all be right here."

She looked back at the doctor and her brothers, "How do we tell him? This is going to crush him. He just found us again," she whispered in despair.

"If I may, these things are never easy, Ms. Love. There's no easy way to do this. We just have to keep him calm and let him know that his surgery went well, and that he's going to be OK. I'll be back in, in a few hours to check on him. We have a dedicated nurse who's going to look after him through the night. She'll page me if anything changes. Y'all should go home and try to get some rest."

"No, we'd like to stay if that's OK, Doc."

"Of course that's OK. Once he is taken out of the ICU, and placed in his room, I'll have the staff roll you all in some beds and some linens."

"Thank you," Penelope replied.

The staff eventually moved Peyton to his room, where he was able to rest, and his brothers were able to join Penelope.

The night came and went, and Peyton woke several times yet would fall back asleep before his sister could speak with him.

The next morning, Dr. Orengo and the staff came into the room to speak with the family. "How are y'all feeling? Can we get y'all anything? Has Peyton been awake at all?"

They just nodded. They were all concerned with the inevitable pain their beautiful brother was about to face. Even in the face of all that adversity, Peyton had been able to find his father, forgive him, and go so far as to save his life. He was the true definition of their last name: Love.

As Peyton began to stir, he opened his eyes and saw a room full of people. He could recognize his sister talking but couldn't make out what she was saying. He saw the doctor on the other side of the room, flipping through paperwork, and a nurse fiddling with some tubing connected to his arm. He could see his two brothers sitting by the window on rollout beds, hugging each other and comforting each other.

The doctor noticed him waking up and walked over to him. "Mr. Love... Peyton, can you hear me? Nurse, what are his vitals? Mr. Love can you hear me?" Dr. Orengo repeated.

"All vitals are normal, his BP is 128 over 90, and he's stable," the nurse replied.

Peyton spoke. "Yes, ma'am, I can hear you," he replied with a crackly voice. "May I please have some water? My throat is very dry."

"Let's get him some water. How are you feeling, Mr. Love?" Dr. Orengo asked.

"Doc, I told you, call me Peyton. We're friends now." He smiled.

"How are you feeling, Peyton? Are you in pain?"

"I'm OK. I'm just a little sore, and my side hurts quite a bit."

"We can give you a little more medicine that will ease your pain."

"Nurse, let's up his meds by ten mics…"

"So, how did it go? Did everything go well? How's my father?" Peyton asked. He looked back and forth from Dr. Orengo to his sister. Dr. Orengo pulled a chair close to the bed and sat down, and Peyton immediately knew something was wrong.

"Peyton, we need to talk, but more importantly, I need you to remain calm and breathe."

Timothy began to cry louder.

"Oh no, Doc. It didn't work? What happened? How's my father? Where's my father?" Peyton tried to sit up.

"No, no, son. Don't get up. Just rest. You need rest. Try not to move too much. I don't want you to reopen your stiches," Dr. Orengo implored.

"Just tell me what's wrong," Peyton exclaimed. He looked at his sister, who had obviously been crying. "Penelope, what's wrong? Where's our father? Is he OK?" Peyton begged.

"Peyton, there's no easy way to say this, but your father came through the first portion of the surgery just fine. As we were implanting the portion of your liver lobe, he arrested."

"Arrested, wha… wha… what do you mean? What does that mean 'he arrested'?"

"Peyton, as we were working on your father and implanting the liver lobe, your father's body was just too diseased and too far gone. His heart began to pump faster and faster, and it gave out. We did all that we could to revive him, but despite our best efforts, there was just too much damage, son. I'm sorry to tell you, but your father didn't make it through the surgery. His ailments were too…"

Peyton erupted into tears, calling out hysterically, "No, no, no this can't be. He promised he'd come through this. He promised we'd be a family again. Penelope, he promised… Penel, Penel, Penel, he… he… he… he promised… he promised." Peyton could barely put together full sentences. He was so distraught.

"Peyton, I need you to calm down. I need you to breathe. Nurse, let's give him some Ativan to calm him down. I don't want him to damage his stitches or reopen his wound," Dr. Orengo said.

Peyton's two brothers got up from the window and hurried over to the bed. The three of them all hugged Peyton. "It's OK, Pey, we'll be a family. We *are* a family," Penelope said.

Dr. Orengo gave way to the family. "I'll give y'all some time, but I'll be right outside should you have further questions."

Peyton began to blame himself as he cried in his sister's arms. "I waited too long to try to find him again. I should've tried harder. I… I should've called. We could've caught this earlier. I made him feel like he couldn't reach out to me. I was so angry. My mom told me to let go of my anger, and I didn't listen. I should have listened. *Why? Whhhyyy didn't I listen?* He's gone now because of me. I've lost him all over again."

"No, Peyton, you did nothing wrong," Penelope replied, tears running down her cheeks.

"You saved him. You saved us," Timothy said.

Peyton wept and wept. He couldn't stop sobbing. There were no audible words coming from his mouth anymore, but his pain was felt, and all his siblings could do was be there for him, as they too were hurting. Peyton was in complete agony, and nothing could console his internal pain. "I'm broken, Penelope. My heart is broken. Why? Why did this happen?" He cried in her arms.

After learning about the story of Peyton and his father, Dr. Orengo had gained somewhat of an attachment to Peyton, because she too had lost her father, after he'd had a kidney transplant, and his body rejected the very organ she had donated.

To see a selfless act from a man like Peyton, in giving his organs to a man who hadn't wanted him almost all of his life, touched Dr. Orengo, even though she made it a point not to get emotionally attached to her patients. "Peyton, Peyton," Dr. Orengo whispered. "How are you feeling, son? Is there anything you need? How's your pain?"

Peyton, not wanting to wake his sleeping siblings, just raised his hand and gave a thumbs-up. "Dr. O, can I see my father? I need to see him before he leaves."

Dr. Orengo nodded. "We can make that happen, Peyton. What else do you need?"

"I need my phone. I need to make a call."

Penelope began to wake up. She saw Dr. Orengo and Peyton talking. "Tim, Jay, wake up." She rubbed her brother's shoulders.

"I need my phone, Penel. Can you grab it for me?"

"Of course, Pey. Me and the boys are going to go and grab coffee. We'll bring you some more water. Do you need anything else?"

"Nah, Penel, I just want to be alone for a bit," Peyton replied.

She kissed him on the forehead, handed him his phone, and walked out along with Dr. Orengo. "OK, we'll be right back, Pey."

Peyton dialed the only person he could think of, the only

person he wanted to talk to at this lowest point in his life: James.

His friend answered. "Peyton, I'm so glad that you called. How did it go? Are you OK? How's your father?"

Peyton had no clue, but James had flown out from Boston the night before to ensure he was there for Peyton when he woke from surgery. Because James wasn't family, they wouldn't give him information on the outcome of Peyton or his father. Therefore, he'd just been waiting in the waiting room. He'd slept at the hospital all night, waiting for information.

Peyton began to cry through the phone. "James, he's gone. He's gone. I've lost him all over again. I feel so alone. I feel so lost. What do I do now? I forgave, I did everything I could to save him, and he's gone, James... He's gone. It's just me now. I'm so alone. Why does this keep happening to me?"

"Oh, Peyton, I'm so sorry for your loss. I can only imagine the pain that you're feeling. But I want you to know that you're not alone. You have overcome so much, and you saw both your mother and father to the end. You carried them both to the end. You made their lives worth living. I love you, and you are *not* alone."

Peyton wept as James spoke. "Your mother will always be in your heart, and now, because of your bravery, your father will always have a part of you, and you will always have a part of them both. You fulfilled your purpose, but you have more to do. Your mother wanted you to forgive your father, and right now, she is smiling down at you. Can't you feel her love, Peyton?" James always had a way of putting things into perspective for Peyton and keeping him focused on the *love* that he brought the world... even in his lowest of times.

"I can feel her love, and I know my father is in a better place. I just feel alone. Like it's just me in this huge world with no one truly with me. I really wish you were here, James. You're the only one besides my mom who's been with me all my life and always loved me, always taught me... I don't know, James. I just feel like I have nothing else. I've given my all, and I have nothing."

"Peyton, I have to go, but I promise to talk to you soon," James replied abruptly.

"No, James, please don't go now... I just, I just, I just need someone to talk to."

"I'm sorry, Pey. I have to go. I have something really important to do," James replied.

"OK, I understand."

As they hung up, Peyton put down his phone and just sobbed into his pillow.

As the sliding door to his room opened, Peyton wiped his eyes, turned over, and there was James...

Shocked and crying joyous tears, Peyton said, "Wait, what... how did you... what... how...?"

With tears in his eyes as he stood at the door, James said, "You didn't think I would let you go through this alone, did you? I told you the day we met, I would never leave you, and I'd always be here for you. That doesn't stop because you're on the other side of the country. I love you, Peyton."

James walked to Peyton's bedside and embraced him. Peyton cried in his arms, but his tears were tears of relief, tears of joy. He'd taken both his mother and his father to the very end, fulfilled his mom's last dying wish, and given all he could to his father.

Peyton was at peace for the first time since he'd woken from his surgery. When his siblings returned, he introduced his brothers to James. Penelope smiled, embraced James, and thanked him for coming out to be with the family. Peyton was finally at peace.

Dr. Orengo walked back in, saw the new face, and asked, "And who's this?"

"Dr. Orengo, this is James Wellington, my speech and physical therapist—"

James cut him off. "No, I'm not. I'm his friend. I'm James Wellington. Nice to meet you, Dr. Orengo, and thank you for taking care of Peyton. It's much appreciated."

"Well, it's nice to meet you." Dr. Orengo shook James's hand. "Peyton, if you're up for it, we've arranged for you to see your father. Are you up for that?"

Peyton looked at James as Penelope grabbed his hand. He turned back to Dr. Orengo. "Yes, ma'am. I'm up for it. I need to say goodbye… *We* need to say goodbye," he corrected himself. "Can James join us, as well?"

"Of course, Peyton. Of course. That won't be a problem."

"We have a wheelchair for you, Peyton," the nurse said. "I'll take you down."

"No, no. I've got this one," Dr. Orengo said as she rubbed Peyton's shoulder.

Unbeknownst to Peyton, for the first time in his life, he had an entire family. James, his mentor, his loving siblings, a doctor who connected with him, the love of his mother within, and his father, whom he'd given all to save… all in the exact same location.

"Here we are, Peyton. Your father's just beyond these doors, waiting. I'll give you and your family some alone time," Dr. Orengo said.

Peyton looked up at Dr. Orengo, "No, Doc, I told you, we're friends now. I want you here, unless you have other patients. Then I understand if you have to go."

"I'd be honored to join y'all, Peyton. Thank you for allowing me to be a part of this."

Love's Final Heart

The doors opened slowly, and Penelope began to cry, so Jay Paul grabbed her and held her tight. "It's going to be OK, Penel. We'll get through this."

"I got him, Doc," James said. He grabbed the wheelchair and rolled Peyton closer. All the siblings surrounded their father. One by one, they said their goodbyes.

Peyton sat, quiet.

"Dad, I want to thank you for being a good man. I want to thank you for teaching me to be a good woman, and I'll never forget the lessons you taught me. I love you, Dad," Penelope whimpered.

"Dad, I have our family now. I have us covered; I'll take care of Penel, and everyone. You rest now. We're going to be OK. I love you always, and I'll be the man you always wanted me to be," Timothy said to his father.

Jay Paul was the youngest son. He was trying so hard to be strong for his siblings, but he couldn't help it. He broke down. "Dad, Dad, I'm not ready for you to be gone. We haven't seen enough baseball games. We haven't tossed the ball around enough. I need you here with me... You once told me that one man can change the world. Well, I want you to know that you changed mine. You made me who I am today, and I won't stop giving my absolute all to the world." Peyton grabbed Jay's hand. "Dad, I love you, and I want you to rest in peace until we meet again," Jay said as he turned. Penelope hugged him as he cried.

Because of his profession, Dr. Orengo had seen many families say goodbye to family members, but this one hit her harder. As she stood in the back of the room, she marveled as she saw a family coming together in the most beautiful way.

"James, can you roll me closer?" Peyton asked.

As he sat next to his father's body, Peyton was silent for a moment. "I don't have the words. For years, all I wanted was to have you in my life. All I wanted was to toss the ball around with you. All I wanted was for you to help make me the man that I should be. All I wanted was you. All I wanted was us.

"I didn't have that, but it wasn't until I woke from surgery that I realized that you gave me the most beautiful thing in life... a lesson in true *love*. You gave me love, Dad. Beautiful, unconditional, relentless love. I want you to know that I truly forgive you, and you did make me the man I need to be. You did give me *us*. You gave me *myself*. You gave me the drive to be someone. You gave me compassion for those less fortunate. You gave me amazing brothers and the most beautiful sister in the world. It's because of you that I will change the world and fulfill my mom's wish for me—to give love to the world. I will always love you, and I will take you with me forever. Rest now, Dad, rest..." Peyton lowered his head.

The siblings surrounded their father, held hands, and said goodbye.

Just before they turned to leave, Peyton said, "Wait, James..."

He turned back to his father, took his thumb, and traced the outline of a heart, the final heart upon his father's forehead! The moment ended with the siblings holding hands, James hugging Peyton, and Peyton's hand on his father's forehead with his heart full of hope.

Green Corduroy

A battered brown suitcase opened, yet it was almost impossible to make out the contents within. Though the outside was covered with random stickers, pins, and obscure markings, the inside contained an old journal, a single sheet of paper, and two photos taped to the underside of the suitcase's lid.

A shaky hand slowly grazed the sole sheet while a soft, arrhythmic sob pushed through the deafening silence. As a man looked up toward the sky, a lone tear raced along the crevice of his nose and continued down his cheek. The tear appeared to travel with purpose, halting only to fill the well created by a dimple of sorrow.

The suitcase closed...

"Sometimes, I just don't understand. I did everything right, just as you said... I found him, Mom, forgave him, and now this. This? What am I to do now?"

Standing up from the dew-covered grass, Peyton slowly walked away from the crowd. Tightly clenching the handle of the suitcase, he walked aimlessly and without purpose, almost as if he had absolutely nowhere to be, or that even the very notion of time had forsaken him.

Walking away, he wiped his free hand on his faded brownish-green corduroy pants. In harmony with his increasing sobs, his steps became slower and without direction before drawing to a halt.

Faint sobs escaped his mouth. White knuckles gripped the antique handle of the suitcase. His grasp got tighter and tighter with each uncontrollable sigh...

Disoriented steps became more staggering as the countenance of sorrow and pain upon his face became overwhelming. He fell back to his knees, suitcase now clutched to his chest, looking back to the funeral.

As the funeral staff began to lower the casket, which threatened to fall from sight, Peyton looked back, as if to give one final goodbye. Only a few words were spoken. Sorrowed gestures and visions of farewell existed within that moment...

He was left standing in the dewy blades of grass with only the tears that filled the corners of his eyes.

As the casket slowly disappeared from sight, the crowd, which was no longer a part of Peyton's focus, began to disperse.

He whispered, "As we say goodbye, thank you... thank you, Love!"

With final embraces, the crowd moved toward their vehicles and prepared to leave the grounds.

Yet one remained, his eyes so filled that tears blurred the casket's final visible moments.

Peyton wept as he opened the old beat-up journal, and read from a torn-out page he had folded and stapled within:

> What is love? A question that has been debated for centuries yet very few have laid claim to a true answer. Can it be found? Does it teach forgiveness? Does it enter and leave our lives, giving us but a snippet of its true form, just to remind us that there is something more out there? Or is it merely the desire to feel an attachment with one other, as we go through this life? The answer is yes, it is all of the above.
>
> It is all-encompassing. It is fear. It is hope. It is the feeling of finally finding the one who understands you. It exists within the fleeting moment of losing one's grandmother after a lifelong example of what a woman should be to a family. It exists within the moment one feels accomplished after crossing the stage of graduation at the ripe age of 42, just because they wanted to set an example for their family. It exists within the short-lived moments of young infatuation, when one first feels the flutters of care and admiration.
>
> However, in its purest form, it exists from the moment a mother feels her child clench to her from within, and the bond of love is created forever. Divine Love!

As a tear fell from his cheek, Peyton kneeled and drew something in the wet grass with his index finger. It could have been coincidence or fate, but the tear dropped directly in the middle of his sorrowful illustration.

His drawing finished, Peyton looked up toward the cloudy blue skies, just sitting there, contemplating life and what his purpose would be from that point forward.

Penelope walked over to Peyton and kneeled down with him. "He's no longer in pain, and you did all that you could. You found us, and now we have each other forever."

"But Penel, why did he have to leave? I miss him so much already, and I feel like I didn't get enough time with him. Sometimes I just don't understand life. I know I'm not like a regular man but—"

She cut him off. "No, you're not like a regular man. You're much better than a regular man. You brought us all together and taught us the true meaning of forgiveness and *love*, and for that, you will always be the man of this family."

Timothy and Jay Paul walked over to Penelope and Peyton, kneeling on the ground. All the siblings hugged each other, consoled each other, and cried in each other's arms.

Peyton had come so far and sacrificed so much. In the end, it was up to him to save his father and his family. He'd had to find his father in order to forgive him, to save him, and in doing so, he'd unknowingly saved himself. His life had come full circle, yet he felt incomplete.

The four of them sat there for what seemed like hours, just talking about their time together with their father. Tears turned into laughs as they discussed touring the city, watching the game, eating breakfast together, and all the terrible dad jokes Mark had told.

Peyton had lost his father again, but in turn, he'd found his purpose and his family. He'd sacrificed all of his life to find meaning in his life, meaning in why he had been born, and he'd finally found it. They were there, then, in that moment, complete.

CHAPTER 18
PURPOSE FULFILLED

Because the siblings all carried their father to the end, they'd built a bond that proved to be quite strong.

Penelope eventually moved to Boston to be closer to Peyton, and Timothy and Jay Paul visited nearly five times a year.

The four had made plans as to who would host Christmas and Thanksgiving over the next several years. They were growing together, learning each other, all while being strong for one another since the loss of their father.

Though Peyton finally had a family, he always felt like a part of him was still missing. And while he'd often put on a nice face for his siblings and James, when he was all alone and the sibling festivities ceased, Peyton still felt a sense of emptiness, a hole he couldn't quite seem to fill.

Months after Mark passed away, Peyton called James and asked him to meet at their favorite hole-in-the-wall breakfast spot, Dariane's Delights. Peyton had always liked this spot because he had a crush on his favorite waitress, Elaine.

After they ordered, Peyton said, "So I wanted to run something past you."

"OK, hit me. I'm all ears," James replied.

"Well... well, I was thinking about trying to adopt a child. Do you think that would be a good idea?"

"Wow, Peyton, that's... that's quite a potentially huge, life-altering decision."

The two sat and discussed the possibility of Peyton adopting a child and if it was the right thing for him to do. James had never been the kind of mentor who'd told Peyton what to do. Rather, he had always been a sounding board for Peyton to bounce his ideas off in a safe space.

It had been nearly eighteen months since that conversation and slightly over a year since Peyton had decided to start the process to adopt.

He'd gone through the entire process and had finally received notice that he was eligible to adopt a child. While waiting for final approval, Peyton fostered a three-year-old girl named Tiffany and a two-year-old boy named Justin. He leaned heavily on his grandparent's wisdom throughout the early days, but quickly gained his parental footing and loved the opportunity to foster.

In both cases, the adoption agency checked in regularly and provided Peyton with all the additional support and resources he required during the trial fostering.

In pure Peyton fashion, he learned quickly and ensured that he gave each of the babies the best home possible.

When he received his notice of approval to adopt, Peyton was over the moon. He had balanced fostering and his career with the help of James and Penelope and was ecstatic to take the next step.

Though James regularly reminded him to make this decision for the right reason, a part of Peyton wanted to adopt in order to fill the hole his parents had left in his heart.

The day was finally here.

Peyton stood in front of a building whose sign read, "Life Change Adoption Agency." There he stood, nearly four years removed from his father's passing, looking at the building in silence.

Overjoyed yet nervous about this next phase of his life, Peyton replayed his parents' words over and over in his head.

"*Love. Love more than I did. The world needs your love. Be the love the world demands!*"

He walked into the building and went to the designated room left on his voice mail, where a middle-aged woman walked up to him, smiling. "Mr. Love? Peyton?"

Peyton smiled back. "Yes, ma'am. That's me. I think we spoke on the phone earlier this week."

"Yes... yes, come on in. I'm Leola, by the way, and I'm so excited this day finally came for you. For us." They shook hands as Leola pointed at a chair for Peyton.

The two sat and talked for a bit, and then Leola pulled out more paperwork for Peyton to sign. "You know, I found it very fascinating that you were interested in an older child. What swayed you?"

"Well, the truth is, Leola, when you told me that the younger kids always get adopted, but the older kids usually just age out of the system, I didn't quite understand it. So, I spoke with my sister and got a better understanding of what you meant. It's so sad that these kids end up not being wanted, for lack of better words. When I understood that, the choice was simple. You see, I was once that child. That child who wasn't wanted. If I can do my little part in this world to change that, I have no choice but to do so."

"Well, Mr. Love, I don't usually get emotionally involved in these things, but I have to say, receiving your email that you wanted to adopt an older child really warmed my heart. We need more people like you... and you, sir, you are changing the world for the better."

"If I may, we need more people like my mother," Peyton replied. "She was the one who taught me to give *love* to the world, giving the love that the world demands."

"Well, I'm sure she's an amazing woman!" Leola replied.

"Yes, ma'am, she was." Peyton smiled.

"Oh, I'm sorry. I didn't know."

"No sorry required, Leola. I'm happy she was here on this earth. I'm happy she decided a long time ago to have me, to teach me, and to make me who I am today."

Ms. Leola reached out, grabbed his hand, and smiled. "You are amazing!"

Their words began to fade as Peyton flashed back to times with his mother. He thought of the day he'd walked his speech therapy trophy to his mother. She'd grabbed his hand, pulled him close, and said, "I'm so proud of you. I wouldn't be who I am today without you, son."

This was the *love* Peyton wanted to give to a child. Even though a part of him wanted to adopt a child in order to fill the hole in his heart, the larger part of him wanted to ensure that a child felt the same love his mother had provided him daily.

"Well, Mr. Love, after your psych analysis, we definitely know that you're fully capable of raising a child. But I have to ask for my own personal reasons, why?"

He looked up and didn't say anything right away... He thought back to the last moments with his father...

"...the world needs your love..."

Bringing Peyton out of his flashback, Leola was calling his name repeatedly. "Mr. Love... Mr. Love, Mr. Love?"

His eyes teared up as he smiled. "Yes, ma'am. Sorry, I was thinking back on something. My reason is simple. The love that I was given for only moments by my father, and all of my life by my mother, I want to give for a lifetime."

Leola smiled. "Mr. Love, I want you to know something from me. We usually tell this to every new adopting parent, but I truly mean it. You are going to save someone today!"

Peyton paused, smiled, and asked, "So when do I get to meet him?"

Love Saves

Peyton's final fulfillment of purpose began when he followed Leola down a long corridor. She looked back at him and asked. "Are you ready?"

"I've never been more ready, ma'am," Peyton replied.

She opened the door and there, sitting at a table, reading a science book, was a young boy. Leola walked Peyton to the table and the two sat down with the kid. "Mr. Love, this is Elijah. Elijah, may we sit down with you?" she asked.

"Yes, ma'am," Elijah replied.

"Hi, I'm Peyton, Peyton Love."

"Hello, Mr. Love. I'm Elijah, Elijah Simon."

"I'll leave you two alone for a bit, but I won't be far if you all need me, OK?" Ms. Leola left the room.

Elijah and Peyton both waved at Leola. "Thank you, ma'am," Peyton said.

As the door closed behind her, Peyton and Elijah both sat quietly for a moment. "So, what are you reading?" Peyton asked.

"I'm reading a science book on the anatomy of the human body," Elijah responded.

"Oh, is that for your homework?"

"No, sir. I just like anatomy and learning about it. I guess I'm a nerd, or so the kids call me."

"Well, that's OK. I'm a huge nerd too. So, what can you teach me?" Peyton asked.

They sat there for about an hour as Elijah shared all that he'd read that day on anatomy.

As Elijah concluded his teachings, Peyton asked, "Elijah, do you know why I'm here?"

"No, sir. I figured you were one of the foster parents who comes for the little kids, but I don't know."

"Well, actually, Elijah, I'm someone who's looking to adopt a child... and, well, if you would have me, I'd love to adopt you!"

Elijah looked shocked. "Me? Really? Why me? Nobody adopts us older kids!" he said, turning to Peyton.

"Well, I'm not nobody, nor am I somebody. I'm just a man who wants to make sure you have a place you can call home. Elijah, I'd be honored if you'd be OK with me adopting you and doing the best I can to give you a great home," Peyton continued.

"Really?" Elijah's eyes filled with tears. "Yes, sir. I'm OK with that, but are you serious? I've been to home after home, and I always get sent back here. This place is OK, but I've always just wanted to be wanted. What makes you want me? What if you don't like me? What if I'm not as brave as you want me to be? What if I'm not what you're looking for? What if I'm not enough?" Elijah lowered his head.

"Elijah, I was once you. Unwanted, cast aside, not knowing when someone would see that I was worthy of love. I've heard all about you, and I know a few things about you. I know you are a great child. I know that you are a great student and that you help all the kids here with their homework."

Elijah nodded as Peyton spoke.

"Look, I can't promise that you and I will get along. I can't promise that we won't struggle as we get to know each other. But I can promise this: I can promise that I will try my absolute hardest to be everything that you need. I can promise that I will listen to you. I can promise that I will learn."

Elijah began to cry.

Peyton wiped his tears. "Elijah, if you honor me by letting me adopt you, I promise to never leave you. Now, I have Down syndrome. Do you know what that is?"

"No, sir, not really."

"It means that I'm a little different. I look a little different from most, and it means that by the world's definition, I was born with genetic deficiencies. Although I don't have what normal people have, I know that I have a lot of love to give, and I want to make sure that you know you are worth loving, and you are amazing. I would be honored to adopt you. How does that sound?"

Leola watched from behind the glass as she teared up, clenching her hands together on her lips. She had been working in social work for over two decades, yet she'd never been a part of an adoption that had touched her so deeply. Her team had been working with Peyton for over a year to ensure he was capable of adopting a child. The state had tested him and approved, but she had never had a person like Peyton look to adopt—and an older child at that.

Peyton exhaled. "I have lived a somewhat untraditional life. I was born with Down syndrome and my father… well, my father left my mother and I before I was even born. My mother was quite the dual parent. In fact, I'd give her a tie on Father's Day and a dress on Mother's Day."

Elijah chuckled. "You gave your mom a tie? That's funny."

As the ice began to break and the two began to carry on a conversation, Elijah became more comfortable. Peyton could see him coming out of his shell.

"Listen, Elijah, I'm not saying that I'd be the best parent in the world. I'm sure there are things that you will need that I just won't have the answer to, but all I can promise is that I will try my very hardest. I don't know your entire story yet, but I'd love to spend the rest of my life getting to know it and hopefully write some new chapters to it. Happy ones!"

Peyton stood up and moved his chair closer to Elijah's.

Elijah had tears running down his cheeks. With these tears of joy, he didn't know if he should cry or laugh.

Through the two-way glass, Leola watched all of this unfold.

"Elijah, a man once told me the world needed my love. Well, I'm offering it to you. Will you give me the opportunity to be your friend, your buddy, your brother, your shoulder to lean on, your confidant, and maybe even one day your dad?"

Elijah looked up at him. "Yes... yes, I would love that." He stood and leaned over to hug Peyton.

At that moment, Peyton thought about the many moments of love and hugs that he'd shared with his mother. He smiled and looked up toward the ceiling with tears in his eyes. No words were spoken... he just smiled and hugged Elijah as the moment ended perfectly.

Suitcase of Passage

A few months had passed, and it was Elijah's first day at his new school. Peyton woke early in the morning and prepared Elijah's breakfast. In his normal chef outfit, a white tank top tucked into his tighty-whities, Peyton was on cloud nine.

Elijah came out of the back room, all dressed, and sat on the couch with a huge smile on his face.

Peyton looked over and smiled. "What? What's that weird smile for?"

"Nothing, I'm just happy. I've always regretted going to

school because I always had to go back to a home where I wasn't really wanted. I mean, they kept me, but I always knew either the family was going to return me, or I would just be stuck at the group home with the other kids." He looked down.

"Pick your head up," Peyton replied. "You will always be wanted here, Elijah. *Always!* I want you to know that when your school day ends, I'll be right there waiting for you! Now, come have your breakfast. You know, they say it's the most important meal, right?" Peyton hugged Elijah as he sat down at the table.

"Ooo yes, what'd you make?" Elijah asked.

"I made you the breakfast my mom used to make. Scrambled eggs, turkey bacon, and my favorite, two slices of wheat toast… with the edges sliced off, of course." Peyton laughed. "All right, buddy. Get it while it's hot." He plated their meals.

Peyton and Elijah sat next to each other and enjoyed their breakfast.

"Now, when you finish your breakfast, go get your books. I have a surprise for you before you go to school," Peyton said with a smirk and a side-eye.

Elijah was excited. "Wow, gifts already?" He ran to his room and gathered his books for school.

When he came back into the living room, Peyton stood there holding a gift wrapped in newspaper with a card taped to it. "Now, this is for you. It's not much, and it won't make much sense now, but someday it will have a lot of meaning to you. It means a lot to me."

Peyton handed it to Elijah, and the two sat on the couch so Elijah could open it.

He took the card that was stuck to the gift, opened it, and read aloud:

> Elijah, here is where our road together begins. I'm so glad to have you with me. You have brought

> me so much joy in such a little time, and I hope to one day bring you just as much joy. Always remember, where broken roads meet forgiveness and LOVE, the journey moves forward, toward greatness forever.

"Thank you. This means a lot to me. It's the first gift I've ever received."

Peyton smiled. "That's funny. It's also the first gift I received from my father."

Elijah unwrapped the gift, and it was the suitcase that Peyton had kept for nearly forty years in remembrance of his father.

"It was my father's, and now I'm giving it to you. All my life, I have kept this suitcase with me because it forced me to work hard, forgive harder, and love everything that I have. I know it's not much, but—"

Elijah cut him off. "It's perfect. Because it means so much to you. Thank you for this."

As Elijah sat quietly looking at the suitcase and rubbing his hands over it, Peyton watched him.

Elijah jumped up and gave Peyton a huge hug and replied, "I love it, thank you. I've received my very first gift from my father on my first day of school."

He kneeled down and began to fill the suitcase with his books for school. As he opened the top, he noticed three pictures taped to the underside of the suitcase's lid. "Who are these people?"

"It's a picture my mom and dad took many years ago, a photo of my father and I at the SF Giants game in San Francisco, and of course, the picture you and I took the day you decided to come live with me. All my greatest days. I wanted you to have them."

Elijah smiled and placed his books and school supplies inside the suitcase.

"OK, hurry up. You're going to be late for the bus."

As Elijah finished packing, he and Peyton walked toward the front door. Before leaving, Elijah turned back to Peyton one last time, hugged him, and thanked him for the gift again.

Peyton looked down at him, took his index finger, and drew the outline of a heart on Elijah's forehead. "Have a great day at school, E!"

He watched as Elijah ran down the stairs to the bus stop, looked back, and waved as he joined the other kids waiting on the bus.

As Peyton looked from the window, he couldn't hear what the kids were saying, but he could see them asking about the suitcase. With a big proud smile on his face, Elijah pointed at the suitcase and gave his explanation.

Peyton smiled as he saw Elijah open the suitcase while all of the kids huddled around. Elijah pointed at the pictures and was obviously explaining what each meant. All the kids were intrigued, and Elijah seemed happy. He was there, surrounded by people that wanted to know him, in the moment, and happy. As the bus approached, Elijah closed the suitcase and turned to wave goodbye one final time.

As Elijah got on the bus, the last thing Peyton saw was the suitcase that had once brought him so much pain being transferred into *love*.

In the final moments, Peyton waved goodbye to Elijah. His life had come full circle. He'd fulfilled his mother's dying wish: "Be the love the world demands." Peyton had worked all of his life to prove to his father that he was worthy of his love. In the end, it was Peyton's love that had not only saved his father, but also saved his own life by saving and changing Elijah's life. He was happy, there, in the moment, and full of *love*.

He looked through the foggy window one final time as the bus drove away, drew the outline of a heart, smiled, and walked away.

Peyton epitomized *down thru love*!

The End

About the Author

Many years ago, H. B. Pierre Simon Jr. mentored a child named Peyton who had Down syndrome, and remembers him as the most beautiful, happy, and lively child he'd ever known. With all of Peyton's challenges, he worked hard to push through them, and even though his father wasn't in his life, he never felt sorry for himself. He and Simon became really close, and Peyton looked to Simon as a father figure, a friend, and someone that cared for him. Ten years ago, Simon told Peyton's mother that he would write a book in Peyton's honor—*Down Thru Love* brings that promise to fruition.

Simon also has a son, Elijah Pierre Simon who inspired portions of the book. He notes, "Elijah's young innocent view of life encouraged me to finish this book which was started nearly 10 years ago. I always wanted to have a project that last forever with my son, and now I do. We have *Down Thru Love*."

In many ways, Simon identifies with the main character. In a previous book he authored, he noted, "There are times in life where life throws us challenges, and seemingly impossible obstacles. However if we face them head on, with no promise of victory, that will be the day we start down our paths of purpose. That'll be the day we live forever."

Printed in Canada